From Twisted Roots

By:

S.H. Cooper

From Twisted Roots

Book Cover by:
Taylor Tate

For the mechanic,
For the detective,
For the scientist,
And for Ma F'n Ma and Dad,
the most delicate of flowers,

Thanks for letting me borrow the best of you so I
could do the worst to you; I love you!

Stories

Fran and Jock

I'm the last in a long line of grandkids on both sides of my family. No one ever said as much, but I'm pretty sure I was an "oops" baby: the result of one too many glasses of wine and a couple over forty who thought unplanned pregnancies were only for teens.

Oops.

By the time I came along, both my grandmothers had already passed away. My grandfathers were elderly and lived in different states. Trying to coordinate travel plans for a family of five, including an infant, was difficult on a budget. Neither of my grandpas were up to frequent trips, so visits were rare and spaced out over long periods.

Both my parents still wanted me to have a relationship with them, so we'd trade phone calls so they could hear my nonsensical baby babble. My grandpas would write me letters for Mom and Dad to read to me, and they'd get crayon scribbles in return.

When I was three, they both began declining in health: first my maternal grandpa, then my paternal one. Fearing the worst, Mom purchased a pair of teddy bears, the kind with recorders in them so you could record a message that would play when the bear was hugged, making sure to save a message from both.

My mom's father died when I was four. A few

days after his funeral, I was given a white teddy bear with bright blue eyes that twinkled from beneath its plaid flat cap and green sweater. When I gave it a squeeze, I heard my grandpa's slightly muffled voice from its stomach.

"I love you, Sadie."

Two years later, after Dad's father passed, I got the other one. It was a slate gray color, and the stitching on its face gave it a rather serious expression for a stuffed animal. A pair of red suspenders held up its tan trousers. I'd fall asleep hugging it. Some years later, with tears in his eyes, my dad told me that he randomly kept hearing Grandpop's voice coming from my room throughout the night.

"I love you, Sadie."

I named my white bear Fran and my gray bear Jock. They sat on a shelf above my bed throughout my childhood. Honestly, I didn't give them much thought; they'd become fixtures of my room, the same way the lamp and dresser were. Every now and again, I'd come home from school to find one of my parents standing beside my bed, looking up at the bears or giving them a little squeeze. Even as time passed, the bears still recited their single phrase without fail.

Aside from those instances, Fran and Jock were little more than dust collectors from my childhood.

When I went away to college, the two didn't make the cut and were left behind while I made my way into the world for the first time. I think my parents were a little disappointed that I wasn't more sentimental over the teddies, but any memories I had of my grandpas were hazy at best and I didn't have the same emotional connection they did.

When Mom gently asked about whether I would like them when I moved into my first apartment, I told her no, that they were probably better off with her.

"Ok," she said. "Well, they'll be here if you change your mind."

I was pretty confident I wouldn't.

The next time I went back to my parents' place was to housesit while Dad took Mom on their long awaited vacation out west. He'd been promising her they'd go for over thirty years. They were both buzzing with excitement, although in typical Mom fashion, she was also very nervous.

"You remember where all the financial documents are in case anything happens to us, right?" she asked from the backseat at least six times on the drive to the airport.

"Yes, in the white bin under your bed."

"And the wills?"

"Fireproof lock box in the back of your closet."

"And th—"

"I think she's got it, hon." Dad said, reaching back to give her knee a squeeze.

Mom harrumphed and sat back. "Just call if you need anything."

"I'll be fine, don't worry! You're only going for a week."

"A lot can happen in a week," she said.

I grinned at her in the rearview mirror, unconcerned. She made a face at me, but seemed to relax.

S.H. Cooper

After I dropped them off, I drove back to their place and started making myself at home again. I tossed my suitcase on my bed and went to the kitchen to cook some dinner and catch up on one of my shows. It had been a while since I'd had a true, completely free week all to myself, and I planned to take full advantage of it. After I ate, I kicked up my feet, stretched out, and commenced "Lazy Lump" mode.

I managed to get almost three episodes in before I started to nod off. I checked the clock over the TV and sighed. It was only just after eleven; was I really turning into an old, early-to-bed woman already? The horror! I rolled off the couch to shut off the TV and all the lights, plunging the house into a deep darkness.

Even in the inky black, I didn't feel even a twinge of nervousness. I'd grown up in the house, I knew it like the back of my hand, and all its creaks and groans were almost comforting. I made my way to my room and flipped on the light.

It had been at least five years since I lived there, but my parents hadn't done much to change my room except to store a few bits and bobs in the closet. They said it was so I'd know I'd always have a place with them. I thought it was because changing it would make the fact that I moved out for good more real. Whatever the reason, I appreciated the familiarity.

As I started to unpack my bag, my eye was drawn to the shelf over my bed. Fran and Jock, ever vigilant, were sitting in the same spots they'd occupied for most of my life. I don't know why, but I couldn't help but smile and reach out to them.

I took Fran down first and gave his little cap a tweak before squeezing him around his stomach.

"I love you, Sadie," Grandpa said.

After putting Fran back, I did the same to Jock, who stared up at me with his usual sternness even as I plucked one red suspender.

"I love you, Sadie," Grandpop said.

It was the first time I'd listened to them in a while. Even if they didn't resonate as deeply with me as they did my parents, I was glad to find their recordings still worked.

A quick trip to the bathroom and a change into my PJs later, I was in bed and fast asleep.

I can't say exactly what woke me. A nightmare, I figured, given that my heart was beating quite quickly, but I couldn't remember any details. I took a deep breath and rolled over, already falling half-asleep again, and found myself face to face with a dark figure on the pillow beside me. I yelped and sat up, grabbing my phone, my nearest source of light, and shining it toward my bed.

Fran was lying on his side beside me.

I let out a small chuckle and gave myself a little shake to dismiss the lingering fright he'd caused.

"Did you fall off the shelf?" I asked him quietly, picking him up. I must have put him back too close to the edge earlier and gravity had done its duty.

I gave Fran a gentle squeeze.

"Get out."

I stared down at the bear and blinked once, very slowly. I must be more sleepy than I realized, I thought. I was hearing things. To prove to myself that it had just been my imagination, I squeezed him again.

"Get out."

It was still Grandpa's voice, but instead of the soft warmth it had always had, it sounded cold, almost menacing. I threw Fran across the room and he hit the wall.

From over my head, I heard Grandpop's more gravelly voice.

"Get out."

I whipped around and looked up at Jock. He was sitting in the same place as always, but now he was turned toward the door instead of facing forwards. Had I put him down like that? I couldn't remember.

"Get out!" Grandpa's voice came from Fran again, louder this time.

"Get out!" Grandpop echoed Jock.

The two went back and forth, their voices getting louder and louder, until I slapped my hands over my ears and leapt from my bed. I wanted to scream, but my voice was stuck behind my fear-tangled tongue. I stumbled across my dark room, chased by the voices from my long dead grandfathers.

"I know you're down there!" Jock shouted with Grandpop's voice.

I froze. Down there? Down under the shelf? I glanced over my shoulder at the gray bear staring silently down from over my bed. I had to get out of my room. I had to get out of the house! I yanked open my door.

"I see you!" Fran said in Grandpa's voice.

I was halfway into the hall, tears streaming down my face. I didn't know what was happening. Was I going crazy? Was I dreaming? All I knew was that my two childhood toys were screaming threats at me and that I had to get away from them. I turned toward the stairs.

"You take one more step, I'll make sure it's your last!" Jock bellowed.

"Get out!" Fran roared.

From somewhere downstairs, a step creaked.

Someone else was in the house.

They weren't yelling at me at all, I realized with a strange mix of confused relief and newly formed horror. They were yelling at the intruder who was making their way up the stairs toward me.

"Get out!" my grandfathers howled together.

Footsteps clamored across the wood floor downstairs. Something fell over in the living room with a loud crash, and again in the kitchen. The back door slammed against the counter as it was thrown open, and a car engine rumbled to life.

I somehow regained my wits enough to run to my parents room and look out the window to the driveway below. An SUV was peeling backwards into the street. It slammed into the neighbor's mailbox, righted itself, and then screeched off into the night.

A heavy quiet had fallen over the house again.

After waiting a few, long, tense minutes, I crept back across the hall and peeked into my room. Fran and Jock were where I'd left them, both completely silent. When they stayed that way, I hesitantly approached Fran, who was lying on his side with his little flat cap beside him. I picked him up and, with trembling fingers, squeezed his stomach.

"I love you, Sadie," Grandpa said warmly.

I put his cap back on his head and gently put him back on the shelf beside Jock. I backed out of the room, watching them the whole time with wide eyes. As I rounded the corner, heading downstairs to the phone, I heard Grandpop's voice trailing after me.

"I love you, Sadie."

The police arrived a bit later, following my frantic call to 911. I filed a report, leaving out the bit about my talking bears, and allowed them to collect whatever evidence they could. Every so often, I found myself glancing at the stairs, almost like I was expecting a repeat of whatever had just happened. It never came, and the cops wrapped it up, leaving me alone again.

I called my parents to tell them about the break in. They immediately wanted to rush home, but I assured them there was no need.

"Really," I said, "I don't think I have anything to worry about."

"We could be on the next plane," Mom insisted.

"No, I'm ok. Whoever that guy was, I'm pretty sure he won't be back."

It took a few more go arounds, but I eventually convinced them I was safe. I felt it too, for the most part. After the initial shock wore off and I'd had time to process what happened, I really was ok. I couldn't explain it, I couldn't tell anyone what had happened without sounding crazy, but I knew it had been real. I knew that as long as I had Fran and Jock sitting on the shelf above my bed, I could sleep easy.

A few days later, the cops found the guy who broke in. He was a coworker of my dad's who'd overheard he'd be out of town. He thought the house would be empty and easy pickings. When he tried to tell them about the two crazy guys upstairs and their violent threats, the cops rolled their eyes and laughed at him. He was very surprised to hear that only a twenty-two year old woman had been in the house during his botched burglary.

When I returned home to my apartment a week later, Fran and Jock were with me. I keep them on the TV stand in the living room now where they have a full view of the front door. Whenever I start to feel a bit anxious about being alone, I'll give each bear a little squeeze and smile as they speak.

"I love you, Sadie."

And now I respond, "I love you both, too."

The Signs Were All There

Women in my mother's family have an unusual relationship with death. We believe in signs and listening when the universe, or whatever you want to call it, tries to tell you something. The night before my great grandmother passed, she told anyone in her nursing home who would listen that she was going home. She said that Daniel, her husband of forty-seven years who had pre-deceased her by five, was coming to get her.

The next morning, the staff found her tucked neatly in her bed, her hair and makeup done as best she could, and a smile on her face. That's how she died.

About a decade later, moments before my mom received the call that my grandma had succumbed to pneumonia, she was stopped by an elderly woman at the grocery store who said, "I'll always be with you."

When Mom asked what she meant, the old woman just pat her arm gently and resumed pushing her cart up the aisle. Mom said that when her phone rang shortly thereafter and her brother told her the news, she wasn't surprised. Underneath the rolling waves of devastation that accompany such loss, there was a sense of peace.

I thought about those stories sometimes, especially during a particularly long and difficult shift. Although we were trained and advised to stay detached, watching a patient take their final breath was never easy. It helped to think that there was some kind of afterlife waiting for them.

On one such shift I should have gone home about an hour before, but a surgery had run long and I was exhausted. Still in my scrubs, I'd stopped into the cafeteria for a coffee, needing a moment of respite before changing and heading home. I'd actually manage to get back before dinner was ready! The sun would still be up for a few hours, so maybe a relaxing walk would be in order. Then I'd be able to slip into the bath; nothing sounded better than a nice, long soak in my claw foot tub.

"Excuse me?"

A girl, maybe nine years old, had come to stand beside my table. She was looking at me shyly from behind a curtain of dark hair, and she had a small white bear clutched tightly to her chest. A visitor pass stuck to her shirt gave her name as Arianna. I did my best to smile through my weariness and put my coffee down.

"Yes?"

"Are you Dr. Drakeson?"

"I am," I replied, trying to covertly look over her shoulder to see if I could spot anyone searching for their child.

"She said she's ok. She's not hurting. She loves you."

A tingling chill ran up my spine. The girl stared at me with a solemn expression, no hint of teasing or mischief sparkling in her eyes. My mouth went dry. I slid from the chair to take a knee in front of her so that I was on her level. "What did you say?"

Arianna hugged her bear tighter and cowered away from me a bit. "I was just supposed to tell you."

"Who told you to say that?"

"Molly."

I learned in that moment what it truly felt like when your heart stops. Every hair on my body stood on end. My throat constricted painfully. I could barely form the words I needed.

"Molly? How do you know Molly? When did you talk to her?" My rush of questions frightened the girl, who took a large step back. Her eyes had the watery look of someone on the verge of tears. We were starting to draw attention, but I hardly noticed. "No, no, you're ok. You're not in trouble, sweetie. I just need you to tell me when you spoke with Molly."

"Just now, when I went to throw the trash away. She was over there."

I knew that couldn't be true. My daughter was home on summer vacation being babysat by her aunt, but I found myself hunting the crowded room for any sign of Molly anyway. Arianna took my distraction as an opportunity to flee back to wherever her parents were, but I didn't care. My coffee forgotten, I half ran from the cafeteria to the locker room where I tore through my purse to find my phone.

"Come on, Candace," I muttered into the mouthpiece while it rang. Any minute my sister would pick up and laugh at me for getting so worked up over nothing. She'd put Molly on and I'd be regaled with tales of their arts and crafts and adventures going down to the community pool.

But the phone just kept ringing.

"Damnit, Candace!" Why couldn't my sister be attached to her cell like everyone else?

I threw the phone back into my purse and hurriedly changed into my "civilian" clothes. A small part of me felt bad about leaving my scrubs balled up on the floor in front of my locker, which I wasn't sure I'd even remembered to close, but I was in too much of a rush to take them to the laundry chute. I tried to call Candace a few more times on my way to the parking garage, but each time it went to her voicemail. My tires squealed as I pulled out from my spot and descended to ground level. I was lucky that there was no oncoming traffic, because I didn't even slow down as I hit the street.

I probably passed the same billboard every day for however long it had been up, but I'd never noticed it before. A red light forced me to come to a rubber-burning halt. I anxiously drummed my steering wheel, urging the light to change, when I saw the sign.

"Do you know where your child is?"

Panic coiled and writhed in my stomach. For a moment, I thought the coffee I'd managed to get down was going to make a reappearance all over my windshield.

"It's just a stupid ad by one of those responsible parenting groups," I said aloud, "Stop looking for signs."

I flipped on the radio to help drown out the dark thoughts shrouding my mind. It was playing a song I'd never heard before, some country lite number sung with a slight twang.

"If I die young, bury me in satin; Lay me down on a bed of roses; Sink me in the river at dawn; Send me away with the words of a love song"

When the singer started crooning about a mother burying her baby, I laid on my horn and blew through the intersection, light be damned. It took a car nearly side swiping me to give me pause and think that maybe I was overreacting.

Maybe the kid knew Molly from school. They were about the same age, maybe she'd seen me picking her up and thought it'd be a funny joke to scare Molly's mommy. And everything else was all coincidental; it was just the result of me being hyperactively aware.

I started to slow down as rational thoughts overtook the hysterical ones. Then I passed a doll lying on the side of the road, her arms and legs thrown askew, her head twisted so that she was facing too far over her shoulder. I might have ignored it, except that its hair was the same shade of auburn red that Molly's was. I was a woman of science and logic, but when the signs were all there, I couldn't ignore them. All lights were optional after that.

The drive from the hospital to home was only ten minutes, but it stretched on for an eternity. I almost let out a sob when I turned onto my quiet side street. The speed limit in the residential area was 25, but I was pushing 60 and even that was with great restraint. I had to get home. I had to see my child.

The thump was so sudden that I barely had time to register it. A flash of color, a scream, and the terrible crunching sound of metal beneath tires.

I slammed on my brakes and skid to a halt about half-mile down the road. I clutched my steering wheel in a white knuckled grip and gasped for breath. My heart thudded painfully in my chest. I could barely bring myself to look in the rear view mirror.

A woman was on the ground in the middle of the road beside a little girl, frantically screaming for help. She held the child, who hung limply in her arms, against her chest. The girl's bike had been dragged for a distance down the street and lay in a tangled mess a few feet behind my rear bumper.

I don't know how I managed to get out of my car. I don't know how I made my way back to the pair before my knees finally gave out and I collapsed beside them.

Streaks of red lined Molly's pale face. Her helmet, the blue Frozen one she'd begged for at the store, was split so that Elsa no longer had a complete face. My daughter's arms and legs were thrown askew, and her head rested at an odd angle against her aunt's shoulder. Candace was screaming, perhaps at me, maybe still just for help, I couldn't make it out. I couldn't touch Molly. I couldn't move. I couldn't do anything except stare at my baby's face.

The ambulance came later; I don't think it took long. They wrapped my little girl in a white sheet and put her on a gurney bound for the hospital morgue. Police tried to question me, but by then the only sound I could make was an animalistic wail. I had no words. As they guided me into a cruiser, I looked back to where Molly had lain. Where her blood still stained the asphalt. Standing on the sidewalk just beyond the police tape, grinning and hugging her teddy bear, was Arianna. She waved as the officer closed the door behind me.

As Long As There Are

Children

Times were different when I was young. Used to be that if the sun was shining, the kids were out. Whatever they got into was between them, their buddies, and their bikes. As long as everybody made it home in one piece without the cops on their tail, there were no questions asked.

That summer, the one when the rumors started, I was finally old enough to tag along with my big brother when he ventured out with his friends. I knew he didn't really want me there; he was only letting me go because Mom told him he had to, but it didn't matter. I was getting to hang out with Billy and his boys, the coolest guys anywhere, in my nine year old opinion.

They were all older than me, twelve and thirteen. They swore and had fire crackers, and sometimes one of them would nab a couple smokes off their parents when they weren't looking. Billy wouldn't let me try any of them, but just standing in the circle while the others took drags made me feel like a real Bad Boy.

It was during one of these sessions, all huddled behind the Woolworth's, trying to look devil-may-care and inconspicuous at the same time, that Mac Stanson brought up the carnival.

"It's out in the woods off the old highway," he said after a short pull from the cigarette. Smoke curled in thin tendrils from between his lips with every word.

"Bullshit," Billy said. I couldn't help whispering the word immediately after with nervous glee.

I'd never said such a grown up thing before. I glanced around with some hopefulness to see if anyone had noticed. They were all too focused on Mac, though.

"No, it's there," he said with a dismissive scoff. "I heard some kids at the arcade talking about it first; they said they heard rumors about it. It's supposed to come around every few years or something like that. But I've got a first-hand account; my cousin's best friend was cutting through the woods to get to the pond last weekend and actually saw it. It looked huge, and there were rides, and he said it smelled like cotton candy and peanuts. He talked to the guy running it, the Barker or whatever, at the entrance, and he said it's open all summer. Free for kids. No adults."

It was the kind of rumor only bored kids caught in a small town summer lull would pay attention to. We were buying into it, hook, line, and sinker. An impressed murmur rippled across the group. A whole carnival with no supervision sounded like utopia.

"So how come nobody's heard of it then?" Billy, still skeptical, asked. I quickly changed my expression to match his doubtful one.

"'Cos it's a secret, shit for brains," Mac said. "It's like...only certain people can go to it. You gotta know about it. Otherwise all the parents would be there too."

"So we know about it, can we go to it?" Kirk Blatts, Billy's best friend and the biggest kid in the whole eighth grade, swiped the cigarette from Mac. Kirk eyed him with a raised brow, a look he'd been trying to perfect for ages. I thought it made him look more confused than anything else.

"We just gotta find it first," Mac replied.

"It's a big carnival in the woods; how hard can it be?" Billy said.

Talk of the carnival went on for the rest of the week. Maps were examined, and we hung out at the arcade and mall trying to overhear more conversations about it from other kids. We were careful not to let our parents in on the planning. We took the "no adults" rule very seriously.

Robert bowed out first. His mom smelled smoke on him when he got home one night and grounded him for the next month. Then Jerry remembered he had a family thing to go to. When the scheduled morning actually arrived for us to bike out to the woods, only Billy, Mac, Kirk, and me were left; my place in the group was shaky at best.

"Noah's not gonna be able to keep up," Mac griped.

"I will!" I promised earnestly, looking to Billy for support. It stung a bit that he didn't immediately jump to my defense.

He frowned, obviously weighing his limited options, and finally shrugged. "He can ride on my handlebars."

"Come on, man," Mac said. "We'd have more

fun without him!"

"Mom says I have to let him come when he wants."

"That's bull—" Mac started to complain again, but Kirk punched him soundly in the shoulder.

"Quit bitching and let's go," he said.

I'd never been so grateful for the big lug in my life.

I perched on Billy's handlebars with a wide grin and held on tight as we lurched out of our driveway. We rode out of the neighborhood, straight down Main Street. Past all the mom and pop shops that weren't open yet, across the wooden footbridge to the old highway. The road was pockmarked with deep, wide potholes that the other two made a game of jumping over. Billy swerved more carefully around them, struggling a bit to keep us upright.

Even at that early hour, the sun was glaring down at us. I urged him to go faster toward the woods and their welcomed shade. He just grumbled at me to shut up.

Kirk skid off the pavement first to sweep down the embankment, followed closely by Mac. Billy and I came last at a more cautious pace.

The bikes had to be abandoned shortly after we crossed the tree line. There was no good path, and it was quickly decided that we'd be better off hoofing it. I stuck close to Billy as we delved deeper into the woods, equal parts nervous and excited. The guys were talking about all the treats they were going to eat and the rides they'd go on, but I just focused on keeping up, determined to prove Mac wrong.

We wandered aimlessly, unsure of where exactly we were going, but certain that we were going to take as long as we needed to find it.

The morning dragged into a sweltering early afternoon and I'd started to lag behind the others. My mouth was dry, my legs were tired from kicking through underbrush, and my clothes were damp and clinging with sweat. It was Mac who was doing all the whining, though.

"I'm thirsty! My feet hurt! It's hot!"

It was hard not to feel smugly superior to him after all the moaning he'd done about me earlier. At least I could keep my mouth shut about how miserable I was. His long string of complaints earned him some sharp remarks from Billy and Kirk, and the three of them started bickering back and forth until I shouted at them to be quiet. Mac was the first to whirl around, ready to lay into me, but my wide eyed smile stopped him short.

"Do you smell that?" I asked.

They all paused and sniffed the air. One by one, their faces lit up.

"Cotton candy!" Billy said.

"Where's it coming from?" Kirk tilted his head up like it might give him a better sense of direction.

Like a pack of hunting dogs, we followed those enticing scents through the trees. They were sweet and warm and thick, the kind of smells that only comes from one kind of place: a carnival.

When we heard the music, distinctly cheerful and tinny, we knew we were going the right way. We started to walk faster and faster until we were running, all of our previous aches and pains forgotten so close to the Promised Land. The woods thinned around us until we spilled into a large clearing, directly beneath a banner featuring a painted-on smiling man in a top hat. Large, blocky letters read: "Welcome!"

We'd arrived!

Beyond the banner, we could see the tips of rides and brightly colored tents poking over a wooden fence. There were music and smells too! It was heavenly; there was no other word for it.

Waiting to greet us, standing tall atop an overturned bucket, was the same man who was on the banner: the Barker. He plucked his top hat off and waved us over with it, smiling broadly from beneath a thin mustache.

"Ah, welcome, welcome!" he said, hopping down to greet us each with a shake of the hand. "Why, you're the first ones here! Lucky you! You'll have the whole place to yourself!"

We cheered and whooped, and the Barker told us to follow him to the ticket booth where he handed us each five tickets.

"These can be used freely on any ride, on any game. Once they're gone, there's a price to pay!" he said with a wag of his long finger.

"Aw, man!" Mac groaned. "We were told it wouldn't cost a cent."

"And so it won't, my boy, and so it won't!"

"But you said—"

"Don't worry yourself about that. Just be mindful of your tickets and go enjoy the carnival!"

That was good enough for us. The Barker ushered us to the gate and we were off, each of our five little blue tickets clutched tight in our fists. It was empty inside, both of workers and other children. The lights were on though, the music was playing, the popcorn popping, and, for a moment, we were the luckiest kids alive.

Kirk ran for the shooting gallery where little wooden ducks with targets on their sides were sitting in front of mounted BB guns. He fed a ticket into a slot on the booth and the two rows of ducks churned to life, going back and forth while Kirk took aim. He missed his first two shots, but the third hit its mark and the unfortunate duck folded down. A siren went off, and a string of lights around the backdrop flashed. The Barker appeared, stepping out from behind the booth to reward Kirk with a lollipop.

None of us knew how he'd gotten all the way back there from the gate without any of us noticing.

We went from booth to booth, each taking turns at the ones that interested us. I spent two tickets trying my hand at ring toss. Billy knocked over milk bottles, Mac popped balloons with darts, and each of us tried the strength test. Every time the lights flashed and the siren sounded, the Barker would be there with a treat for the victor.

The tilt-a-whirl was next, and then we were rushing toward the small Ferris wheel and its half-dozen seats that would lift us just high enough to see over the tents.

I can't say if Mac really meant to trip me or if we just collided with one another and I ended up going down. Just before we reached the ride though, I found myself flat on my back and seeing stars after smacking my head against the ground.

He barely paused to glance down at me. He laughed once, then shoved his ticket into its slot and got into one of the slow moving buckets after Kirk. Billy shouted a nasty cuss after him and crouched beside me.

"You ok?" he asked, probably more worried he'd get in trouble if I was hurt than he was about me.

"I think so," I said.

I sat up, gingerly touching a hand to the back of my head. I scowled down at the ground, trying not to cry like a big, fat baby, when I heard this terrible creaking: the squeal and protest of old metal. It seemed even louder now that the music had become fainter and more disjointed, like a cassette tape about to tangle. Looking up, I realized right away where the sound was coming from.

The Ferris wheel, which had only a moment before been gleaming steel, was little more than a rusted, skeleton of its former self. It had stopped rotating, and sitting in two of the warped buckets were Kirk and Mac. They were laughing and pointing like they thought they were high overhead instead of still at ground level. The creaking sounded again every time they shifted their weight.

Billy was still asking if I was sure I was ok, unphased by any of it.

"W-what happened to the ride?" I looked to my brother in confusion, and he returned my stare, equally baffled.

"Huh?"

"The ride! It's all wrong; it's old and broken!"

I pointed at it, desperate for him to realize that something wasn't right. He looked over shoulder, but his expression didn't change. By then, the others were hopping out of the buckets and heading over to us.

"What's with him?" Kirk nodded down at me.

"He tripped," Billy said.

I wasn't even bothered that that wasn't what happened at all. I was too busy looking around at the carnival. There were no lights, no music except that ghostly, off key melody coming from somewhere in the distance. Even the smell had gone, replaced by that of mildew and rotting wood. I leapt to my feet, turning in circles. I only grew more upset, more frightened, when I saw the state of things.

Tents were dirtied and torn. The rides were run down and unusable. Stalls once filled with food and sweets were empty, except for remnants of packaging that looked like it had been nibbled on by rodents. All of the brightness and good cheer had been washed away by age, and sun, and decay.

The other kids didn't notice and were still walking toward the spinning swings.

"This is my last ticket," Mac said

"Mine, too," Kirk held his up.

"I've got two more," Billy gloated.

"It doesn't matter, he said we could still do stuff after we use them all," Mac was quick to remind them.

I tried to call after them, to tell them that the swings they were climbing into were just cracked plastic on dangerously groaning chains. I couldn't find my voice though. They sat on the broken-down ride, their hands raised over their heads, hollering and carrying on as if they were swooping around high in the air.

The Barker was standing opposite me on the

other side. Instead of the tall, slender man with the thin mustache from before, he was faint and hollow. His skin was tinged grey beneath his threadbare red coat and collapsed top hat. When he saw me staring, he pressed his pale lips together in a grim, pleased grin.

I was still screaming when the guys got off the swings a few minutes later.

"God, what's his issue?" Mac said.

"Maybe he needs a nap." Kirk laughed at his own joke.

"Stop being assholes," Billy snapped, and then to me, he said, "What's your deal?"

"I wanna go! Something's wrong!"

I tugged at his arm pleadingly, and he shot me a look of derision that normally would have turned my stomach. Now I just wanted to get out of there.

"I have one ticket left. I'm going to use it."

"Billy, please!"

While we argued, Mac and Kirk had become distracted by the carousel at the center of the carnival. I remembered seeing it when we first came in: finely painted creatures, both real and fantasy, threaded with shining brass poles and dancing up and down invitingly as they circled 'round and 'round. Now they were chipped and broken, their colors faded, and their poles tarnished. It was clear their dancing days were long behind them.

That didn't stop the pair from bypassing the ticket slot and climbing on their chosen steeds: Mac on a white leopard with only three legs, and Kirk on a horse with half its head smashed, leaving a jagged, splintery crater on one side where an ear and an eye should have been.

"You're sure we don't need a ticket for this?" Kirk asked uncertainly, even as he swung his leg over the horse's back.

"The ride's still going, so who cares?" Mac replied dismissively. "Hey, Billy, get your ass up here! There's a little pink unicorn with your name on it!"

My brother flipped him off, but told me to stay put and moved as if to join them.

"Billy, I want to go," I whispered again, clutching the back of his shirt.

"Noah," he said warningly.

"Please," I continued to hold tight, afraid to be alone, and even more afraid of letting my brother get onto that decrepit ride.

"Get off, man, we're not done yet!"

He yanked himself away and started toward the carousel. A surge of panic propelled me forward. I'd hit my head and it made everything change for me, so I could only hope the same would be true for Billy. I didn't give myself time to stop and think what might happen if I was wrong, or the world of pain I'd be in when he was done with me. I just swung my fist as hard as I could at the back of my big brother's head.

It connected with a crack, and he stumbled to his knees with a surprised, pained cry.

"You little shit!" he shouted, grabbing at his head.

He started to push himself up again, and I shuffled back a few steps. My eyes went from him to the carousel where Mac and Kirk seemed to think they were riding in a circle. Then back again as he whirled on me, his own fist raised to return my blow. He froze before it landed, his mouth falling open.

"I don't...what happened?" his voice was soft, mystified, and afraid. I grabbed his arm again, tugging him toward the exit.

"You see it now too, right? We gotta go!"

"B-but the guys," Billy, still in a daze, glanced over his shoulder as Mac called his name again.

"Where are you two going?" Mac cupped his hand around his mouth and twisted on the leopard as if the ride were taking him away from us, over to the other side, and he were about to lose sight of us.

"Mac, Kirk, you gotta get off there! We gotta go! Now!" Billy's voice cracked with agitation. Instead of heeding his words, the others laughed at him. "Guys!"

His warning was followed by another crack, but this one wasn't from him. It was a sharp, wooden snap. Then another, and the leopard that Mac was riding suddenly faced him, its head rotating completely around.

The snarl it released was heard by all of us.

Mac shrieked. Kirk swore. His horse with its half face had done the same as the leopard. They tugged at the safety belts around their waists, shouting for us to help them. We started running toward them to help them off the ride, but the gate at its entryway slammed shut in front of us. Billy grabbed the back of my shirt and hauled me back again.

From the carousel, there was another snarl. Another snap, and the guys were howling.

The creatures, the horse, and the leopard, had all opened their mouths to reveal row upon row of all too real looking teeth. They sank those fangs into Mac and Kirk's forearms. Kirk struggled, yanking and kicking, shouting at the top of his lungs. Even with his size and brute strength, the horse's jaw remained firmly shut.

Mac could only scream.

There was a long, agonized groan of gears and wood. Slowly, the carousel started to turn. Mac and Kirk yelled for us again, begging us to help them off. I looked to Billy for guidance. He had gone ghostly pale, his lower lip quivering. He jumped when I touched his hand.

"I'm scared, Billy!" I cried.

The others rounded the carousel, disappearing from view. We still heard them screaming.

Screaming.

Screaming.

When they reappeared a moment later, their arms had vanished up to their elbows down the throats of their mounts.

The Barker was standing between them, smiling in delight.

"Join us, my boys!" he said, throwing his bony arms wide. "There's plenty of room for everyone!"

"Go, go, go!" Billy had me by the wrist and was pulling me away.

My legs didn't want to work. I couldn't tear my eyes away from the Barker, who didn't even try to stop us.

"Do come back soon, my boys!" he shouted over the piercing, anguished screeches of our friends. "We'll be here, we'll be waiting, and we're always hungry! As long as there are children, there will be a carnival!"

Billy half carried me the rest of the way back to the bikes. He didn't look back, didn't slow, he just kept moving, making sure I was with him every step of the way. When we reached the embankment, he shoved me ahead of him, telling me to go and that he would be right behind. I sobbed and begged him to stay next to me, but he had to get his bike. It was an impossibly long climb back to the highway, and every few seconds I had to look back to make sure Billy was still there.

Once we reached the top, we scrambled onto the bike, him in the seat, and me on the handlebars. He pedaled as fast and as hard as he could back to town.

Mac Stanson and Kirk Blatts were never seen again.

When the woods were searched, they did find the remnants of a carnival. Nothing but broken down rides and empty, half rotted booths and stands. They combed through it with careful precision, going through every structure. There was no trace of Mac, Kirk, or any Barker.

"It hasn't been used in decades," we were told. "It's abandoned. There's nothing out there. It's more graveyard than carnival."

The cops weren't wrong about that. It was a graveyard, for Mac and Kirk and all of the other kids who had chased rumors of a secret carnival into the woods.

We tried to tell them that. It needed to be destroyed, but that never happened. It was too much work, too much red tape, and eventually the disappearances of our friends were forgotten, and the carnival remained.

Not that I really thought removing the items would remove the Barker. He was darkness, an infection. I'd felt it even as a child. All we could do was warn as many people to stay away as we could.

Things were quiet for a time, peaceful, even, until about fifteen years later. A little girl went missing near those woods. Billy and I just looked at each other, and we felt the same sick certainty.

It was active again. It was back.

Because as long as there are children, there will be a carnival.

Her Last Call

When my mother told me that Catarina was coming to stay with us for a few days, I immediately started going through all the stages of grief. First, I tried to deny that it was going happen. Mom just replied that I'd have a say in house guests once I started paying half the mortgage. That made me angry, so I gave her the silent treatment, pouty glares and all. When she seemed amused by that, I moved to bargaining; I told her I'd do all the housework for a month if Cat didn't come. I got a pat on the head, taken up on my offer to clean more. Oh, and by the way, she was still coming.

Depression and acceptance occurred at the same time. I was miserable while I cleaned my room, making space on the floor for the air mattress that my cousin would use, grumbling loudly the entire time.

"Cheer up, buttercup," Mom said as she passed my door. "It's only for a week."

A very long, very frustrating week in which I would have to share my sanctuary with one of my least favorite people. Mom knew how I felt about Cat; I was very vocal about it, but it didn't change the fact that she let my aunt and uncle drop her on our doorstep every time they went out of town. I was convinced they viewed their yearly vacation as a much needed break from their daughter, but

Mom said that was a terrible thing to suggest. I wasn't allowed to verify whether it was true.

"You're both a bit older now. Maybe you'll have more things in common." Mom was an eternal optimist. "Just try to be nice."

The moment Cat stepped into my room, I knew this visit would be no different than any other. She threw her things onto my bed, gave me a disinterested once over, and pulled out her phone. Only two years separated us, but Cat had quite the Queen Bee complex and couldn't be bothered with someone so beneath her as fourteen year old me.

Before bed that night, Cat took the invitation to make herself at home to the next level. She convinced mom that the air mattress would be too uncomfortable and cause her back pain, so I was forced to switch. Cat watched me get settled on the mattress with a victorious smirk, and I wanted nothing more than to bean her in her face with whatever was closest at hand. While I struggled to find a comfortable position, she reclined against her pillows and blasted obnoxiously loud music from her phone.

I'd only just managed to get Catarina to turn off her music, shut off the light, and agree to sleep, when her phone rang. Instantly I was sitting upright again, one of my pillows in hand, aiming at my cousin.

"Don't you dare answer it," I said in warning.

She scoffed and I was reminded, once again, why I disliked her so strongly. I launched the pillow at Cat's face, but she smacked it aside and flipped me off before answering her phone. To annoy me further, she put the call on speaker.

"Who is this?"

"Catarina?"

"Who's asking?"

"Th-this is Virginia Press, from school?" There was something odd about the way the girl spoke: a nervous, twitchy energy that made me uncomfortable.

"Virgin?" Cat asked incredulously. "How did you get my number? Why the hell are you even calling me?"

"Because there's something I need to-to say to you."

"This couldn't, like, wait until Monday?"

"N-no, I need to say it now."

Cat heaved a put upon sigh. "Fine, whatever, but when you're done, delete my number. I don't need weirdos like you calling me and pretending we're friends."

"Th-that's your problem," Virginia said, her voice thick with trembling emotion. "You treat people like crap! You say what you want, you hurt our feelings, but you don't care!"

"This is why you cal—"

"Shut up!" The girl was shouting into the phone. "You always get to do the talking, but it's my turn now! You're a horrible person, Catarina! You're nasty, and mean, and you make everyone who isn't just like you miserable!"

The shock that crossed Catarina's face was delicious. I doubted anyone had ever spoken to her that way, and I was only too happy to have a front row seat when it finally happened.

"You've made me miserable for so long. I know it was you who made everyone start calling me Virgin. I know it was you who photoshopped those pictures of me, and I *know* it was you who started the rumors about me being a lesbian. I can't go into the locker room or bathroom anymore without people screaming that I'm trying to look at them!"

Catarina mimed a yawn at me. I scowled. This poor girl was obviously hurting, and Cat couldn't have cared less.

"People started calling my house and telling my parents. My dad wanted to throw me out!"

"Not my problem, Virgin," Cat said.

"It is, though. This all started because of you. I never did anything to you, and you've made everyone hate me!"

"No I didn't. They hated you because you're just such a fucking freak."

"That's ok." Virginia's voice became eerily calm. I thought I could hear wind whistling in the background. "It's not going to be anyone's problem really soon."

"What?"

"I just wanted to tell you...I wanted you to know so that you never doubted it...this is all your fault."

Virginia started to scream.

It was so loud, so full of fear. It went on and on for what felt like minutes, muffled only by the sound of wind whipping wildly by. Cat fumbled to pick up her phone, desperately trying to end the call. I wanted her to so badly, but her hands were shaking and clumsy.

The screaming ended abruptly in a heavy, wet thud.

We stared at one another, eyes wide, speechless and pale. The phone crackled a couple of times, then went quiet.

"Did she...?" I couldn't bring myself to ask the full question.

Cat gaped dumbly, her mouth opening and closing. She just kept shaking her head in disbelief.

"Girls?" We jumped when my mom knocked on the bedroom door. "Everything ok in there?"

Before Cat could answer, I sprung up and pulled the door open to throw myself into Mom's arms. She pat my back comfortingly, obviously confused. When Cat didn't answer her, she tipped my tear streaked face upwards.

"Baby? What's wrong?"

"I think she killed herself!" I cried.

"What? Who?"

"The girl on the phone!"

We both looked over to Cat, who had taken on a greenish tint. She ran from the bed, shoving past us on her way out to lock herself in the bathroom. We listened in stunned silence as she vomited violently.

Cat didn't come out for hours. She refused to speak to us through the door, so it was up to me to tell Mom what happened. She was horrified and, for a moment, I thought she'd be sick too. She collected herself quickly though, telling me to try to sleep in her bed while she took care of things. I lay awake the rest of the night, unable to get Virginia's terrified shrieking out of my head.

The police found Virginia's body the next morning at the foot of the water tower. They said she used a pair of bolt cutters lying nearby to get through the chain link fence. Then she'd climbed all the way to the top.

That's why I heard wind when she was talking, I thought numbly as we watched the story unfold on the news. Whe was already up there.

After it got out that her last call had been to Cat, I'd thought for sure she would be shunned for her part in the girl's death. Cat's friends rallied around her though, blaming Virginia for "putting Cat through such an ordeal". They said it was so cruel for Virginia to do such a thing when Cat had only ever played harmless pranks.

I was floored by their response, angry that they were turning Virginia into a villain, but there was nothing I could do. I'd never met the girl, hadn't even known who she was prior to that night. She'd just been another upperclassman lost in our crowded school.

Cat seemed to recover from it all very quickly. Her parents offered to come back early from their vacation, but she declined. She was fine — better than fine, actually relishing in the extra attention the situation brought. I overheard her tell and retell the story multiple times, treating it like some kind of spectator sport. I was disgusted by her behavior and, after so many days, I told her so.

"*She* called *me*. I have every right to tell my story."

"Your story? Her death isn't *your* story! You're such a bitch!"

We started to argue, calling each other names and making catty remarks aimed to hurt. We were getting louder, more heated, and I was sure we were going to resort to physical fighting when her phone rang. It helped break some of the tension. I slumped back in my chair at my desk, watching her with narrowed eyes. She tossed another insult at me before answering.

"Who is this?" she demanded.

I watched the color drain from her face. She hung up quickly.

"Who was it?" I couldn't help asking.

"N-no one. Mind your own busi—"

The phone rang again.

She glanced down at it, but didn't answer. Her expression was agitated. The ringtone kept playing, an endless loop of some Lady Gaga song, long after it should have gone to voicemail. Cat threw the phone on my bed and backed away toward the door. I could see the caller ID read "Unknown".

"What the hell, Cat?"

"Don't answer it," she said.

But whoever was calling wasn't going to be ignored. There were only so many times I could listen to the same few lines of a song before I snapped. She tried to stop me, but I lunged at the phone and answered it.

"Hello?"

"Catarina?"

That voice. I knew it instantly. I don't think I'll ever forget it.

"Virginia?"

"Th-this is Virginia Press, from school?"

Cat snatched the phone away from me and hung up. She was shaking, caught somewhere between fear and fury.

"It's a prank," she said. "Some sicko trying to make me feel bad."

Her phone went off again. This time she answered immediately.

"I don't know who this is, but if you don't knock it off, I'm calling the co—"

"Shut up!" I could hear Virginia's voice shouting. "You always get to do the talking, but it's my turn now! You're a horrible person, Catarina! You're nasty, and mean, and you make everyone who isn't just like you miserable!"

Cat released a frightened sob and again cut off the call. We looked at one another, uncertain and afraid. Then down to the phone as it rang again. Cat tried to decline the call, but it didn't work. It kept ringing.

"Give it to me!" I said, tearing the battery out of the back.

The screen didn't even flicker.

Ra-ra-ooh-la-la! Want your bad romance!

Cat and I bolted from the room, leaving both phone and battery on the floor behind us. As we ran through the kitchen, the house phone went off. When that was ignored, my own phone followed suit. I tore it from my pocket. The caller came up as "Unknown". I chucked it over my shoulder, and we ran out of the house, tears streaming down our faces.

Mom came home to find us huddled on the front steps, shaking and crying and unable to tell her why. When she tried to get us back in the house, we begged her to take us over to Cat's and stay there for a while. She refused until we told her what was going on.

"Virginia's been calling!" I finally shouted.

Mom was immediately sympathetic. She sat

between us, an arm around each of our shoulders.

"What you've been through was very traumatic, girls. I'm so sorry for that, but you know Virginia can't be calling."

"She was though!" I insisted.

Mom kissed the top of my head. "It was probably just someone who sounded like her and you got scared. That's ok."

"But she said the exact same things!"

"Our brains can trick us when we're afraid, baby, that's all."

"Cat, tell her!"

I looked pleadingly at my cousin, who just shook her head. She'd calmed considerably since Mom came home. Now she looked annoyed at me. "I can't believe I let you get me so worked up over nothing. Your mom's right."

I'd never felt so betrayed. Before I could argue further, Mom handed her car keys to Cat and told her to take me to the pizza place and grab some dinner, her treat. She was too tired from work to join us, but would watch a movie with us when we got home. The last thing I wanted to do was spend more time with Cat, who was now a liar on top of everything else, but I was told in the Mom Voice that it would be fun and I was going.

Grudgingly we agreed, knowing full well Mom wouldn't have it any other way. Mom gave us each a twenty dollar bill and told us to call if we needed anything. She didn't know we both left our phones home.

"Why did you lie?" I asked angrily after we got into the car.

"Because she's right! You were getting scared

and I let it get to me. It was probably a telemarketer or something. I should have known better." Cat didn't look at me as we backed out.

"You were scared first! You heard her. You know it was Virginia! We even took your battery out!"

"Drop it!" she snarled and I shrank away.

We sat in glum silence for most of the ride. Cat kept her eyes locked on the road ahead. Her hands curled into white knuckled fists around the steering wheel. I'd just started to think that maybe they were right and I'd imagined it all. Maybe it really had just been some woman who happened to sound like Virginia. Then the radio clicked on.

"You've made me miserable for so long. I know it was you who made everyone start calling me Virgin. I know it was you who photoshopped those pictures of me, and I *know* it was you who started the rumors about me being a lesbian. I can't go into the locker room or bathroom anymore without people screaming that I'm trying to look at them!"

The car swerved dangerously with Cat's surprise. She pulled over sharply and slammed a hand down on the radio's power button, shutting it off. We didn't look at each other, didn't speak. We just sat there. There was no denying what we'd heard. After a moment of silence, Cat pulled back into traffic and we continued on to the pizza place. The radio stayed off the rest of the way there.

If I tried to speak, Cat would cut me off with a quick, "Shut up!" and I eventually gave up. She parked across the street from the pizza place, shot me a dark, frightened look, and climbed out. I followed mechanically behind.

We'd just been seated at a table and given menus when the restaurant's loudspeaker crackled noisily.

"I just wanted to tell you... I wanted you to know so that you never doubted it...this is all your fault."

Virginia's screaming flooded the room, swallowing all other sound. The other customers went quiet, casting confused looks around while the employees scrambled to shut off the PA system. It didn't matter. I knew what was coming and I threw my hands over my ears so I didn't have to hear it again: the dull, meaty sound of Virginia's body hitting the ground.

Some of the other customers were getting upset, demanding in raised voices to know what was going on. A few got out of their seats and went to the counter, where the unfortunate cashier could only hold up his hands defensively and offer an apology.

Despite my ears being covered, I could still hear Virginia's voice on the loudspeaker.

"... this is all your fault... this is all your fault... this is all your fault."

Cat was gripping the edge of the table, her breathing shallow and quick. She reminded me of a small animal looking to escape a predator. When the screaming started again, she leapt up from her seat and ran from the restaurant. She didn't stop or even slow down. She just ran out into the road, trying to put distance between herself and the sound of Virginia's voice.

I doubted the driver had any time to even see

Cat, much less to avoid her. I could only watch as my cousin bounced off the hood of a passing car and was thrown beneath the wheels of an oncoming SUV.

She came back into view, lying very still in the middle of the road with her back to me. Virginia's screaming immediately stopped, just as mine began.

The December Tapes

Every year on December 12th a new one would arrive. Always in the same bright Christmas wrapping, always unmarked, always left on our front porch.

They started coming a year after my sister, Libby, disappeared.

She was last seen walking home from the elementary school in her favorite bright purple jacket with the faux fur hood. It was only a couple blocks, a walk she'd made hundreds of times. Our mom was standing at the foot of our driveway to keep an eye out for her. No one knows for sure what happened in the ten minutes it should have taken Libby to get home; we only know that she never made it.

I remember lying in bed that night, listening to my dad trying to keep his voice steady while he spoke to the cops. Mom made phone call after phone call to Libby's friends, and our neighbors, and all the local stores, just in case she'd decided to take an uncharacteristic detour and lost track of time.

Our quiet life quickly became media fodder. It was surreal and upsetting to see my nine year old sister's latest school portrait grinning at me from the TV screen on the evening news, to hear her name spoken on the radio. My parents gave interviews and pleaded for anyone with information to come forward, which only resulted in dead ends and prank calls. There were reporters stationed outside our house for a week, just waiting to pounce with their invasive questions.

Slowly, the attention began to fade. A missing girl only kept people interested for so long. When no new leads appeared, they moved on. The reporters gave up first, then the cops, and then our neighbors, until at last only my family was still looking.

"We'll keep it open, but inactive," we were told over the phone by a sympathetic sounding desk sergeant. "It" being my sister's case file. She didn't even have a name to them anymore.

The first year after Libby disappeared went slowly. My parents did their best to keep things normal for me, but it always felt thin, fragile, strained. Normal now meant pretending I didn't notice Mom staring at the seat where Libby used to sit every night for dinner. It meant tiptoeing back down the hall so my dad didn't know I saw him standing in the middle of her room, her favorite stuffed toy hugged against his chest. It meant dreading her birthday and holidays because they were now razor sharp reminders of loss.

It meant trying to cope without my little sister, and there were some days I wondered how anything would ever feel right again.

Then on December 12th, exactly one year after she went missing, a package arrived on our doorstep.

It was wrapped in sparkly red paper and tied off with a bright purple ribbon. There was no card or name tag attached, just the box, but Mom brought it inside anyway. She figured it was from one of our neighbors just trying to spread a little Christmas spirit. It was the first gift we'd gotten. She put it aside and set about making dinner, careful to keep her back to me so I might not notice she was crying. I noticed anyway, and any tiny speck of holiday cheer I might have been feeling was swept away.

The package sat on our kitchen counter, unopened until dad got home.

"Go ahead and open it, Phin," Dad said with a tired smile after asking what it was.

With as much enthusiasm as I could muster, I tore into the wrapping paper and pulled open the small cardboard box within. Sitting inside, nestled on a bed of red and green tissue paper, was a cassette tape.

Curious, I ran to my room for my boombox and lugged it back to the kitchen. I popped open the front and dropped the cassette into its player, filling the room with my sister's terrified, desperate screams.

"Mommy," she wailed from the speakers. "Daddy!"

We all sat in stunned silence for a moment before my dad leapt at the boombox and tore the tape out.

I listened to that cassette many times in the following days. First from just outside the kitchen, when my parents played it in full after they thought I'd gone to my room, and then a second time when the police came. Snippets were released to re-generate interest in the case, and I heard them again on the news and the radio. Once again, Libby

Helmer was a household name for another couple of weeks. No matter how many times I heard it, though, it never got any easier.

Libby screaming for our parents, the gut wrenching fear in her voice, the way she sobbed and begged to go home, and behind it all, a soft voice that just kept saying, "Shhh, shhh."

Nothing came of it except more heartbreak. There were no prints, no DNA, nothing to trace the package or its contents. All we were left with was Libby's terrified voice.

The only solace we could take from it was the possibility that Libby was still alive somewhere. Mom and Dad redoubled their search efforts and upped the reward offered for Libby's safe return. Another year came and went without any new information, until December 12th was upon us again.

For the second year in a row, we received another cassette tape.

"Hi Mommy and Daddy and Phin," Libby said from the boombox once we'd gathered enough courage to hit play. She sounded tired, the kind of tired that resonates from deep down; the kind no kid should be familiar with. "I miss you. I hope I can come home soon, but I don't know. I think about you lots. I hope you think about me too." Her voice cracked, and I bit down hard on the inside of my cheek to keep from doing the same. "Smiling Thom says I've been a good girl. He wanted you to know that."

The tape ended.

Again, we went to the police, and again, nothing came of it. Even with the inclusion of a name, this *Smiling Thom*, they weren't able to dig up anything that might help us find Libby. All we had to hold us over for another year was her sad, small voice.

The third tape arrived, right on time, the next year. Libby's voice sounded a little older, but it was still recognizably her's.

"Hi, it's me. You remember me, right? I try to draw you lots so I don't forget you, but it's getting harder. Smiling Thom says that's just the way it goes. I asked him for a picture of you, but he hasn't brought me one yet. He said if I was really good, he will, and I've tried to be. I dunno if he will though. I want to go home. Smiling Thom said maybe next year. He says that a lot. I love you."

It hit me then that it was getting harder for me to remember her too. Not just what she looked like, but the sound of her voice, the things she liked, and the way she laughed. While my parents played and re-played the tape, desperately listening for any clues about Libby's whereabouts, I went and dug out her baby book. I spent the rest of the night studying her face and all the little notes that Mom had put in the margins.

I fell asleep with the book clutched against my stomach, tears staining my face.

It was another long year with no answers.

For four more years, we waited for December 12th to arrive with a strange combination of hope and horror. We fed off those tapes, used them to get us through another 365 days with the belief that Libby was still alive. We dreaded them too, but we dreaded the December 12th that we opened our door to find nothing even more.

Every tape followed a similar pattern: she'd tell us she missed us, that she wanted to come home, and that she thought about us. In some tapes she'd ask questions like whether we still thought of her. She'd tell us that Smiling Thom said she'd been good again.

She sounded more different in every one: older, more articulate, but always sad, always tired. It was like listening to my sister grow up in sound bites when I played the tapes back to back.

There was never anything new in them. We kept bringing them to the cops, but it felt more like a hollow effort each time. Dad finally stopped notifying the cops altogether; we gave up on them the same as they'd done with Libby.

"We're not giving up though," Dad said. "We're just on our own now."

Another year passed. We put up posters, we shot local commercials, we gathered volunteers and combed wider and wider areas. It was obvious that those who joined us were doing it more for solidarity than out of any actual belief we would find Libby. Even when we played the tapes for people, they didn't seem quite convinced that the girl they were hearing was my sister

Eight years since Libby disappeared, and the only people who still thought she might come home were me and my parents.

Until we got the tape that year.

Mom stood over the table, staring at the still wrapped box for a long moment. Her eyes were glassy, her lips trembling. She shook her head.

"I can't," she said weakly. "I can't listen to another one. I don't even know her voice anymore.

What kind of mother am I? What kind of mother doesn't even recognize her own child's voice? Just take it away; put it back! Put it back! I don't want it in this house!"

She started to sink to the floor. Dad hurried around the table to catch her.

"Just do it, Phin!" he shouted over his shoulder.

The pain I saw on both their faces, still so raw after so long, drove me to grab up the box and run to the front door. I dumped it back on the porch and left it to sit in the gathering snow. I didn't think about it at the time; if I had, I would have hidden the box in my room or just tucked in a drawer somewhere. In that moment, though, I just did what Mom said. I got it out of the house.

Once Mom calmed down, I had no doubt that I'd be told to retrieve it again. We'd listen to it the same as we did with all the others. Neither of my parents would miss the chance to hear their Libby's voice.

It was only an hour later when I was instructed to go get the tape. Mom apologized, saying that she was ready. When I opened the front door, the package was gone though, and no amount of searching made it reappear.

We assumed some opportunistic low life looking to steal Christmas gifts had taken it. We tried to console one another with reassurances that there would be another tape the next year, but it didn't really help. Mom blamed herself, I blamed myself, and Dad was just caught up in his grief over not getting to hear his little girl. We thought about filing another police report, but after all the previous dead ends, we decided against it.

We'd just have to try and wait until the next December 12th.

We didn't put up posters, or launch search parties, or do anything else to look for Libby that year. It was too exhausting, too expensive, too heartbreaking. Mom was especially fragile after the loss of the last tape. There was nothing we hadn't tried, and it had all ended in failure. We just needed some time to recoup and collect ourselves before we began the search again.

I was woken up the morning of the next December 12th by a muffled thud coming from downstairs. It was early, still dark, and I almost rolled over and went back to sleep until I remembered what day it was.

I was up and out of bed instantly.

My parents' bedroom door was still closed. Their light was off when I hurried past on tiptoes. I was relieved, in a way. It was always hard to get the tapes, but seeing what it did to my parents just made it harder. If I could listen to it alone first, it might make it less horrible somehow.

It didn't occur to me until I was opening the front door that the tapes had only ever arrived the evening before. By then I'd already seen the package, and I knew immediately that something was very wrong.

Instead of a small box, this one was large. Very large. It was still wrapped in the same bright paper and tied off with a purple ribbon, but this year, there was a card on top. I instinctively closed the door behind me before moving toward it. It felt like I was doing something wrong as I reached for the card.

Only 9 years before you gave up. I had hoped for better from you. She was such a good girl.

The message was written in thin, slanted letters, ending in a hand-drawn smiley face.

A slow boiling queasiness started in my stomach. I let the card slip through my fingers to the ground. I grabbed the edge of the large box and started to peel back the paper. The box beneath was plain white and covered by a lid.

I paused, panting, sweating despite the cold. My heart hammering against my chest, I fought back the bile rising in my throat.

I could only bring myself to lift the lid ever so slightly, just enough to peek inside. Just enough to see the thin brown hair and pale face with its slack jaw and sightless eyes staring back at me from within a bed of red and green tissue paper. Just enough to see the edge of a bright purple coat wrapped around her emaciated body.

Just enough to see that Libby had finally come home.

Smidge

The steak was the first thing to go missing. I'd left it to defrost in the fridge overnight, but by morning, only the empty plate remained. I asked my husband Connor about it, but he said he hadn't touched it. Our seven year old son Jamie was so thoroughly grossed out by raw meat that I didn't bother questioning him. It was a mystery I wasn't sure would ever be solved; the kind that would no doubt be a funny story to tell at family get-togethers in the future.

Then the sausages vanished a few days later, followed by a couple of chicken quarters some time after that. A whole spiral cut ham I'd been planning to cook for Connor's birthday dinner followed.

"I swear, babe, I don't know what's going on," Connor said, gazing down at the empty space where the the ham had been.

We decided it could only be one of two things: either we had a very single-minded thief breaking in every couple of nights, or Jamie had suddenly gotten over his aversion to raw meat.

"But what would he even be doing with it?" I asked.

I couldn't imagine why a seven year old would start hoarding food out of the blue. He was well fed at every meal, had access to snacks when he asked for them, and never went to bed hungry. It baffled both of us.

Connor shook his head. "Only one way to find out."

When Jamie came home from school that afternoon, we all sat at the kitchen table, our usual spot for serious Family Discussions. Jamie kept his gaze on his lap where his little hands twisted nervously around one another.

"I think you know what we're going to ask you," Connor said.

Jamie half-shrugged.

"James." Connor tapped the tabletop with his index finger. "Look at us."

Our son glanced out of the corner of his eyes at us, guilt stamped across his features.

"You wanna tell us what's been going on with the meat?" I asked, matching Connor's stern but still gentle tone. When Jamie didn't answer, I added, "We know you took it."

"Sorry," Jamie mumbled.

"We just want to know why, little man," Connor said. "This isn't like you. You hate even looking at raw meat!"

"It's not for me," Jamie replied.

"It was for all of us," I said.

"But we had a lot, and he didn't have any. He didn't like when I tried to give him leftovers!"

"Who?" Connor and I frowned toward one another.

"Smidge."

"What?"

"Smidge lives under the house and likes meat. He's good and doesn't bother anybody!"

Connor and I exchanged another glance, this

one tinged with relief. A stray animal hiding under the house was far preferable to some of the other possibilities that had popped into my head.

We asked Jamie if Smidge was a dog or a cat, maybe even a raccoon. He was either unable or unwilling to give us an answer.

"He stays in the back, in the shadows. It's hard to see him, but he makes happy noises when I visit and he likes when I talk to him."

After assuring him we weren't mad at him *or* Smidge, Jamie opened up a bit. He'd seen something crawling under a gap in the lattice work on the porch when he was playing outside a couple weeks before. Just a brief glimpse, and with all the infinite wisdom of a child, he'd decided to follow it. He claimed it dug a deep hole in the far corner where it was darkest and mostly stayed there when he visited.

"He growled at first, but I kept talking to him and then I fed him. Now he likes me!"

"When do you go visit him, kiddo?" I asked.

"After you and Daddy are in bed. It was so I could feed him! He was very hungry."

Connor and I made Jamie agree to stop bringing food to Smidge and put an end to their nighttime visits until we determined exactly what the critter was. Jamie pouted and kicked his feet, but promised he'd keep his distance from his newfound friend. To keep him honest, we even went through the fridge and made note of what was there, just in case anything went missing.

"What do we do, call animal control?" I asked while Connor and I got ready for bed.

"Not yet. I'll get under there in the morning,

see what it is. If it's a dog or something, maybe we can consider keeping it."

"I dunno," I replied doubtfully. I didn't want to get stuck taking on all the responsibilities of a pet that should have been Jamie's.

"He's already done a pretty good job keeping it fed," Connor pointed out with a cheeky grin.

I rolled my eyes and told him to turn off the light.

The next morning, I took Jamie to school while Connor crawled under the house to see if he could locate the mysterious Smidge. A tiny kitten, black and fluffy and purring wildly, was waiting for me in the bathroom when I got home.

"*This* is Smidge?" I laughed as it rubbed against my ankles. "Jamie thought this little guy needed a whole ham?"

"I guess," Connor said. "Cute, isn't he?"

"Adorable."

"Jamie must have been cleaning up after him because there's no bones or anything left under the house. Thank God; I can only imagine what that would have smelled like."

"And the hole?"

"It's just where he said it was. Looked pretty deep, probably been used by other critters before Smidge. I'll fill it when I've got more time, but I really have to get to work."

We traded quick kisses before he hurried off to change and leave.

Smidge turned out to be a clingy, affectionate kitten who yowled every time I left the bathroom. I made some calls and found a vet who could see us in short order. Smidge was less than thrilled when I zipped him up in an old handbag and drove him over.

He was given a few shots, a thorough exam, and finally declared completely healthy. I was surprised to find how happy that made me; I'd only had him for a short time, but I was already falling in love. It was hard not to when he looked up at me with those big amber eyes, his whole body rumbling with never-ending purrs. I had a feeling it was going to be an easy choice when it came to deciding whether to keep him.

Back at home, I put Smidge in the bathroom. I set out to kitten-proof our house as best I could before running to the store for some supplies. I snapped a picture of Smidge in his new bed once I got back and texted it to Connor. He replied almost immediately.

Soooo I guess we have a cat now lol

I sent him another picture of Smidge flopped over in my lap as confirmation.

Jamie was going to be thrilled!

I could barely contain my excitement when I went to pick Jamie up from school. I almost blurted out that we'd found Smidge and that he could stay, but decided it would be more fun to let it be a surprise.

Smidge's cries for attention from the bathroom greeted us as soon as we walked in the front door.

"What's that?" Jamie asked, looking to me.

"Go look!"

With less enthusiasm than I had expected, Jamie went to the bathroom and opened it up. Smidge came darting out immediately.

"We found him!" I said, scooping the kitten up

S.H. Cooper

to offer him to Jamie. "We're going to keep him."

"Who?" Jamie looked from me to the kitten and back.

"Smidge?" I replied with some uncertainty.

"That's not Smidge. He's bigger than that."

"But he was under the house, near where you said…"

Jamie dropped his gaze. His hands started to wring in front of him, his tell that he was trying to hide something.

"What is it?"

"Nothing," he said, but it was hardly believable.

"Jamie," I pressed in my Mom Voice.

"I found the kitten last night," he admitted slowly. "It was in the front yard."

"You were outside again?"

"Yeah."

"James!"

"Sorry! But I knew Smidge would be hungry and—"

"We talked about this!"

"But I didn't give him any of our food!"

"Then what were you doing out there?"

Jamie hung his head and shuffled his feet. I had to keep probing and prodding until he finally broke down and answered me.

"I was checking on Smidge and telling him I was sorry that I didn't have food. Then I found the kitten and I… put it under the house. For Smidge."

I couldn't stop my mouth from hanging open.

My son, my little man, had tried to *feed* a live kitten to whatever was under the house?

"He must've still been full from the ham

~62~

though," Jamie mumbled.

Not knowing what else to do, I told him to go do his homework while I started dinner. I couldn't wait for Connor to get home so we could talk this over together. Kitten Smidge wound around my feet, meowing and purring and kneading at my pant legs. I stared blankly down at him, wondering what had been going through Jamie's head.

Connor barely managed to get through the door before I grabbed his arm and dragged him to our room, telling him what our son told me.

"He wanted Smidge to eat the kitten?" Connor paused in the middle of removing his tie.

"Yeah, that's what he said."

"I... don't know how to feel about that. I mean, it's not like he was torturing it or anything."

"I know, but it's *weird*, isn't it? For a little boy to try and make one animal eat another?"

"It's nature, I guess? I don't know, Audrey. It definitely feels weird. Look, let's have dinner, think a bit, and regroup after. We can talk to him once we've figured things out better on our end."

It was a quiet meal. Jamie seemed to sense the tension and kept his head down while Connor and I were lost in our own thoughts.

I wondered if I was overreacting. Was it the big deal I was making it out to be? Then I'd look down at Kitten Smidge, threading himself through chair legs and swatting playfully at our toes, and I'd wonder how Jamie could have looked at that same creature as food? I *knew* that animals eating animals was, as Connor said, nature, but that didn't make me feel any better about it.

When we were done, Jamie asked if he could

go play with some of the other neighborhood kids.

"Yeah, just don't go under the house, ok? Not until your dad and I can check out the real Smidge."

He nodded and darted outside.

Connor and I remained quiet while we washed dishes. I absently watched Jamie running around the house with Maya and A.J. from next door. He looked so carefree and innocent in the orange glow of dusk.

He didn't understand what he was doing. He was just trying to take care of Smidge, whatever Smidge was, and that wasn't a bad thing, really.

A dog, probably. Hopefully.

Connor came to a similar conclusion by the time we'd taken a seat in the living room to discuss it.

"Kids are impulsive. They don't think things through. It wasn't about hurting the kitten, it was about helping Smidge," Connor said.

"I think so, too. We just need to talk about what he should have done differently."

It was going to be an odd, possibly uncomfortable, conversation, but we both knew we had to have it. We sat back with matching sighs, glad that we could navigate through this often strange land of Parenthood together.

We were feeling better, more relaxed, like we had a handle on things. Then the screaming started.

We almost tripped over each other running out the door.

By the time we rounded the corner it was coming from, it had stopped.

Jamie pulled himself out from under the

house. I grabbed him by his shoulders, looking him over for any sign of injury.

"What is it? What happened?" Connor and I asked.

"I wanted to show them Smidge," he said with an eerie calm.

"Who? Maya and AJ?" Connor started to look around. "Where are they? James?"

Jamie looked toward the gap in the lattice work.

"Oh God," Connor breathed, "are they under ther—"

His question was cut off by the sound of wet tearing. Then long, slow crunching.

Connor staggered back a step and I had to put a hand over my mouth to keep from being sick.

Jamie looked solemnly up at us: so carefree, so innocent.

"Guess Smidge wasn't full anymore."

The Ringing In My Ear

I remember the day I started to lose my hearing. I remember it because two things happened the day before: I'd received a particularly painful numbing injection at the dentist's office, and my daughter was raped and left for dead in a dumpster just outside her college campus.

We got the call at 4 AM. Being woken like that by a shrill ringing in the otherwise quiet dark is something no one should have to experience. You know before you pick up that something life changing is about to be dropped in your lap, and all you can do is let it happen.

"Mr. Barrister?" the voice on the other end said. "I'm sorry to call at this hour. It's about your daughter."

I'll never forget those words, or the icy way they wrapped around my heart. My daughter, my baby girl. I looked at my wife, she looked back at me, and she knew. If I never again hear the sound she made then, I will consider myself blessed.

In the flurry of packing and finding a flight to Emily, amid all of the gut wrenching worry, I didn't even notice it at first. It wasn't until we were in the air and Helena was whispering prayers under her breath that I heard it: a high pitched keen in my left ear that came in short beeps. It reminded me of hearing test tones.

I stuck my finger in my ear and wiggled it around, trying to lessen the sound. It remained: incessant, irritating, and beeping.

It was pushed to the back of my mind the moment we landed. We raced from the airport to the hospital where Emily was lying unconscious with a row of machines standing vigil at her bedside. I'd seen them countless times before, I knew what they each did and why they were attached to her. They were strange mechanical monstrosities in that moment however, making her look so small and frail.

As we sat there, stroking her hair and telling her how we loved her, I had a flashback to the only other time Emily had been in a hospital. She'd been six, maybe seven, and it was bedtime. She wanted to stay up longer like her older brother, but I told her to stop jumping on her bed and to settle down for sleep. I turned my back for just a minute, I don't even remember why, and she slipped. Blood poured out of a nasty gash over her eye where she'd struck the headboard, then suddenly she was screaming.

After we'd calmed her down and got a look at the wound, we'd agreed she'd need stitches. While Helena got her dressed, I called the hospital where I worked as an anesthetist to let one of my doctor buddies know I was coming. Helena stayed home with our son while I took Emily in.

"Is it gonna hurt?" Emily had asked from the backseat. She was staring at me in the rearview mirror, one eye covered by the cloth she pressed against her forehead.

"No, I'll make sure it doesn't."

"How?" My little girl, ever the skeptic.

"Remember how we talked about how Daddy makes people go to sleep for his job?" It had become something of a joke in our house; better behave or Daddy'll put you to sleep...*forever*!

"Yeah?"

"Sometimes I only make *part* of a person fall asleep. That way the nice doctors can make them better and they don't even feel it!"

"You're gonna do that to me?"

"Yep."

"And you're gonna stay with me the whole time?"

"Of course."

She barely winced when I injected the local anesthetic, and she'd fallen asleep during the actual stitches.

Emily was a tough little girl.

She was a tougher young woman.

It took her three days to wake up this time. The hearing in my left ear faded until the only thing I could hear with absolute clarity was that high pitched ringing I'd first noticed on the plane.

Beep. Beep. Beep.

I couldn't worry about it just then. Not when my family needed me so badly. I didn't mention it to anyone.

Emily's recovery was a slow process. She claimed not to remember who attacked her, and she couldn't offer any description or statement to the police. She was tightlipped about what happened, even with her mother, with whom she'd shared everything. My carefree, forever smiling daughter was now haunted, and every time she looked at me, there was such pain etched deeply into her eyes.

I'd never felt so helpless or hollow.

After she was released from the hospital, she quietly withdrew from school and moved back in with me and her mother. She spent most of her days shut in her room.

All the while, the deafness and ringing in my ear continued.

Beep. Beep. Beep.

I put off going to get it checked out. I figured it was some kind of screw up from the dentist's injection and that there wasn't much that could be done anyway. It would be almost impossible to prove.

My focus was entirely on Emily and helping her in any way I could, my own issues be damned. We got her into therapy, we researched healing techniques, we devoted ourselves entirely to her physical and mental health in every way she would allow. It took months before she started to smile again. Then the night terrors started to recede, and, piece by piece, our Emily started coming back to us.

We'd just started discussing whether she felt comfortable enough to return to school when things began to unravel.

Emily came to the hospital where I worked to have lunch with me. We sat in the cafeteria, our trays of food untouched while we talked about what courses she might take. She was in the middle of telling me about a genealogy class she was interested in when she froze mid-sentence, the color draining from her face.

"Kiddo? You ok?"

I followed her fixed stare back to the register line where a trio of people were waiting to pay for their food. I looked back to her.

"I need to go," she said suddenly.

"What's wro—"

"Love you, Dad."

She practically ran out of the cafeteria.

I turned back to the three at the register. Two I recognized, the chief of medicine and an oncologist, but the third I didn't know. He was a young man around Emily's age, and the passing resemblance he bore the chief led me to believe he was a relative of some sort, probably his grandson.

The longer I looked at him, the louder the ringing in my ear became.

Beep. Beep. Beep.

When I got home that night, Emily was sitting on the back porch, staring vacantly while our dogs wandered about the yard. She jumped when I opened the slider and took a seat next to her.

"You ok?" I asked.

"Yeah," she said.

The silence that fell between us was heavy.

"About today..." I started to say.

"Victor," she said quietly.

I didn't say anything, afraid to interrupt and cause her to shut down again.

"He goes to the same university. We had a biology class together." Every word sounded like it was being torn forcibly out of her. "We found out we're from the same area, so we talked a few times about classes and how you and his Grandpa work for the same place. Then we...traded pictures and stuff."

"And stuff" was clearly things that no father ever wants to think of his daughter doing. I just nodded.

"It was going too fast, so I...I told him I wanted to just be friends again. He didn't like that. He told me if I didn't do what he wanted, he'd share the pictures I sent him." Her voice cracked, and she turned away from me. "That's illegal now in a lot of places, and I said I'd make sure he got in trouble. He got angry."

Victor cornered her outside a club and tried to get her to go home with him. When she refused, he became violent. He dragged her into alleyway and attacked her.

"He said if I ever told, he'd share all of our texts so people would know I wanted it. He said he'd make sure you were fired, and that your career would be over." Emily was shaking with sobs. "His grandpa's the chief of medicine, he could've done it!"

I pulled her in close and held her while she cried. No matter how much I tried to tell her that we needed to call the police, she refused.

"I can't, Dad," she said. "He has texts and pictures. No one would believe me."

The next day at work, I went straight to the chief of medicine's office. I didn't know what I was going to do or say, I just had to do *something*. I had barely knocked on the door when he called me in.

Before I could speak, Dr. Gladson looked up and said, "Oh, good, Martha found you. I wanted to talk to you about my grandson, Vic. He's having surgery this afternoon, nothing too serious, but I'd like you to be his anesthetist. I'd ask Taylor, but he's already scheduled."

I almost said no. I almost shouted that his damn grandson was a monster. I almost told him I'd sooner see him dead.

Instead, I took a deep breath and said, "Of course."

"Good. It's at 2:30 with Dr. Lim."

As I turned to leave, the ringing in my left ear seemed so loud that it was almost throbbing.

Beep. Beep. Beep.

At 2:30, as promised, I was seated at the head of the surgery table behind the ether screen. Victor, a good looking kid with a cocksure attitude about him, was lying in front of me.

"Hello, Victor," I said.

"Hi."

He wasn't at all nervous, which told me he didn't know who I was. It didn't surprise me. Not many people bothered to learn the anesthetist's name.

"Is this your first surgery?"

"Nope."

"So you know how anesthesia works?"

"Count back from ten, yeah."

"Yes."

I made small talk while I set up, asking him about where he went to school and what he was majoring in. When it came time to put on his mask and count down, I asked him one more question.

10

"I think you might know my daughter."

9

"Yeah?"

8

"Yeah. Emily."

7

"Oh yeah, I think so."

6

"She ever tell you what I do for a living?"

5

"Maybe?" He was getting drowsy.

4

"I put people to sleep for a living, Vic." I was whispering.

3

"Huh?" He was struggling to stay awake.

2

"Sometimes permanently."

1

The beeping in my ear was especially loud. I slowly realized that it was echoing. I looked up at his heart monitor, sitting not too far over my head. It beeped in time with the ringing in my ear.

Beep. Beep. Beep.

The surgery went well for about twenty minutes, until Victor experienced a sudden drop in blood pressure. The shock to his system sent him into a violent seizing fit. The surgeon was barking orders, demanding this and that to stabilize the boy.

But there was nothing that could be done.

Anesthesia overdoses can be such terrible, tricky things. The staff struggled to revive him, and I made a show of doing the same. The steady rhythm of the ringing in my ear changed for the first time.

Beep. Beep. Beep. Beeeeeeep.

Victor was pronounced dead at 3:02 PM.

At the same time the heart monitor was turned off, the ringing in my ear ceased. Sound returned in a loud, almost painful burst.

I was glad for the surgical mask as they covered Victor with the white sheet.

No one could see that I was smiling.

Through The Peephole

We got the Peephole doorbell camera at my husband, Reg's, insistence.

It started when we both got promotions at work. With it came pay raises, which then meant we could afford our very first house together. It was a cute little bungalow on a street of similar starter homes. The house would require some effort and elbow grease before it reached its full potential, but that was fine by me. Anything was better than the apartment we were getting out of.

Along with the upgrade in our living situation, we also had a bit of play money left over. Reg was finally able to get himself a noisy little car that he could compete in amateur races with. We were both excited for him to be able to pursue one of his longtime interests, although it did mean he'd be going out of town on a pretty regular basis to participate in events.

Between the new place and his travel schedule, Reg worried about me being nervous on my own. It didn't help that we had a few instances of ding-dong-ditch shortly after we moved in. The perpetrator was always gone by the time Reg opened the door, but it still put him on edge.

I rolled my eyes a bit at his concern. The area was known to be pretty safe, and I had two dogs and a cat-who-thought-he-was-a-dog to keep me company. He suggested getting a doorbell camera for his own peace of mind, and I went along with it.

If it made him feel better and helped discourage pranksters, then I didn't see an issue.

The device was actually pretty neat. It linked up to an app on our phones that alerted us when someone triggered the motion detector or rang the bell. Then we could bring up a live feed on the screen to see who was there and speak to them through the Peephole's intercom. It also recorded any activity, allowing us to go back and review it later.

It certainly came in handy for checking on deliveries and making sure we didn't open the door to any faith peddlers. It seemed to solve our pesky problem with late night doorbell ringers too. We didn't have any more "mysteriously" vanishing visitors for the next couple of weeks.

When it came time for Reg to do his first full weekend race, it helped put him at ease to know I wouldn't have to open the door to any strangers.

"If all goes well, I won't be back until Sunday evening," he reminded me again as I helped him load his equipment into the back of his car.

The sun wasn't even up yet and I was still half asleep, but he was practically thrumming with nervous, excited energy.

"I know," I said, suppressing a grin, "but if you mess up, you could be home as early as tonight. No drug fueled orgies with hookers for me then, got it."

He made a face and I returned it. Then we kissed and he climbed into the car. I cringed when it roared into life. The unnecessarily loud metal beast was right at home on the track, but a bit less welcome at 5:30 am in the suburbs. I shooed him off, still hearing the growling and popping in the distance even after he'd turned off our street. I shook my head, hoping he'd not woken every neighbor in a five mile radius.

I was met inside by our dogs, Beauty and Merry, and our cat, Goblin, all crowded around the door and impatiently waiting for breakfast. It was certainly hard to feel the least bit alone when I was surrounded by so many wagging tails and nudges for attention. After feeding them, I went back to bed, grateful to Past Me for deciding to take that Friday off so I could enjoy a nice, long weekend.

It didn't get much more exciting than that for the most part. I remained in my PJs long after I finally got up for good, ate far too much junk food, and watched terrible reality TV shows in between going into our fenced backyard to play with the dogs. Reg and I texted throughout; he'd update me on his race times and his current standing, and I'd encourage him and send him pictures of the pets in return.

It was an entirely lazy day, one of the few I allowed myself, and it was glorious.

That night I snuggled on the couch, Beauty at my feet, Merry on my lap, and Goblin curled in a little ball on my chest. I was watching a chick flick, a guilty pleasure that I only partook when my husband wasn't home. My conversation with Reg had drifted into silence, as it usually did when he became caught up with his buddies or was working on his car, and I'd left my phone on the kitchen counter. I absently stroked Goblin along his back and allowed myself to get caught up in the cute, but contrived, movie I'd selected.

We'd made it about halfway through the film when Merry's head shot up off my knees and turned sharply toward the front door. His ears perked forward. He was stiff, attentive, listening for something. Then came a soft growl from the back of his throat.

Beauty, woken by her brother, followed his gaze. After a moment, she got up and slowly approached the door. She sniffed around the threshold briefly, the hair all along her spine rising as she was backed away. Head still held low, she also started growling. Even Goblin, never one to pay attention to visitors, was sitting upright on me and staring unblinkingly.

"What is it, babies?" I asked softly, not entirely concerned with their behavior.

There'd been a raccoon lurking about the last couple of weeks. I thought it might be wandering about outside, just close enough to the house to get the dogs going.

When Merry growled again, louder and more forceful this time, a nervous knot began to twist in my stomach. Beauty came to stand beside the couch again, her hackles still raised. She looked up at me and whined. I laid a hand on her head in an attempt to reassure her.

The doorbell went off and I jumped. It seemed even louder by how unexpected it was. I Immediately suspected the same damn ding-dong-ditchers who'd been harassing us before we installed our Peephole.

"Hey, Elaina?" Reg's voice came from outside, soft and apologetic. "You awake? I locked my keys in the car and can't get in."

I relaxed immediately with a relieved exhale. The race must not have gone his way and he'd been eliminated in the first stages. Unlucky for him, but I was always happy to have him back earlier than expected.

"Doofus," I replied loudly enough for him to hear. "I'm coming."

I started to pick Goblin up, but he sank his claws through my top and into my chest, clinging to me. Merry and Beauty launched themselves at the door, pawing and snarling madly.

"Get down!" I shouted at them, trying to untangle myself from Goblin's painful clutches. "Damnit! Hold on, Reg. The kids are being nuts!"

The more I tried to disentangle myself from Goblin, the more he clung to me. He started yowling in defiant protest, which only drove the dogs deeper into their frenzy.

"Get off!" I snapped at the cat, who hissed in my face in return.

I finally managed to peel him off and set him down on the couch, although I was sure it hadn't been without some bloodshed on my part. I took a step toward the door. As I neared, Beauty turned and whined pleadingly. Merry kept right on barking and clawing at the door with all his forty pounds of fury.

"One more sec, babe," I said, reaching for Merry.

He turned and snapped at me, his teeth barely missing my fingers—the first time he's done that in all his eight years. I drew back, my hand held protectively close to my chest, gaping at him in shock. He went right back to practically attacking the door.

Reg rang the doorbell again.

"It's freezing out here, let me in!"

But I couldn't stop staring at Merry. Then at Beauty, huddled at my side. Over my shoulder at Goblin, perched on the arm of the couch, poised as if he meant to jump on my back.

Then it occurred to me. In all of the noise and commotion, I hadn't heard Reg's car.

That loud, rumbling, popping piece of junk that should have announced his arrival from blocks away.

"Elaina!" Reg yelled again, but this time, I took a step away from the door.

With Beauty pressed so close to my legs that I almost tripped, I tiptoed over to the kitchen counter where I'd left my phone to open the Peephole app.

The front of the house was dark except for the single solar spotlight pointed at the door. It was dim now, but still enough to illuminate Reg's familiar frame standing in front of the doorbell. I watched as he lifted his hand, balled into a fist, and brought it down against the door.

"Elaina!"

It was my husband. It had to be. Why, then, was I suddenly feeling so uneasy? Why were our animals, who had never been anything less than thrilled when he came home, suddenly turning on me?

I minimized the app and dialed Reg's number. While it rang on speaker, I returned to Peephole, watching him intently. He was standing there with his hands shoved into his jacket pockets, shifting his weight from foot to foot.

He was still standing just like that when Reg answered his phone.

"Hey, babe, what's up?"

"You're not home," I whispered. It wasn't a question.

"No, I'm doing well! We just finished and I qualified for tomorrow's round. Why? What's up?"

On the screen, the man outside my door rang the bell again.

"Elaina?" Reg's voice sounded concerned. "Was that the doorbell? Is someone there?"

"Yeah," I could barely get the word out.

"Who?"

"You."

I'm not sure he really heard what I said because of how quiet I'd become. He must have heard how loud Merry continued to be, but I'm certain he recognized the raw fear which crept into my tone.

Reg told me to hang up and call the cops. He was a few hours away, but he'd be home as soon as possible. I tried to argue. I didn't want to stop talking to him, but he assured me that I could call back as soon as the cops were there.

As I was hanging up, a long, slow series of knocks sounded against the front door.

"Elaina," I heard the man say in Reg's voice. "Let me in."

"I'm calling the cops!" I shouted back over Merry's wild barks.

"Let me in."

When I glanced down at my phone again, I

saw Reg's face: white and blank, filling up the screen, almost as if he was staring through the Peephole.

Almost as if he was staring at me.

He looked so much like my husband that I might have second guessed myself, even after our phone call, had it not been for his eyes: two black voids where Reg's hazel ones should have been.

A scream, high pitched and short, escaped me before I clamped my mouth shut again. The man straightened without expression and rang the doorbell again.

"I promise I won't run away this time. I've waited so long for you to be alone," he said. "Open the door, Elaina."

Run away this time, I heard him say over and over again in my head.

All those previous nights when someone had rung our door and run. We'd assumed it was bored kids, just harmless, but annoying, fun. We thought it was a prank.

Now the only thing I was certain of was that it was anything but a joke.

"Go away!" I screeched at my phone, which sent both Merry and Beauty into a renewed fit of howling.

Goblin hissed and swiped the air with his claws.

The man with my husband's face looked down at the Peephole again, turned, and walked slowly out of view.

I gripped my phone in both hands, studying the screen with a thudding heart.

Everything outside was dark and still and

quiet. Then the tapping began against the front window behind the TV. The soft *tink, tink* of nails against glass.

In one movement I shoved my phone in my pocket, grabbed Goblin under one arm, hauled the still barking Merry under the other, and called for Beauty to follow me as I ran for the bedroom.

Behind us, the window erupted inwards.

I slammed the bedroom door closed and tossed Goblin onto the bed just long enough to lock it. I could faintly hear the sound of more glass shattering while I called 911.

I barely started to tell the operator what was going on when something slammed into the bedroom door, causing the heavy wood to rattle in its frame.

"He's in the house!" I screamed into the phone. "Please, hurry!"

Merry and Beauty stood side by side in front of me, teeth bared, ears pinned back. Goblin was on the nightstand behind me with his back arched and claws out. The door shuddered again. I pressed myself against the side of my bed, pleading with the dispatcher to get someone over to us.

A long crack spider-webbed its way up the middle of the door under the third blow.

I grabbed the dogs to keep them from charging at it and held them close even as they struggled to get in front of me.

I screamed. Somewhere in the distance, a siren sounded, almost as if in response. And then another.

The assault on my bedroom door stopped.

There was no trace of any man, one with Reg's

face or otherwise, in the house when the cops arrived moments later. Just me, my pets, and a number of broken windows and a badly damaged bedroom door to tell the tale.

They believed readily enough that someone had attempted to attack me. They even believed that he'd been watching the house, ringing the doorbell and then hiding to check who answered. They had a harder time believing it was someone almost identical to my husband with empty eye sockets.

When I pulled up the Peephole footage to prove it, all we found was a blurry, barely decipherable video with the shadowy outline of a person standing outside my door. Even the audio was too garbled to make sense of.

Reg was the only one who took me at my word, even when I couldn't rationally explain what I'd seen. He stopped racing for a time, and we moved far from that house. It helped, but I still wasn't satisfied with all the questions I'd been left with. I was mostly scared, but angry too: angry over the violation, the invasion, and the loss of security. I couldn't truly put it behind me without at least trying to understand what actually happened.

I looked around online and went to the local library to research the history of the house, but there was nothing particularly noteworthy. It was built in the 50s and had traded hands a number of times since its completion. None of it struck me as particularly odd; it was small, needed some work, and was a bit far from town for a lot of folks. It didn't take me long to run through the list of available resources, but none of it helped much.

In a last ditch effort, I looked up the person we'd bought the house from, Marcia Dunberry. I was able to locate her through social media and sent her a message explaining what happened, asking if she could help me understand. I hesitated before hitting send, well aware that this message looked like the ramblings of someone with only one foot in reality. I had to be honest if I wanted answers though.

I checked my messages constantly over the next few days, anxious for her response. It was slow coming, and when it finally arrived, it was very brief.

Hello, Elaina. I'm sorry for what you went through. I can't say I'm surprised to hear it, though. I wanted to tell you when you bought the place, but the realtor told me not to. That house is sick. It's built on a graveyard from the 1900s, the previous owner told me so. There's an energy there, something bad. It wore my son's face like it wore your husband's. It doesn't stop when you leave. It just bides its time. I think I'm finally free. Please don't contact me again. Good luck.

When I went to reply, I realized she had blocked me. All I was left with was a lingering chill.

We have security cameras and lights all over our property now. Every door and window is reinforced and lined with locks. Peephole is still installed on our front doorbell, and Merry and Beauty and Goblin are forever at my side. Even so, I haven't managed to shake the feeling that something is watching from outside. Waiting.

I don't ever answer the door anymore. Reg does, but only after checking Peephole.

And if he's not home, I listen for the loud pops and roars of his race car, which he started driving regularly so I always know when he's coming.

So I'll be ready when it knocks again.

Death's Choice

I tried really hard to get my kid out of my neighborhood. When he was born, I made all the promises my old man made me when I was young.

You're not gonna live like this.

You're gonna be better than me.

You're gonna be somebody.

But what does an eighteen year old know about getting anybody outta anywhere? I couldn't even get myself out. Me and my girl lived in my mom's basement while we tried to get our shit together for little Abel's sake, but it was never gonna work. My girl was younger than me, she didn't want to be a mom, and she split when Abel was only a couple months old.

My mom sat me down and told me, "Boy, I'm not raising your child, so you best figure out what you wanna do. Man up or drop him at one of those safe places where he can be adopted and get himself a real family."

I knew it killed her to say that. Mom loved Abel even more than me, I think, and the last thing she wanted was to lose her grandbaby. Abel was my son though, and my responsibility.

I dropped out my last year of Highschool and started working a couple part time jobs. It was the real fucking American dream: fifty to sixty hour work weeks and still not able to make ends meet. The only reason I kept going was my little boy. The world just seemed to be getting shittier around us, but I kept clawing my way up; I didn't hang out with my old friends, didn't get involved in any of the old shit I used to do, just kept looking ahead and working my ass off.

Things started to get better when I met Shayla at one of my janitor jobs. She had a kid around Abel's age and wanted out of the neighborhood as bad as I did. We got together, started figuring out goals and saving money, and we thought we were really gonna do it.

Closest we came was when Abel was about eight. Shayla and I had gotten married a couple years before and could finally afford to rent a place of our own a few blocks from my mom. It was still in the same neighborhood, but closer to the edge. Shayla got a real good job working as a secretary in a law firm, and I was digging ditches for the city. We were finally managing to get by with some money stashed away for the future. We could almost see a way out.

I'd told my boy to stay away from the older kids a few houses down. They were no good, I'd say. They were dangerous. I didn't tell him it was because they were messing around with a gang, one of the reasons me and Shayla wanted out in the first place, but I probably should have. Maybe it would've stopped what happened.

I'd been at work on a Saturday, overtime to afford a birthday present for Shayla's daughter, so I only got to hear about it after it happened. Abel had slipped out of the house and gone to hang out with the "cool" kids down the road. It had only been a minute, shouldn't have been long enough for anything bad to happen, and it was broad fucking daylight.

Didn't stop some rivals from driving by and taking shots at the group. At my son.

He took two in the back before he hit the ground. The two that had been meant for the "leader" he'd been standing in front of.

By the time I got to the hospital, Abel was in surgery. Walking into the hospital was like a dream. Nothing felt real: not the hugs from my mom or Shayla, not the updates from the doctor, nothing. I sat in one of those hard plastic chairs against the wall, put my head between my knees, and I prayed for God to spare my boy.

Shayla and Mom went to the cafeteria to get coffee while we waited, but I stayed there, staring at the doors and wanting some kind of answer.

When someone stepped between me and the doors, I looked up, angry and grateful at the same time. I needed an excuse to vent and scream and fight, and this bastard had offered himself up without realizing it.

"Hey!" I snapped, but then I froze.

The figure before me was tall and covered in a heavy robe of black. Its hood was pulled low, hiding his features, but I was sure that a skeletal smile lurked in the shadows. All he was missing was a scythe.

I blinked.

The robes became brightly colored in blue and red, and flowers wrapped around the skeletal figure. Beads draped around the skull and its tall headdress.

Another blink. Now it was a Chinese man with

a long black beard in official looking robes and a cap.

Every time I blinked, the figure would change: a small Indian child, an old, haggard woman with wild hair, a large black dog. I'd never seen most of them, but I knew what each was called.

Santa Muerta
King Yan
A Yamaduta
Banshee
Black Shuck

All different names for the same being.

Death

"No." I don't know if I was denying what I was seeing or trying to ward off the creature in front of me. "Oh God, oh please, no!"

It turned toward me, a hundred faces in a single form. Trying to focus on any one shot lightening across my brain. It wasn't real, but at the same time, it was the only thing that was real. I was going insane with grief; it was the only explanation, but I didn't care. If there was any chance I could save Abel, I was going to try it.

"Not my boy," I begged. I was miraculously alone in the hallway, speaking to something that probably wasn't even there. "Anyone else, just not Abel."

It continued to stare.

"Please..."

Slowly, it lifted a hand, one minute boney, then dark skinned, then old, young, a paw, and touched my forehead.

I wasn't me anymore. I was someone else. Someone angry, so full of hate—there was a gun in my hand. It felt heavy and familiar. I was fearless. I was hot blooded, out for revenge.

I was Abel. Older, no longer an innocent child. Flashes of a life whirled before me: drinking, drugs, love and loyalty bought with blood. The colors of the gang he'd been with when he was shot waving like a flag over it all.

Everything went black for a moment. My eyes were opening as someone else. A pastor, filled with peace and generosity. The beloved leader of a congregation, a pillar in the community, a husband, a father, a friend.

A reformed gang member who changed his ways and escaped a life of violence after being shot in a drive-by on a Saturday afternoon in broad fucking daylight.

My body jerked sharply. I was back in my own skin. The figure still in front of me, its endless eyes all staring, waiting.

"They're both in there?" I asked weakly.

The figure remained silent and still, but I knew. My boy and that piece of garbage were both in surgery, but only one would make it out.

"You can't know that will happen," I said with a defiant shake of my head. "My son is a good boy! I'm getting him out of here! It won't happen!"

It tilted its head slightly.

"Y-you, don't know. Abel is good. Abel is...he's good."

I started to sob while it continued to stand in front of me, waiting, expectant.

"My boy," I whispered. "Save my boy."

Then I was alone again.

Carter Wright died on the table five minutes

later. He was sixteen years old.

Abel survived.

I don't know what I saw in the hospital or how real it even was. I don't know why I was given the choice when it shouldn't have been mine to make. I tried to go to different churches and temples to have it explained, but no one could help me understand.

Even without that knowledge, I told Abel he'd been given a second chance and not to waste it. It never made a difference. First he lost his innocence by force, and then he willingly gave up the rest by choice. He wanted revenge. He knew who could make it happen, and he was going to get it whether I liked it or not. I had to kick him out when he was eighteen after he pulled a gun on Shayla in our home.

Despite my best efforts, and all the love we gave him, and all the attempts we made to change things. Despite trying to move, to separate him from what was always outside our door, he was never my little boy again.

He became everything that I'd been warned about.

And now, almost fifteen years later, not a day goes by that I don't regret the choice I made in the presence of Death.

The Quiet Neighbor

Just about the first thing anyone new to the neighborhood learned was to avoid Bud Filimore. Cantankerous, territorial, and fueled by what seemed to be a deep-seated hatred for just about everything, he was the kind of man that childhood nightmares are made of.

He'd only lived there a few months longer than us, but by the time my family moved in across the street from the Filimore house, his reputation was already firmly established. When other neighbors came by with their cookies and casseroles to welcome us and saw me and my brother, just nine and eleven, they'd pull my parents aside and offer hushed warnings.

"Keep them away from that nasty little man across the way," Mrs. Devin said. "He can't stand children."

"My son, Bill, swears Bud tried to run him down in his car!" Mr. Crane said.

"He'll look for any excuse to yell at them. He says the most terrible things," Mrs. Paul said

My parents thanked them, but I don't think they quite believed them. My mom especially wasn't fond of gossip, and she tried to take rumors with a grain of salt until she could make her own decisions. She didn't have to wait long.

My older brother, Scotty, and I were outside tossing a baseball one Saturday morning when

Scotty tossed it too hard and high. It sailed over my head, bounced in the street, and rolled to a stop at the very edge of Mr. Filimore's yard. Both of us had overheard our neighbors warnings and were hesitant to even look at the house, much less approach it.

"Go get it, Liz," Scotty said, nudging my shoulder.

"But you threw it," I replied.

"So? You missed it!"

"I couldn't reach!"

My whining had no effect. He pushed me toward the road and, after checking both ways, I began to creep toward our ball.

I almost reached it. Just a couple more steps and it would be within my grasp, but the front door of the house flew open first.

"What the hell are you doing?" A stout man with thin, graying hair came bursting outside to stomp across his lawn toward me.

"M-my ball," I tried to say, pointing to it.

"You brats throwing things at my house? Think it would be funny to break a window?"

"N-no," I glanced over my shoulder to see Scotty half-poised to run. I whimpered.

"Get outta here," Mr. Filimore snapped.

"Can I just—"

"No!"

Before I could react, he'd scooped up the baseball, which had barely even touched his grass, and stormed back inside. The whole front of his house seemed to shake with the force of his slammed door.

It was the first of what would be many run in's

with everyone's least favorite neighbor. Our parents tried to talk to him about his behavior, but he just told them to keep their noisy little shits off his lawn and away from his house if we didn't want trouble. Dad thought about calling the cops on him, but as Mom became fond of saying, there was no law against being rude. We were told to just be more careful.

"He must not have always been such a bull," Mom said over dinner about a month after we'd moved in. "He's married, you know."

Dad scoffed at the idea. "Oh yeah? How do you know?"

"Dolores Devin was by again for a chat and it came up. Bud wears a ring, and she said she sees Mrs. Filimore looking out the windows from time to time. The poor woman never comes outside. She thinks she heard Bud say it was cancer once."

"Poor lady, sick and married to *that*," Dad said.

"Terrible, isn't it? But it does explain a bit about him. He's just trying to keep things quiet and peaceful around his house."

"Yeah, sure," Scotty muttered. Mom frowned at him.

"He's probably very sad and lashes out without meaning to."

"He's an asshole," Scotty said.

"Language," Dad warned, "but yeah, he is."

Whatever his reasoning, we all agreed it would be best to just try and avoid Bud Filimore.

Scotty and I were extra careful to keep all our toys well within the confines of our own yard when we played outside. I couldn't help but keep a wary eye on the house across the street, just in case he decided to be extra crazy and we had to run for it.

That's when I started to notice Mrs. Filimore.

Almost every time Scotty and I were out and I happened to glance at their house, I would see the tall, slender figure outlined behind the sheer curtains in one of the upstairs windows. I couldn't get a very good look at her, but I figured it couldn't be anyone but the missus; Mr. Filimore didn't have anyone else.

She never banged on the window or shouted at us like her husband. She'd just stand there, watching us. I liked to imagine that she was a nice lady; a quiet neighbor who just enjoyed seeing kids at play.

I remember mom saying Mrs. Filimore was sick and I felt sorry that she was trapped in her house with her horrible husband. I tried to be nice and smile and wave once. Just once. Mr. Filimore appeared on his front stoop and yelled at me for being a pest until I retreated inside.

When I peeked out the living room window later, Mrs. Filimore wasn't in her usual spot anymore.

Eventually we got used to Mr. Filimore glowering at us as he drove slowly past, his short temper and his loud voice. It was such a regular thing that our fear turned first to caution, then only to eye-rolling dismissiveness.

"Bud doesn't own the street. You kids go out and be kids. If he has a problem with it, I'll deal with him," Dad said.

After that, we started to be a little less careful with our things and a little more free with our laughter. We lost a few balls to the Filimore yard, one or two frisbees, but nothing we really cared too much about. Nothing until Scotty's remote controlled helicopter.

It had been a birthday present, and we were both eager to try it out. As soon as we finished supper, we raced out to the front lawn where Scotty prepared the helicopter's first flight.

Under my brother's inexperienced and clumsy guidance, the helicopter lifted slowly from the ground and staggered drunkenly through the air. In his excitement to keep it aloft, Scotty didn't even realize it was heading right for Filimore's yard until it was too late.

"Scotty!" I tugged at his arm to try and turn it off course, but that only made things worse.

The little helicopter took a nosedive straight into the hedges under Mr. Filimore's bay window. Scotty frantically wiggled the controls, but the helicopter's blade was stuck fast in the thick greenery.

As if he'd been waiting for us to slip up, the front door flew open and he practically pounced on the toy.

"What have I told you?" he bellowed.

Before we could argue, he'd already disappeared back into his house. Upstairs, the curtain fluttered just so, and I knew Mrs. Filimore was watching. I wanted to call up to her and ask her to get the helicopter back, but Scotty grabbed my wrist and dragged me behind him to find Mom and Dad.

When our parents went over later, he refused to come to the door.

"Don't worry, kids," they assured us, "next time we see him, we'll sit down and have a real discussion about this."

That wasn't enough for Scotty though. I followed him up to his room and sat on the end of his bed. He paced back and forth, ranting about how unfair it all was. He was fuming and furious, and he wanted his birthday present back now.

"But how?" I asked.

He paused, his gaze sliding to his window and the house beyond. "We're going to take it."

It was a childish, simple, stupid plan with no thought to consequence or punishment; we were going to break into the Filimore house and get all our things back.

"We'll do it when he goes out next. I can figure out how to get the lock open—it can't be that hard—then we just have to find our stuff."

"What about Mrs. Filimore? She never leaves!"

"You can distract her or something, I don't know. We'll figure it out."

"I dunno, Scotty," I said uneasily. I didn't want to disrupt a poor, sick lady for a few toys.

"Don't worry. We'll just be in and out. She probably won't even notice we're there."

I doubted that, but I had a hard time saying no to my big brother.

Scotty put his plan into action the very next afternoon. We were playing a game of horse in the driveway when Mr. Filimore's garage opened and his car chugged to life. He was wearing his customary scowl as he drove by. The moment he turned the corner, Scotty chucked our basketball aside and bolted across the street.

I checked to see if Mrs. Filimore was in her window and, when I saw no sign of her, I followed.

Scotty's idea of "getting the lock open" turned out to be using a small rock to break the window pane on the door above the latch. It was something he'd seen in a movie or something. I Immediately had images of flashing red and blue lights and handcuffs, and my stomach turned sharply. My brother whispered that it would be fine.

"He can't prove it was us! Everyone on the street hates him."

He sounded so confident that all I could do was nod. Scotty reached carefully through the broken glass, careful not to cut himself, and found the deadbolt. It clicked out of place and he pushed the door open, letting us into Mr. Filmore's house.

I clung to the back of Scotty's shirt as we tiptoed across the kitchen. It was spotless, obsessively so, and smelled of cleaning supplies. Every window had something tacked over it; old blankets and towels blocked the bright afternoon sun. The gloomy darkness made the room seem small and oppressive.

I swallowed hard and forced myself to follow Scotty. Every room was the same; fastidiously clean, organized, and shrouded in shadows. The bay window that he spied on us from had a little hole cut into the heavy velveteen material, just big enough for someone to peek out. I could just picture him sitting on his plastic covered couch, watching us, waiting for us to get too close. It was enough to make me shudder.

We cleared the whole downstairs pretty quickly, but there was no sign of our things.

"Shit," Scotty hissed. "He must keep it upstairs."

"But Mrs. Filimore..."

"Just stay close and stay quiet, ok?"

I nodded, too nervous to say anything else.

We'd only climbed a few steps when the floorboards on the second floor creaked. Scotty immediately pressed himself against the wall and motioned for me to do the same. We listened to the soft padding of footsteps crossing from one room to another.

"Scotty," I whispered, grabbing at his sleeve with both hands, "let's just go!"

"No, he went too far this time! I'm going to get my helicopter."

Door hinges squeaked from somewhere upstairs. The footsteps stopped.

Scotty pulled his arm from me and scampered up the remaining steps. Reluctantly, I followed.

We found a guest bedroom first. It was all muted colors and magazine quality furniture, void of any warmth or personality. Like it was just set up for show, never intended for use. At least it was a bit brighter up here; the windows only had a few layers of sheer curtains over them. Enough to obscure visibility, but still let in light.

The second room was obviously Mr. Filimore's. It was the most lived in looking room of them all; at least there were some pictures on the walls and personal items on the nightstand. The bed was meticulously made, and all the clothing, most of which was masculine, hung neatly in the closet. There weren't even stray hairs in the brush on the vanity.

I wondered how someone could live in such a cold, lifeless house.

There was only one room left upstairs, the one Mrs. Filiman must have gone into. Its door stood half open. Scotty and I traded a look: his determined, mine silently pleading to go. He took a step toward the door. I shook my head and grabbed at the back of his shirt again. He brushed me off and placed the flat of his hand on the door, pushing it open slowly.

The room was almost empty except for a large vanity against one wall. A framed wedding picture was on it, and I recognized Mr. Filimore despite being younger and thinner. In front of the vanity, posed on a tall stool, was a mannequin.

She was wearing what I thought of as a 50s housewife dress, white with little pink and green flowers all over it. She wore a string of pearls, and a blonde wig carefully combed back into a bun. Her featureless face was fixed on the mirror in front of her.

Scotty's brow wrinkled, showing the same confusion I felt. We both heard Mrs. Filimore walk into this room, but there was no one here.

"Let's just go," I begged, a cold sweat starting to trickle down the back of my neck.

Scotty shifted his weight, obviously torn; the floorboard beneath his feet groaned.

The mannequin's head turned sharply toward us.

Scotty leapt back with a yelp, an arm thrown out protectively in front of me.

"Liz," his voice was trembling, "run."

I stumbled back down the hall on legs that

didn't want to work. I could hear Scotty stomping along behind me and, behind him, a rapid skittering.

We skid at the top of the stairs, and I grabbed the railing to keep from falling headlong down the steps. While I righted myself, I dared to glance back down the hallway.

It was empty.

"Where'd it g—"

Something thudded against the ceiling.

We both looked up and screamed.

The mannequin was crawling, spider like, over our heads. She wrenched her head completely around, turning her blank face toward us. Flitting toward the wall, she started to descend, facing us the whole time.

I was still screaming when Scotty hooked his arm around my waist and hauled me down the steps. We crashed at the landing, tripping over one another. We could hear the click of fiberglass on wood as she pursued us. I was crying, scrambling on my hands and knees across the floor. My brother was shouting for me to get up and go. He grabbed the back of my shirt and practically threw me down the hall.

Scotty started shrieking.

I spun. The mannequin was crouched on the last step, one arm outstretched. She had her fingers wrapped around Scotty's ankle. They were tightening, tightening, until his bones started to crunch beneath her grip. He kicked at her with his other leg, but it did nothing. She started to drag him back toward the stairs.

"Scotty!" I screamed, but before I could move,

he looked up at me and shook his head furiously.

"Liz," he could barely get the word out through the fear and pain which masked his face, "run!"

I wanted to stay. I wanted to grab his hand and pull with all my might and drag him out of that house with me. He was shouting again though—run, run—over and over, until the words became a garbled mess of howling. I always did have a hard time saying no to my big brother. His terrified cries chased me out the same door we'd come in through.

It was the last time I ever saw my brother.

No trace of Scotty was ever found. My parents searched. Police searched. There were dogs, and special agents, and tons of time, money, and energy put into trying to find him. None of it mattered. It was as if he had simply vanished. Bud Filimore wasn't a suspect very long; with no evidence and no history of any criminal record, he was let go. Scotty was dubbed a missing child, reduced to a single box of paperwork that was all too soon moved to the cold case stacks.

No one believed me when I told them what really happened. They all said Scotty must have been kidnapped on our way back from Mr. Filimore's house. They said I was too young to really understand it, that I had gotten confused and, in my fear, made up some story using the scary thing I'd just encountered.

"Mr. Filimore's mannequin belonged to his late wife, Sharon. He kept it after she passed because it reminded him of her. Sometimes he'd move it around, put it in a window, but it wasn't alive. You understand that, right, Liz?" My therapist was fond of asking.

I told her what she wanted to hear, even if I knew it was a lie. The adults preferred it that way; it was easier for all of us. Maybe that's why I never showed anyone the note that was taped to our door, typed and anonymous, which read:

I tried to keep you away.

I didn't think it would have changed anything.

I knew, though, and I never doubted myself or the fact that Scotty sacrificed himself for me. Up until Mr. Filimore packed and moved a few years later, I would sit in my brother's room and stare out the window at that house. I'd watch the second story window, waiting for the telltale dark figure to appear behind the curtains.

Waiting for the quiet neighbor that everyone said didn't exist.

Going to Grandma's

I only ever spent one night at my grandma's house. It was all I needed to know I never wanted to set foot there again.

By the time I was born, Grandpa had passed away and Grandma had sold the house they'd spent 40 years in. They left the place where they'd raised their two sons and made all of their marital memories to return to her childhood home. The three story Victorian had been built by Grandma's own grandfather, passed down the family line until, after the death of her brother, it wound up in her hands. She told Dad it felt right to go back and spend her remaining years in the house she grew up in.

The family tried to convince her that it was too big, too much work, too dangerous, but Grandma's mind was already made up. I remember the day we helped her move in: cold and gray in early December. It smelled like snow. As soon as we'd finished unloading the few belongings she'd chosen to bring from the truck, she ushered us back outside.

"I'm tired and I still have a lot of unpacking to do. It'll go faster if I do it myself," she said.

"We could help, Mom." Dad tried to offer, but Grandma shook her head firmly.

"I'll have you lot back around once I'm settled. I'd really like some time alone to get reacquainted with the old place."

It was an unusually abrupt dismissal for a woman who always kept an open door policy before. Dad said later that he thought she was just getting emotional over being back and didn't want us to see. It made sense, really. From what Grandma had told us, the house was still very much the same as it had always been. The furniture, the flooring, the wallpaper; even some of the light fixtures were originals to the house. Dad was sure she just needed some time.

But Grandma's previous open invitation wasn't re-extended.

Instead, she came to us. For the first time, Christmas was held at our house. She visited for her birthday in February, and again for Easter and the Fourth of July. All the holidays and events that she always insisted on hosting were now bounced back and forth between my house and my uncle's.

"I'm too old for that sort of thing now." She laughed when we asked her about the sudden change. "It's time for me to put my feet up and let you guys do all the work for me."

My parents worried about her up in that big old house all by herself. It was on a sizeable piece of property bordered by woods, and the closest neighbor was a nice little walk down the road. No matter how much they tried to insist on visiting, Grandma wouldn't have it.

"I've got the girls around today for cards," she'd say. Or, "I'm in town for the afternoon, maybe next weekend."

Next weekend came and went, and then the one after that, and the one after that, until almost a full year went by. Dad made brief, drop in visits during that time and, while everything seemed ok at the house, Grandma never let him stay long. When he finally demanded to know why, she put her foot down and told him that she didn't have to explain her desire for a little privacy.

The family was a bit strained after that. Dad thought maybe Grandma was starting to get a little affected by age and it was making her pull away. Alzheimer's had taken his father in a long, terrible process. I was only eleven, but I could see how scared Dad was of going through that again. Mom did her best to comfort him, but I saw the same worry in her eyes.

Grandma didn't come down to our house to go trick or treating with us that Halloween, but she showed up at Uncle Rusty's for Thanksgiving. While still not quite herself, things started to feel a little more normal.

It was just after that when the fire happened.

I was woken up late at night by the screeching smoke alarm in the hallway. I'd barely managed to sit up before my mom burst into my room, ripping me out of bed along with my comforter. She hugged me to her chest, put it over both of us, and ran for the front door. There was a flash of heat and the smell of acrid burning. Then we were outside in the cold, clinging to each other.

Dad stumbled out a few minutes after, coughing and wheezing and clutching one arm. He'd stayed behind to try and put out the fire, but it got away from him and he'd been burned trying to get outside.

There was nothing we could do but stand in

our front lawn and watch our home be consumed by the growing flames.

Grandma arrived just after the fire trucks did. Mom called her from a neighbor's house, and she'd made the usually thirty minute drive in half that. Dad was being loaded up in the back of an ambulance when she arrived and, after being reassured he wasn't seriously injured, she hurried over to me and Mom.

"Please, Eunice," Mom begged after Grandma made sure we were ok and smothered us in kisses. "Larry needs to go to the hospital, and I want to go with him. Take Sheila back to your place, just for tonight. We need you."

I never thought I'd see Grandma hesitate to babysit me. She frowned and glanced from my mom to me before nodding once.

"One night," she agreed, but it was obvious that she didn't want to.

The drive to Grandma's was quiet. I sat in the backseat, still in shock, tired, scared, and hurt that Grandma didn't want me. She kept her eyes on the road and her lips pressed together in a thin line. When we pulled into her long gravel driveway, she finally broke the heavy silence.

"You ok back there?"

"Yeah," I said quietly.

"Good." Another pause. "I know tonight was scary, but Daddy is going to be fine. He just had to get his arm looked at."

"Oh."

I saw Grandma look at me in the rear view mirror. "You must be very sleepy, huh?"

I shrugged.

Grandma seemed like she wanted to say something more, but she just forced an ephemeral smile and parked the car.

She held my hand all the way up to the front door, and then into the foyer. She was reluctant to let me go. While she took off her coat, I took the opportunity to look over the entryway: all hardwood and pale, striped wallpaper. An antique chandelier hung overhead, its dim light barely strong enough to ward off the darkness. The hallway before us was narrow, with one side leading up a stairwell and the other lined with doors that branched into other rooms.

I shivered, already creeped out by the unfamiliar shadows which seemed to lurk in every corner. I'd never been afraid of her old house. I wished immediately that we could have gone there instead.

I wished I could go home.

Tears sprang to my eyes at the thought of my house, now a charred shell, and I sniffled.

"Sheil?" Grandma said from over my shoulder. "You want anything to eat or drink?"

"No," I said.

I really just wanted my mom and my dad, to be back in my own bed and for everything to be normal again. I knew my parents would want me to be brave and behave for Grandma, but the mounting realization of what we lost and how shaken I was quickly overwhelmed me. I started to cry, despite how hard I tried to control it,.

Grandma took me by the hand again and led me to the living room, a neat and formal room with more antique furnishings. We cuddled on the couch, and she reassured me that everything would be ok. I curled up against her side and cried myself to sleep.

I woke up some time later in pitch blackness. It took me a long moment of near panic to remember where I was. Grandma had tucked a blanket around me, but wasn't on the couch with me anymore. I sat up a bit, blinking and rubbing my eyes until they'd adjusted as much as they could.

Dark shapes loomed in the shadows around me. I recognized the shape of a high backed chair next to the couch, the outline of a grandfather clock against the wall, and a coffee table in the middle of the room. I was starting to calm down, telling myself only babies were afraid of the dark, when a floorboard creaked behind the couch.

I turned sharply, half expecting to see Grandma coming into the room. There was nothing. With a whimper, I lay back down, grabbing the blanket to tug it all the way up to my chin. I squeezed my eyes shut. It was just my imagination. Just like Dad and Mom were always telling me after nightmares.

I didn't have to be afraid.

"Have you come to play?"

The whispered question sounded like it was only inches from my face. It sounded like a little girl. My eyes flew open, but again, there was only darkness. I pressed myself as far back into the couch as I could and gripped the blanket tight.

"We like to play," came another girl's voice, thin and soft, this one down by my feet.

"Won't you be our friend?" A third asked quietly from behind the couch.

"Get up!"

The blanket was ripped away, and I squeaked in terror. I wanted to scream, but my throat was tight and my voice frozen.

"Wake up!"

A hand, small and cold, grabbed at my ankle. I yanked it away, and a ripple of giggles echoed around the room.

"Play with us!"

The girl's voices were getting louder, less playful in their demands despite the wicked laughter following their words. I felt fingers twist around my ponytail, jerking my head harshly back.

"Silly cow! Stupid girl!"

Someone was tearing roughly at my nightshirt. A stinging slap landed across one cheek. Nails dug into my ankle and pulled at my leg again. Clawed hands scratched at my face, my arms, and my chest, with more pulling at my hair.

Their hollow, mirthless laughter surrounded me.

I curled up into the tightest, smallest ball I could manage and I started to scream.

A light came on in the hallway and the attack stopped all at once.

Grandma was next to me, touching my face and my hair, saying something, trying to calm me down. I couldn't hear her over my own terrified shrieks.

The next time I saw myself was in the hotel mirror. Grandma took us there after I'd run out to the car and refused to go back into her house. Long, vicious red lines ran down one cheek. My forearms and one of my legs had them too, marking where

I'd been scratched. The hem of my shirt was stretched and torn. My hair was a gnarled mess from where fingers had tangled in it.

Grandma didn't say anything for a long time. She cleaned me up as best she could, bandaging the cuts and putting ice on the fast-forming bruise under my eye where I'd been slapped. She rubbed my back in small, slow circles.

"I'm sorry, Sheila," she said at last, her voice quiet and heartbroken. "I tried to keep you away. I was only gone for a moment to use the bathroom. I didn't think it would be long enough..."

I could only stare at her. The fear I'd felt, so absolute, was still coursing through me. I thought if I opened my mouth to speak, the only thing that would come out would be more screaming.

"I'm sorry," she whispered again.

Every family has a skeleton or two in their closet; the kind of deep, dark secret that's shared in hushed tones behind closed doors. That night, I found out that my family was no exception.

Grandma told me that my great, great grandpa had built the house she was now living in not as a family home, but as an orphanage for girls. The community viewed him as an upstanding citizen, a near saint for those poor unfortunate children, and they lavished praise on him for his selflessness. By all appearances, he was a philanthropic soul who created a home for those with nowhere else to go and no one else to care for them.

Although Grandma was vague with the details, only saying that Great Great Grandpa had done very awful things, I came to understand years later just what she truly meant.

Far from being the kind, generous man that he made himself out to be, he had collected these girls for himself. He used and abused them in every terrible way imaginable. His wife knew, but he had given her a lavish lifestyle and a son, and she let him do as he pleased so long as he kept it out of sight and away from their boy. His appetites were sick and sadistic, and some girls had a tendency to go missing while in his "care". They were initially dubbed runaways.

But those girls had never left.

Once he was done with them, they'd be cut up. Parts were dropped into vats of boiling lye, and whatever remained was buried in the basement.

He was forced to stop ten years after he began when people started to take more notice of just how often his girls went missing. His wife was faced with a loss of status and reputation should he be found out.

More than three dozen girls between the ages of five and thirteen went missing in those years.

Grandma had heard him admit to all of it in his later years, when his mind was slipping, and he claimed the little girls were waiting for him. By then, he was already a very elderly man close to death and his crimes were decades old. Going to the police seemed pointless. The family agreed to let sleeping dogs lie.

"When he was alive, they stayed hidden; my father never experienced anything supernatural and I never saw them when I was a child. After that horrible man died, however, strange things would happen, although only to the kids. It was almost playful, at first, but as the years went on, it got more aggressive. The boys would get bite marks and scratches when we'd visit my father, but nothing like you have now. It seems like...the longer they're trapped there, the angrier they become."

Grandma believed they were afraid of adults and only went after children. It was jealousy, she supposed, or a desire to inflict the same pain they'd felt. Either way, it was too dangerous for kids to be there.

"That's why I told you not to come. I didn't want any of this to happen. I've been trying to find out how to help them. To free them. I've had religious ceremonies and cleansings. I've searched for their bones. Nothing worked, and I can't sell the house knowing they might hurt someone."

She thought that her presence would be enough to keep them away, and that a five minute bathroom visit wouldn't be enough for them to cause me any harm. She hasn't realized how eager they'd become.

"Don't worry, Sheila," she said, holding me close. "I'll never make that mistake again."

I wrapped my arms around her and held on tight, trembling. She didn't need to worry about making "that mistake" with me though.

I already knew I'd never set foot in that house ever again.

The Aftermath of Murder

On March 12th, a teenage girl from my town went missing on her walk to school. Leona Joy Vans was 15. She was a cute kid who played clarinet for the Highschool band and volunteered at the nearby animal shelter on weekends. She dreamed of going to college for music and getting a position with an orchestra. It was impossible not to know these things — her parents were all over the news for days, pleading with anyone to come forward with information. No one had seen or heard anything.

Search parties were organized, a few of which I joined with my mother and brother. The town was thoroughly combed for the girl. We walked through woods, divers dragged the nearby lakes, and cadaver dogs sniffed their way in circles. No sign of Leona.

It went on for a week. Rewards were offered, tearful pleas from friends and family were broadcast on every local channel, candlelit vigils held, and everyone was still holding out hope that she would somehow make it home safely.

On the seventh day after her disappearance, that hope was snuffed out.

I was driving home from work, which took me passed the street my mother and brother live on, when I was overtaken by a cop car with lights and sirens blaring. I pulled over to let it pass and checked my rear view mirror to see two more speeding along after it. I got back on the road and trailed more slowly behind them until all three turned sharply onto Hamilton, my family's street.

I tried to dismiss it as coincidence. Hamilton had a lot of houses, and they could be going to any one of them. A cold sweat still broke out across the back of my neck. I glanced in my rear view mirror at the fast fading street sign and shook my head. No need to be foolish. When the uneasiness refused to subside, I turned up my music. It did little to drown out the niggling little voice that was demanding I turn around.

"They're going to Mom's house!" it said.

No, they wouldn't be. There was no reason for them to.

I made it another mile before making an illegal u-turn and heading back. Sometimes you just can't shake that intuitive feeling that something is very wrong.

I was only planning to drive by and prove to myself that everything was fine; no one would even know I was there. Except all the neighbors who were standing in their yards, watching as officers taped off the street and my mother's yard. Cop cars and an ambulance were parked all along the street in front of her house, their lights still flashing. Mom was standing on the front stoop with an officer. I'd never seen that expression on her face before: some terrible combination of horror and deep cut sorrow that aged her immeasurably.

In a daze, I pulled into a nearby driveway. Ignoring the incredulous looks from the homeowners, I left my car running while slowly approaching the police tape on with leaden feet.

"Sir, please return to your vehicle." A cop was suddenly in front of me, holding up a hand.

"That's my mom," I said.

"What?"

I pointed dumbly to the house.

"Caleb!" Mom shrieked more than called my name. She was tearing across the lawn toward me, oblivious to the stares from her neighbors. She almost collapsed into my arms.

The cop helped me catch her and lower her to the curb. She sat and shivered, groaning my name over and over again. I held her against my chest and rocked with her, back and forth, completely at a loss. I looked helplessly to the officer, who had stepped back to give us some room.

"Did something happen to Art?" I asked.

Mom wailed at the sound of my brother's name.

"Mom? What happened?" My throat was tightening with panic. "Where's Art?"

There was no getting through to her. Whatever composure she had was gone, and she could only sob hysterically.

"Somebody tell me what's going on!" I demanded. The flurry of people continued to move around us, and I got no immediate answers.

A gurney was wheeled out of the house some time later. The unmistakable black bag lying atop it nearly made my heart stop.

"Mom!" I pushed her back to arm's length, my fingers digging into her flesh. "Is that Art? What happened? Talk to me!"

My shouting must have startled her enough to

bring her halfway back to reality. She touched my face gently and shook her head, tears streaming down her cheeks.

"Leona."

It was a while before the cops would speak to me. I had to wait until Leona's body was put into the back of the ambulance and taken away and they'd finished up photographing the crime scene and collecting evidence.

Crime scene. Evidence. I could hardly wrap my head around those words. They'd made sense once; now they sounded foreign and difficult to comprehend. Nothing about this made any real sense.

When I finally managed to speak to someone, details were fleeting. All they would tell me is that they received a 911 call from my mother saying she'd found Leona's body in her attic.

"We'll know more after the autopsy," was a popular phrase.

They let Mom back in long enough to pack a suitcase under intense supervision. They only let her leave once I provided my address as where she'd be staying. She wasn't even allowed to take her car as they hadn't searched it yet.

"Don't leave town. Either of you," we were told as we crossed the street to my car. The neighbor had been nice enough to shut it off for me and leave the keys in the ignition.

Mom didn't speak again until the next morning. We were sitting at the kitchen table with breakfast and coffee in front of us, untouched.

"She was in your dad's old trunk. The brown one with all the stickers on it," she said numbly. "I went up to get the Easter decorations, and there was this awful smell..."

"Mom," I put my hand over hers and she gripped it tight, "where's Art?"

"I don't know. He went out in the morning to run some errands after I said I was going to decorate. He never came home."

"He knew you were going to the attic."

She turned her dark rimmed, sunken eyes to me. "He knew I was going to find her."

We stopped talking after that.

The month that followed was a hellish one. Art remained missing, but people needed someone to blame, and we were the best thing. We answered and re-answered the cops' questions and offered all the information we had, but it never felt like enough. It was as if they thought we'd eventually break if they just kept applying pressure. We had nothing left to give them: no secrets, no involvement, nothing.

It didn't matter.

Mom was quietly let go from her workplace two weeks after Leona was found. She was told that her performance had been slipping and she was unfocused, but we knew the real reason. Her friends stopped calling for the most part, and she didn't get invited out anywhere. The only time her phone did ring, it was the police with more questions. Either that or unlisted numbers calling to tell her she was a monster, a whore, blaming her for what Art had done.

She stopped leaving my house except to go for more interrogation; the stares and whispers were too much for her to handle. We got toilet papered and egged on more than one occasion, and one particularly bold bastard spray painted "Murderer!" across the front of my house.

It only got worse once the autopsy results came back and were leaked. Leona had been tortured before she died: raped, cut, choked, beaten, and finally stabbed half a dozen times in her chest and stomach. There was some evidence that she'd still been alive when Art put her in the trunk where she succumbed to her injuries alone in the dark.

The calls got worse. Mom had to shut her phone off. My car tires were slashed and all of the glass was smashed. Rocks were thrown through the house windows. Reporters started lurking on the edges of my yard, and any time we so much as looked outside, they'd start screaming questions. They demanded to know if we'd heard from Art, if we knew where he was, or if we thought he was capable of something like this.

The last one was the worst. I'd never been close to Art since I was eight years older than him, but we'd gotten along okay. He seemed shy and nerdy as a teen, but he had friends and a social life. I'd worried a bit about him as an adult—he was an unemployed 22 year old who lived with our mom—but he'd been taking some online college classes and never gave any signs that he was unhappy. At least not when I was around. He'd certainly never shown any indication that he would do something like this.

A journal found by the police proved otherwise. In it, Art documented his anger, his depression, and his loneliness. Women were a source of constant frustration for him that morphed into a confusing combination of vulgar hatred and idolization. I found out he resented me for my success and thought our mother favored me while looking down on him. He wrote that she was "just another bitch", and he couldn't wait for her to die so he could get his inheritance.

When the cops read that to Mom, she got up, gathered her things, and left the station.

"It really is my fault," she said to me on the drive home. "How did I miss so much?"

No matter what I said, she wouldn't and couldn't stop blaming herself.

I started hearing her move around in the night. Often she'd just cry, sometimes it sounded like she was pacing, other times I'd hear her talking. It was always quiet and muffled by the wall between us, but it still kept me up. I didn't tell her that though. I thought she might be praying and didn't want to interrupt.

In the mornings, she'd come to the kitchen looking older than the day before. She seemed to be shrinking into herself, her shoulders hunched and head bowed. I swear her hair was graying more every time I saw her.

"Maybe we should see someone. A therapist or something to help us," I suggested gently over breakfast.

"That wouldn't help."

"It could."

"No."

"Mom —"

"I don't want to talk about it!"

She slammed her spoon onto the table and

shoved her chair back. I tried to apologize, but she left the room, her robe hugged tightly around her thin frame.

I left for work, clouded with grief and worry, and dwelled on thoughts of mom and Art and Leona all day. I was at a loss and felt completely isolated, which caused ripples of guilt to stir. I struggled with wanting to reach out for help as part of me believed we didn't deserve it. Maybe we should have noticed what was going on with Art; maybe there was something we could have done to stop it. I didn't know what, but *something*. Had we just buried our heads and ignored the warning signs? Could we have saved Leona?

I got home that evening in time to see someone running away from my house, a mask pulled over their face. They flipped me off as I drove up, disappearing around the side of my neighbor's house across the street. They'd left a present for me though: a burning bag of feces on my welcome mat outside my front door. I smelled it before I saw it. I ran inside for the fire extinguisher and found Mom huddled in the entryway, sobbing hysterically.

"Are you ok?" I asked. "Did he do anything to you?"

"I can't live like this!" she cried.

"I'm sorry, Mom. We can move. We don't have to stay here."

"It wouldn't matter!"

"A change might be good for us!"

"No!" She stood up and grabbed me by my shoulders. "She'll follow, Caleb. She won't stop. I hear her crying all the time! She wants to go home and she can't and *I can't help her!*"

I tried to make sense of what she was saying, all while very aware of the fire still burning on my doorstep.

"Who, Mom?"

"Leona! Don't you hear her? I try to talk to her, but she doesn't stop. All day, all night, she cries and asks why I let him hurt her. She asks why I won't let her go home!"

"Whoa, no, Mom, no, she's not. She's not here." I tried to hug her, but she shoved me back.

"Don't patronize me!"

"I'm not! I know you're having a hard time, I am too—"

"She blames me, Caleb, and I think she's right. I knew Arthur had some trouble. I tried to get him to talk to me, but he wouldn't. I should have done more, Leona knows that. I know that!"

"Listen to yourself! It's guilt, not Leona, Mom. I feel it too, ok? I should have been around more after Dad died. I should have helped more."

"She hurts so much. She hurts and it's my fault."

"No, Mom—damnit, I need to put that out. Just wait a minute."

I ran past her to the kitchen for the extinguisher, leaving her standing there looking like a lost child.

"I tried my best with both of you," she called after me. "I love you both so much."

"I know, Mom." I shouted over my shoulder while I read the instructions on the canister. "Love you too."

I hurried back to the front door and aimed the extinguisher's nozzle at the base of the flames. I squeezed the lever, showering it in a burst of white, until the fire had died. I looked down at the mess in disgust and turned back to Mom, only to find the entryway empty.

"Mom?" I said.

Bang!

Thud.

The silence that followed rang in my ears. I walked slowly to the bottom of the stairs and looked up, but I couldn't make myself go up to the second floor.

I sat on the bottom step, staring out my open door at the burnt bag of shit: an apt metaphor for what my life had become. I tried my best to ignore the smell of iron drifting down from my bedroom. I was still sitting there when the police came, no doubt called after someone heard the gunshot. I stayed there after telling them what had happened and where to find my mother.

Curious neighbors were standing in my yard, craning their necks to see inside. I got up, sickened by the gawkers, sick for my mom, furious with my brother, and kicked the door shut. There would not be any more shows from the Graham family for them to watch.

I didn't watch them take Mom out in the same kind of black body bag they'd brought Leona out in. I didn't watch them load her in the ambulance and drive her away. I barely spoke to the cops, who were mercifully understanding.

I just sat on my living room couch, drinking from a bottle of scotch. I was trying to figure out if I could really hear the sound of a young girl crying, or whether it was just my grief and my guilt playing tricks on me.

The Gift That Keeps On

Giving

Most little girls don't dream of growing up and spending their days surrounded by human blood.

My sister was not most little girls.

When we were young, our dolls spent as much time in quarantine with terrible illnesses as they did at tea parties. She enjoyed dissecting our stuffed animals and labelling their bits of fluff as if they were body parts. I suppose that our parents could have been worried about their youngest child and her unusual fascinations, but where some saw "Future Serial Killer" burning in neon colors above Leah's little head, they saw "Scientist". As far as they were concerned, she wasn't hurting anything. She was just trying to learn, and there was certainly nothing wrong with that.

While we both enjoyed more conventional hobbies, like gaming together or taking trips to the beach, Leah never wavered from her more morbid interests. We frequently visited the science museum, especially if there was an exhibit on anything having to do with the human body. She had me watching all kinds of true crime and medical shows.

Nothing, however, captivated her like blood. Its properties, its functions, what it contained; it drew her in the same as a good novel did me. If it weren't for Leah, I might never have even known my own blood type, much less what kinds of diseases or genetic traits could potentially be floating through my veins.

It never failed to amuse me when new people heard her talking about various biological functions and fluids with such passion. Most quiet, pretty girls didn't care for those things, their polite, slightly uncomfortable smiles said.

Like I said, my sister was not most girls.

It came as no surprise to us, then, when she went to college to study biology with a special focus on genetics and hematology, the study of blood. It was even less of a surprise when she landed a lab job running blood tests shortly after graduating. The only crux was that it was over a thousand miles away in a small New England town. We'd never been more than a couple hours away from one another.

"Don't worry about it, Jackie," she told me when I started getting emotional over the distance. "You can visit whenever you want!"

I took her up on that offer barely a month after she left when we both had an extended holiday weekend. She'd always been my best friend, and it was hard adjusting to the fact that she was no longer within driving distance. She took my clinginess in good cheer and welcomed me into her apartment with a pizza, a daiquiri, and an air mattress on her living room floor.

The long weekend flew by much faster than I

thought possible. During the final afternoon of my trip, I was feeling sentimental all over again. Before I had to leave, I insisted that we stop somewhere so I could get her a gift to commemorate my first visit.

"Fine," Leah conceded after I'd spent our entire lunch nagging her about it. "But don't get carried away, ok? It's really not a big deal."

I made a face at her. "It is to me. I don't know when I'll see you again."

"Uh, next time we video chat? Probably right after you get home tomorrow?"

"Just shut up and let me buy you something, ok?"

She rolled eyes. I rolled mine right back, and then we looked up where the nearest thrift shop was. We both liked wandering through second hand stores; you could find some real buried treasures if you just dug around enough. Whatever we ended up finding wouldn't be too expensive, which would keep Leah happy.

I hadn't really expected much when we first walked through the shop doors. It was a small place and a lot of what they had was tacky or simply not Leah's very particular "Hint of Goth" style. On a whim, I left my sister flipping through a rack of t-shirts and wandered over to the jewelry case. Inside the dimly lit glass box, they had some rather gaudy rings, a few bracelets, and a couple of necklaces lined up on a display board.

It only took one, brief look to know exactly what I was going to get my sister.

I called over the bored looking cashier and pointed to the necklace in the middle. She unlocked the case and scooped the piece up to lay it across the top of the glass in front of me. It was perfect for Leah: a silver pendant, long and slender, ending in a red, teardrop shaped gem which hung from a thin chain. It reminded me of blood on the end of a needle.

"How much?" I asked.

"$50, and you'll get a little certificate of authenticity and stuff to go with it," the cashier said.

"Certificate?"

"Yeah, it's historical or something, donated by a local family."

After I paid, she put the necklace into a small cardboard jewelry box and dug the certificate out of one of the drawers beneath the display case. Both went into a plastic bag that was handed to me. With the present in hand, I tracked Leah down and waved the box enticingly in front of her face.

"We can go; I found your gift."

I made her wait until we were back in the car before letting her open up the box. The moment she saw it, her eyes went wide as I had hoped. A genuine, thrilled smile spread across her lips.

"It looks like a blood drop!" she exclaimed with more excitement than most would have gotten from such a comparison.

While she worked on getting it latched around her neck, I grabbed the certificate, which she'd let fall on her lap along with the bag.

"It's supposedly an antique," I said. "According to this, it belonged to an herbalist who 'practiced healing arts' back in the mid-eighteenth century and was passed down in her family from then until now."

"Sounds like a load of bull," Leah scoffed while she studied her reflection in the visor mirror.

I blocked her view with the paper and waved it around until she took it from me. "But look, it's got an official looking seal and signature and everything!"

"I'm sure a beloved family heirloom, certificate of authenticity and all, is really going to end up at Andy's Secondhand Goods instead of in some safety deposit box. It's probably not even real."

"You never know," I said, grinning. "So what do you think? You like it?"

"I guess I'll keep it," Leah replied with an exaggerated, put-upon sigh.

She gave herself one last look in the mirror, and flipped it up. We headed back to her apartment to enjoy one last night of sisterly bonding over cheesy 90s sitcoms and margaritas.

I left the next evening with promises of another visit sometime soon, reminding her to text or call whenever I landed. I told her she was sounding more like our mom every day, and she flipped me off all the way to the security gate. My flight home was noisy and crowded. I was all too happy to bid it and all of my fellow passengers a not-so-fond farewell when we finally touched down a half hour past our scheduled arrival time.

It took me another two hours to get home and, by then, it was well past my bedtime. I sent Leah and our parents a text to let everyone know I'd made it and stumbled into the shower for a quick rinse before flopping into bed. It took no time at all to fall asleep, and I stayed that way until well into the next morning. Travel never really did agree with me.

After I'd rubbed the sleep from my eyes, I groped along my nightstand for my phone. New text notifications filled my screen.

Mom had sent a couple hearts back. Dad gave me a thumbs up. Leah, though, had sent me a string of short messages back to back.

K glad you're home, she'd sent the night before.

Earlier that morning, she'd sent more. *Had such a weird dream last night about Gary, the jackass shift lead I've told you about.*

We were talking in the lab, and this huge black spider crawled out of his mouth mid-sentence. I tried to tell him because he hadn't even flinched, but he just got louder and louder until I stopped.

More spiders started coming out of his nose and ears and he had a couple legs poking out from behind one eye.

I mean, it was kind of cool, but also creepy.

I snorted in amusement and shot back, *Only you.*

Once I could finally bring myself to leave the comfort of bed, I spent the majority of my day playing catch up on all the laundry and cleaning I'd not done before I'd gone up to visit Leah. Not exactly the ideal last day of vacation before heading back to work, but it had to get done. My sister helped break up the monotony with more texts and silly pictures from the lab. She even managed to snap a stealthy one of Gary, a middle aged man with a paunchy belly and receding hairline, so I could better imagine what she'd seen in her dream.

Don't be a creeper taking pictures of people without them knowing :p, I sent.

Just imagine spiders on his face. Do iiiit!
No thanks. That's more your thing than mine.
You're no fun.

Yeah I know, I replied, giggling at myself. It was 2pm and I was sitting in my living room in pajamas, folding socks.

No fun indeed.

Both Leah and I were used to her weird nightmares, something she'd experienced regularly since she was a little girl. I barely gave this latest one any thought that day, or even the next, until she mentioned having another, similar dream. This time the spiders were more aggressive, biting Gary and leaving bloody fang marks across his face and down his neck before disappearing into his shirt. The third day, when she sent me a photo of herself, asking if she'd managed to successfully conceal the dark circles under her eyes, I started to get a little concerned.

What's up? I asked between steps in my own makeup routine.

Another dream.

When she didn't elaborate, which was unusual for her, I prodded until she gave me a brief synopsis.

Gary again, more spiders. They'd eaten half his face and throat. Didn't sleep well, gonna grab a coffee before work.

I frowned at the screen. Leah didn't often lose sleep over her dreams; she actually enjoyed them most of the time, but this recurring one seemed to be getting to her. I scrolled back to her photo and clicked to enlarge.

She was pale beneath her makeup, even by her

normal ivory standards. Her eyes had a slightly sunken look. She'd done a good job bringing some color back to her cheeks, but if you knew her well enough, it was obviously just one tiny degree off from natural. She looked exhausted.

The pendant I gave her gleamed from her throat.

My gaze was drawn unconsciously from my sister's unsmiling face to the spot over her shoulder. There was something about the dark apartment behind her, a murkiness, that seemed out of place somehow. I chalked it up to it still being early and her not having turned many lights on. I set my phone aside in favor of a mascara wand.

As I often did when Leah was feeling down, I flooded her phone with cute pictures of kittens and puppies, plus the occasional deceptively adorable cartoon with a morbid caption. When I didn't receive any response, I blamed her job for actually making her do work and headed out to start my own day.

By the time I could check my phone again during my lunch hour, Leah had sent me a number of replies.

Something's wrong with Gary. He came in this morning and half his face was a little puffy, like he slept on it all night. Now it's looking really red and swollen.

A half hour later, she followed up with, *He just got a really bad nose bleed all over my station.*

Then another, a little while after that. *omg Jackie it's like he's got golf balls under his skin on his face! They just started appearing and keep growing! Wtf!!!*

The last text in the series just said, *Gary had a seizure. Doesn't look good.*

Leah didn't freak out easily. This was the same girl who cheerfully shared stories from her internships over the dinner table about finding body parts along railroad tracks. To be able to actually read the panic in her texts was enough to get my heart rate up. I stepped out of my office break room to call her.

"What's going on?" I asked as soon as she answered.

"We don't know; an ambulance came and took him away," she said. There was an unsettled quietness to her voice.

"You ok?"

"Yeah, I'm fine. I think. It's just so weird."

"It sounds like it."

"Not just what happened, Jackie. Where, too. On his face, I mean. It was...it was where I saw the spiders in my dreams. Everywhere they ate away, that's where the welts or whatever appeared."

"Coincidence," I said quickly, before she could start overthinking it in her already agitated state. "Maybe you noticed something different about him without realizing it, and your subconscious was trying to tell you."

"That's bull and you know it," she replied with a strained, short laugh.

"Maybe not."

We sat in silence for a while, both of us unsure what to say next.

"I gotta go," she said at last. "I'll talk to you later."

"Take it easy, ok? Call if you need anything."

"Ok, Mom."

It was unfortunate and frightening what happened to Gary. The lab thought he might have come into contact with something and had a severe allergic reaction, but nobody really believed that. Nobody knew what to believe, least of all Leah, who spent the next few days dwelling on the spider-filled dreams that ceased as suddenly as they began.

Gary passed away three nights later with an official diagnosis of chordoma, a rare type of bone cancer that occurs in the skull. It was rumored that the autopsy showed evidence that the cancer had been brewing for a while, but there was no accounting for its freak, aggressive nature or the rapid onset of symptoms. Most were still satisfied just to have some kind of answer.

Leah might have been, too, if the dreams had stopped.

I had a nightmare about Carlotta last night, she texted me early one morning before my alarm had gone off.

In this one she'd heard a loud buzzing coming from the other lab tech's head while they worked side by side.

In the nights that followed, the buzzing continued, and a bloody, ragged hole began to form in the side of Carlotta's head, just above her ear. It continued to grow, chewed away from the inside out, until dozens of red wasps poured from the gaping wound and filled the lab with their incessant, rumbling buzzing.

Leah tried to say that it wasn't bothering her, but I could see how tired and tense she was in her photos. I also couldn't help but notice how, no matter how well lit the area was, there seemed to be a shadowy haze across the background; it was like some kind of strange filter. The only thing that stood out against it was the red jewel of her necklace.

I didn't bring it up to Leah, though; she had enough on her mind without having to worry that her phone camera might be on the fritz.

Four days after Leah first dreamed of her co-worker, Carlotta put a pistol to her head, just above her ear, and pulled the trigger.

"Her family said she'd been struggling with depression for a while, but they thought she'd been getting better," Leah told me on her way back from the funeral.

"People hide things too well, sometimes."

"Something's going on, Jackie," she said grimly. "I've dreamed of people twice now, and both times they've died in a way similar to my dreams."

"I know," I reluctantly replied. "It's weird, but…"

"But what can I do about it," she finished for me. "I don't know."

"Me neither."

I wished I could help ease her mind and give her an explanation for what was happening, but we were both equally lost. She sounded so worn out when we hung up, so unlike herself. I almost started to cry.

I was woken late that night by my phone ringing on my bedside table. I felt around for it and practically dropped it against my ear with a sleepy,

"Hello?"

"I had another one," Leah was shaky and breathless. "Addy, my supervisor, there were maggots! They were falling out of her mouth and burrowing from her stomach. Something's going to happen to her!"

It took almost an hour to get Leah calm again. She wanted to call Addy then and there, at one in the morning, to warn her that she was mere days away from death. I finally convinced her that might work against her. At best it would make her seem like she'd gone off the proverbial deep end, at worst, coming across as threatening her boss.

I booked a ticket on the first flight out at 8am the next morning before we'd even hung up.

Leah met me at baggage claim. She was drawn and jumpy, sliding the teardrop pendant along its chain with nervous energy as I walked up. The hug she gave me was the tightest I'd ever received.

"I'm not crazy," she said after we'd gotten into her car.

"If I were going to worry about your sanity, it would have happened a long time ago starting when you decapitated my teddy bear to see if he had a spine," I said. I was relieved to see her crack the faintest of smiles.

We let the ride lull us into silence until we got back to her apartment. Somehow, it just didn't feel like the kind of conversation one had in a car. It was too big, too deep, too serious. She paced the living room once we'd gotten inside, and I perched on the arm of her couch, my arms folded over my chest.

"I don't even know where to begin," she said.

"I was fine. Wo were Gary and Carlotta, and now all…" she waved an agitated hand, "this."

"I still think it could be coincidence. You noticed subtle signs, your brain did the math when you weren't looking and spit it out as dreams."

"Come on, Jack, you don't believe that. If you did, then why come all the way here?"

I shrugged helplessly. "Something must have happened. You saw something or heard it, a trigger of some kind."

"Nope," she shook her head. "Gary was the same dick as always. Carlotta was looking forward to her cousin's wedding in a couple of weeks."

While she spoke, she constantly fiddled the pendant. The light glinting off its red stone drew my attention, and I watched it pass repeatedly between her fingers.

Hadn't I given her that necklace shortly before all this started? Hadn't she been wearing it constantly since she received it? And hadn't that gem managed to still shine in all of those photos that seemed to have a dark film over them?

She must have noticed that I was distracted; she paused and followed my gaze to the necklace.

"What?" she asked, looking back at me.

"I was just thinking about what had changed before your dreams began and, well…"

"You think my necklace has something to do with it? That's…that's…I want to say that's stupid, but it makes about as much sense as anything else."

"Where's that certificate that came with it?"

We found it, folded up and tucked away in her kitchen junk-drawer after tossing through her living room and bedroom. The description on it was short, little more than what I'd read off in the car on the first day. It belonged to an eighteenth century herbalist, including a line thanking the DeWitt family for the piece.

With nothing else to go on, we latched onto the name.

Q quick internet search revealed a slew of DeWitts in the area. Only one branch of the family had articles dedicated to their wealth, philanthropic efforts, and their old ties to the community. They seemed like the best place to start looking for answers.

Most of the family members named in the articles were unlisted, which wasn't surprising given their prominent social status. The youngest daughter, Eloise, was an attorney however, and she had a website complete with contact information.

"Should we call?" Leah asked with a hint of nervousness.

"No," I was already inputting the office address into my phone. "Come on, it's already two. I want to make sure we get there before they close."

The Dewitt & Siegfield Law Firm was an imposing, modern building. The receptionist we met inside was an imposing, modern woman, all angles and sleek. She eyed us all the way across the lobby with a polite, but suspicious, stare. I guessed she didn't see such casually dressed people wandering in very often.

"We're here to see Eloise DeWitt," I said, keeping the question out of my voice.

Direct and confident, that was what these sorts preferred. I hoped.

"Is she expecting you?" The receptionist's

S.H. Cooper

expression didn't change.

"No. We're here to discuss an heirloom donation she made; it will only take a moment."

Beside me, I could hear Leah's pendant sliding back and forth along the chain.

We were told to take a seat while the receptionist put a call back to Ms. DeWitt. I kept expecting us to be told that she wouldn't see us, to be dismissed. The receptionist hung up and simply returned to her work without another glance toward us. We sat stiffly on the leather couch, glancing between each other and then back at the receptionist, silently debating if we should ask what was going on.

I was on the verge of getting up to approach again when the door beside the reception area beeped. It was pushed open by a petite woman with silver streaked hair and a stern countenance even when she was smiling.

"Ms. DeWitt?" Leah spoke for the first time since our arrival.

"You two must be from the Heritage Society. I apologize for keeping you waiting, I didn't think our meeting was until tomorrow." She held the door open for us, and we walked through without correcting her. "My office is the third door on the left."

She took her seat behind a large oak desk covered in files and paperwork and waved us into two chairs opposite her. She was still smiling while we got settled, until Leah was facing her with the necklace hanging in plain sight. The way her lips thinned and her shoulders squared was slight, almost imperceptible: the practiced control of a

~140~

courtroom attorney.

She knew something.

"We're sorry to just drop in like this," I started to say, hoping to ease into the topic of the necklace, but Leah cut me off.

"We're not from the Heritage Society, we're here because of this," she jabbed a finger toward her neck. "Your family donated it to a secondhand store and, ever since I put it on, weird shit has been happening. I want to know why."

"I'm sorry, I don't know what you're talking about," Eloise replied primly, her hands folding atop her desk.

"Bull you don't," Leah argued.

"Ms. DeWitt, we just want to know—" Again I tried to speak, and again I was interrupted, this time by Ms. DeWitt.

"I just told you, I don't know anything about that trinket."

"And I told you that's bull," Leah, driven by sleepless nights and fear, slammed her hands on the desk and stood over her.

"Do I need to call security?" Ms. DeWitt was reaching for her phone. I grabbed Leah's wrist to drag her back into her seat.

"We don't want problems, ok? We just want to know what's going on. If you're worried about us repeating anything, we swear, anything you tell us stays here. My sister just needs answers—" I was beginning to wonder why I bothered at all; Leah started talking over me mid-sentence.

"People are dying! And if it keeps happening, you better believe I'm going to find a way to tie it back to you and your whole family!"

This was not the approach I had hoped to take. Ms. DeWitt studied Leah's reddened face, weighing her options behind a slight frown.

"How many?" Ms. DeWitt finally asked. "Have died, I mean."

"Two so far," Leah relaxed slightly. "I had dreams for three days before both, and now I'm having them again about a third person."

"You're lucky then. It took my family years to put the pieces together. We lost over a dozen while that...thing was in our possession."

"So it is the necklace that's causing it, then?"

"No," Ms. DeWitt sat back and peered at the pendant from over the top of her glasses. "It's what's in the stone."

Eloise DeWitt was one of the last in a long line of descendants of Maeve Bringwell. According to their extensive family history, she'd been, as the certificate of authenticity had said, an herbalist who specialized in the healing arts. What it left out, however, was that she practiced in blood as often as she did herbs. Every remedy she provided, be it a poultice or potion, was said to contain blood. Sometimes it was her's, sometimes it came from family members of the afflicted or animals she had sacrificed.

She recognized that there was power in blood: a restorative property that she was able to tap into in times of need.

Her gift was twofold. In addition to her use of blood, Maeve also had what came to be called the "healer's sight". She could see physical ailments that no one else could. Pregnancies, internal growths, rot; Maeve could pinpoint it all with total accuracy.

She said that it came to her in her sleep, whispered by the Lord's angels so that she might tend to His flock.

When anyone dared to say that it was witchcraft or claimed she communed with Satan, Maeve would stand in the town square, reading from the bible and reciting prayers to prove that she was as God-fearing as any other good, Christian woman. It was simply her gift, and she gave it freely to her community.

Even in the face of adversity, she continued her work. She was the reason they made it through poxes and diseases that wiped out nearby towns, and she was the reason that children became adults and adults became elders.

And her husband was the reason she was put to death.

He, along with a handful of others, including her father and brother, had grown to fear Maeve as a consort of the devil, and they conspired against her. They gathered while she slept one night and slipped into her bedroom where they stabbed her over and over again.

She did not die right away and, in her final moments, she splashed her blood upon them and cursed them to have her sight without the power to help or heal.

The legend said that her blood drops hardened into rubies upon contact with her killers. For weeks after, they would fall from their pockets and roll out of their shoes, marking them for their role in her death.

"Supposedly, the nightmares followed, like the

ones you had. They would see their loved ones being eaten alive by insects and animals and, shortly after, those same loved ones would die of sudden onset maladies. Maeve's husband, possibly beset by guilt, started wearing one of the rubies around his neck until he hung himself some months later. That is the pendant you're wearing now."

Ms. DeWitt nodded at Leah. "It's been passed down for generations. Now whoever wears it sees as she did, but is unable to help or heal. If you're around someone with an existing condition, physical or mental, it exacerbates it rapidly and in a matter of days, they succumb. I lost nannies to it, my brother, a teacher... The list goes on."

"There was a darkness in Leah's photos since she put it on," I said suddenly. "What is that?"

"I've always assumed it's Maeve. She becomes most clear right before a death, as if it makes her stronger. I've seen it happen many times in my own photos." Ms. DeWitt's voice became distant, fogged by memories.

"And you just gave it away?" Leah's voice quivered with a barely controlled rage I'd never heard before.

Ms. DeWitt's smile was razor thin. "It doesn't matter. Give it away, try to destroy it, bury it, burn it. It always finds its way back. An eternal curse against the family that betrayed her."

My sister yanked the necklace and it fell away with a soft snap. She hurled it at the older woman as she shoved herself to her feet.

"Good," Leah hissed. "You deserve it."

I followed Leah back to the car, and we sat

there for a long time, just staring at the office building.

Leah never had another dream like those she'd experienced while wearing the necklace.

She learned later that her supervisor, Addy, was rushed to the ER with a ruptured appendix that same day, but she survived.

We didn't talk about what happened often. There wasn't much left to say. No one would believe us, but I knew Leah still struggled with some guilt afterwards. Instead of dwelling and being dragged down by it, though, she used it as motivation to return to school. She earned additional certifications in blood work and genetic studies and became a genetic counselor, helping people test for predisposition to hereditary issues and early detection.

Maeve Bringwell had known the importance of blood. She knew there was power in it, and she'd used it, for better and worse, both in life and in death.

Leah knew that power, too, even as a kid.

It was what drew her to it.

Although she would never admit it, I think Leah felt a kinship to the misunderstood Maeve, at least to the person she'd been before her murder. In her own way, Leah has chosen to continue seeing things that Maeve saw: the things that blood shows us if we know where to look. And like Maeve, Leah uses her power to help those around her heal.

Ring Once

I'd never been good in storms, but I was even worse in hospitals. When the choice came to visit Nana, my ma's mother, or stay home and brave the thunder and lightning on my own, I only hesitated for a moment before making my decision.

"You sure you don't want to come, Hannah?" Ma asked, hovering uncertainly in the doorway leading to the garage.

Dad was already out in the car waiting for her.

"Yeah," I said.

I didn't add that this was my attempt at facing my fear of thunderstorms head on. I was thirteen already; it was time to stop being such a baby. Besides, I'd have Thaddeus, our five year old Lhasa Apso, with me. It wasn't like I'd be totally alone.

"Ok, we have our beepers if you need to reach us." Ma shifted the large photo album in her arms and continued to linger. "We'll only be a couple of hours."

Behind her, the garage door creaked open and the car started: Dad's signal that he was getting impatient.

"I'll go with you next time. Tell Nana I said hi."

Ma planted another quick kiss on my head and checked just one more time that I was *sure* I wanted to stay home before finally leaving. I watched my parents pull out of the driveway from the living room window. I tried to ignore the fat, angry clouds gathering overhead, grabbing Thaddeus to head to my room to read.

The storm broke only moments later.

The first peal of thunder had my little dog pressed against my side. The second had him shivering so hard that my whole bed vibrated. I cuddled him close and whispered soothingly to him, hoping that he didn't notice how I jumped with every rumble or flash of white lightning. I tried to distract us both by reading aloud.

It worked for a while; I was so focused on the story that the howling wind and pounding rain became background noise. Thaddeus continued to shake, but between keeping his face buried in my side and (I like to think) the sound of my voice, it became more intermittent, only occurring when thunder actually rolled. I had thought we could ride out the whole storm together that way.

A particularly bright flash of lightning followed by the immediate sharp crack of thunder proved me wrong.

I squealed, Thaddeus whined, and we both bolted from my room, leaving my book face down and forgotten on the bed.

"I was hungry anyway," I grumbled, trying to save face as we hurried down the steps toward the kitchen.

I turned on every light on the way down. It made me feel better, less alone, less like Mother Nature was going to burst through my windows. Thaddeus stuck close to my feet while I went from the pantry to the fridge and then back again, trying to decide what I wanted to snack on.

The phone ringing shrilly from its place on the wall beside the fridge made my heart skip a beat.

It rang just once, then went silent.

I swallowed hard and looked down to Thaddeus, like he was the one who had been startled. "It's just the phone, it's ok," I told him.

He licked his lips and wagged his tail once in response. I knew he just wanted a bite of cheese (there was no storm big enough to make him not want cheese), but I took it to mean he agreed that we were fine. It had probably just been a misdial or something, and the person hung up when they realized their mistake.

I put together a little plate of tortilla chips and cheese, some of which went to Thaddeus, and stuck it in the microwave to melt. Once it was done, we took our snack and went to the living room to watch cartoons at a high enough volume to block out the storm.

A few minutes after we'd sat down, the phone on the living room table rang.

A little less on edge this time, I reached for it and plucked the receiver from its cradle.

"Hel—" I started to say, but was cut off by the dial tone.

I frowned and set the phone back down. Maybe the storm was messing with the lines or something. I thought I remembered Dad saying that could happen when the weather got bad.

"Nothing to be scared of," I said to Thaddeus.

He draped himself across my lap, his eyes fixed on my nachos. I giggled and, bleeding heart that I was, gave him one. When a gust of wind rattled the nearby windows, we huddled closer together and I turned up the TV even more.

We made it part way through an episode of my show before the phone went off again. This time I only sat up slightly to look at it.

It stayed quiet after that single ring.

I tried to dismiss it like I had before, but a line of goosepimples had started to creep up the back of my neck which I rubbed roughly. Don't be a baby, I repeated to myself a few times. It's just the phone. I tried to pay attention to the TV again, but every few seconds I'd find my eyes slipping back to the phone.

The next time it rang, about ten minutes later, the lights overhead flickered.

Just once. Another single ring, then silence.

The storm outside continued to batter the house, and the lights dimmed again before coming back on fully. My heart was pounding in my chest, and I suddenly had the urge to use the restroom. I gave Thaddeus a quick pat and leapt off the couch to run down the hall to the bathroom.

I was in the middle of washing my hands when the lights went out. The bathroom was plunged into total darkness.

I whimpered and groped for a towel to dry my hands, then for the handle. There were flashlights in the junk drawer in the kitchen. I just had to make my way down the hall to them. My trembling fingers closed on the doorknob, and I started to pull it open at the same time the phone rang.

It echoed once throughout the dark and the quiet.

I froze, too afraid to move forward. It was dumb—I knew it was dumb—but the high pitched trill of that phone was almost enough to have me bursting into tears. Why did it keep ringing? Who was it? What did they want?

It's someone who knows I'm home alone, a panicked voice cried out in my head.

Thaddeus whined from the living room. He was alone and as scared as I was, and I had to get to him. It was the only thing that got me moving again. I bit my lip, bowed my head, and charged down the hall to the kitchen. The junk drawer was thrown open, and I felt around wildly until I found one of the flashlights there. I switched it on and followed its thin beam of light to the living room.

Lightning lit up the house around me for a second, quickly followed by a deep growl of thunder. I forced back a sob and, in a shaky squeak, called for Thaddeus. He whined again and I shined my flashlight around the room until I found him.

He was sitting at the foot of the table the phone was on, staring up at it.

As soon as the light landed, it rang again. Just once.

"Thaddeus!" I shouted as if I was afraid something was going to reach through the phone and grab him.

He continued to look up at it, his ears perked forward. He whined again.

I darted across the room and knelt to pick him up when I heard something: a thump on the front porch right outside the door. My flashlight was on it instantly, just in time for the lock to start turning.

The door swung inward and I started to scream.

"Hannah! Hannah, calm down!"

It took me a moment to realize that the figures in the doorway, dripping wet and featureless in the shadows, were my parents. They'd come in through the front door since there was no power to open the garage. I dropped the flashlight on the floor and Thaddeus and I ran to them. I fell into my dad's arms.

"What is it? What's wrong?" he asked. I looked up at them, ready to tell them all about the storm and the phone, but the words died in the back of my throat.

Their eyes were red and puffy, and Ma's face was twisted with an expression I'd only ever seen once after her dad's accident three years prior. An ugly sinking feeling filled my whole body. For a moment, the strange calls were forgotten.

"Nana?" I managed to ask.

They hugged me tightly between them. It was all the answer I needed.

"She'd been real sick for a long time, baby girl," Dad said so Ma wouldn't have to. "We thought we'd have more time with her, but she suddenly got worse today and...we were with her in the end. That's what matters."

I wanted to say something nice to Ma, something that might have helped her feel even a tiny bit better, but my tongue had become thick and clumsy. All I could do was cling to her and cry in the doorway.

Behind me, the phone rang just once.

I stiffened and, to my surprise, so did my mom. I looked up at her and saw that she was staring over my head, right at the phone.

"It's been doing that for a while," I was now

angry at whoever was playing the prank instead of scared. Ma didn't need to be bothered right now!

"What, ringing?" Dad asked. He guided Ma the rest of the way into the house so we weren't standing half in the storm and shut the door.

"Yeah, just on—"

"Just once," Ma whispered in disbelief.

"How'd you know?" I asked, my eyes widening.

Ma crossed the dark living room and took a seat on the edge of the couch beside the phone. She never stopped looking at it.

"After I moved out of my parents' house for the first time, I lived an hour away. I'd visit every other weekend and each time I left, Ma would ask me to call them to let them know I made it back to my apartment safely. I did it for a long time, until I met your dad," Ma's voice cracked and she ran her fingers down the receiver. "I'd let the phone ring just once to let them know all was well. She'd call back and let my phone ring once too. She said it was to say got it, thank you, and I love you."

Dad sat beside her and put an arm around her shoulders. She took a deep, shuddering breath.

"Do you think...do you think it's Nana?" I asked.

"It can't be, honey," Dad said gently.

No sooner had the words left his mouth than the phone rang again, just once. The same signal Ma had used for years to let her family know that she was safe. That she was home.

Ma and Dad exchanged a look.

"Abby," Dad said as she reached for the phone.

"She rang once, George. Now it's my turn," she said with the ghost of a watery smile.

Instead of arguing, Dad took her hand and gave it a squeeze. He released it so she could dial her mother's phone number for the last time.

She held it up to her ear just long enough for it to ring once.

Just long enough to say got it. Thank you. I love you.

After she hung up, the phone didn't ring again.

Airsekui

I knew the way to Grandpa's by heart.

An hour up the highway, then another on small country roads. When you start seeing signs for the Native American reservation off to the right and some for the nearest town on the left, you've got exactly twenty minutes left. Then it's just past the same three billboards for anti-abortion, a missing person, and a divorce attorney that hadn't been changed in at least five years.

The edge of Grandpa's property, a massive farm that seemed almost endless when I was young, was marked by a fence with a bright pink corner post. On the days he knew I'd be visiting, he'd tie a balloon to it and we'd ride out to get it on his tractor after saying our hellos. We'd continue on to visit the pigs and the goats and the cows. He only kept a few of each, mostly for my benefit, and they were all fat and happy and friendly.

His "real moneymaker" was his corn: acres and acres of it that ran behind his house. I wasn't allowed to play in the corn fields unsupervised—he and my parents thought it was too dangerous and that I could get lost or hurt among the stalks—but that didn't bother me much. I much preferred to spend time with my favorite goat, Sally Mae, a young white doe who would chase me around and gently headbutt me for chin scratches and carrots.

I didn't even mind that his old TV only had

five channels. There was always something to do outside, a chore to be done, somewhere to explore, an animal to play with, and I could keep myself busy from morning until night.

Grandpa loved having me (I liked to think I was his favorite out of all seven grandkids), and I loved going. When my dad had a big conference out of town that he wanted Mom to go with him for, it was a no-brainer where I'd end up.

"You're going to be good for Gramps, right, Hazel?" Dad asked, glancing at me in the rear view mirror as we passed the pink post with a foil "Welcome!" balloon waving above.

"Yup!" I agreed readily.

"What do you think you guys are gonna get up to this weekend?" Mom half turned in her seat toward me with a smile.

"I'm gonna play with Sally Mae and go down to the creek and help milk the cows and pet the pigs and —"

My "to do" list took us all the way to Grandpa's front door, where he met us with a broad grin and a big hug for each.

"Thanks again, Pop," Dad said. "You're sure you don't mind? Keeping an eight year old entertained on your own for four days can be tough."

"I'm up for it," Grandpa assured him. "We'll have lots to keep us busy, right Hazelnut?"

I nodded enthusiastically as I hauled my little suitcase up the porch steps. I was ready for my parents to be on their way so I could start living the farm life. Mom chased me and scooped me into a tight embrace, which I returned briefly before wriggling for freedom. My parents had never left me for so long and, and now that it was time to say goodbye, it was obvious they were having second thoughts.

"She'll be fine." Grandpa laughed. "We both will be! But if she doesn't behave, I'll just drop her in the middle of the cornfield, no muss, no fuss."

After they'd finally left, I dumped my things inside and grabbed Grandpa's offered hand to head out to the tractor.

Once we retrieved the balloon and I had its ribbon tied securely around my wrist, we zoomed (as well as one can zoom on a tractor, anyway) over to the pig pen. He let me throw some feed into the trough. When the pair of pigs, Gretel and Fat Babs, came trundling over, I crouched between them and stroked their sides while they munched. The rotund sows leaned into my hands with satisfied snorts.

Afterward we stopped by the cow and goat enclosure, which was just a large fenced in area where the seven of them could roam free. As soon as she heard the tractor approaching, Sally Mae came bounding toward the gate, bleating loudly and tossing her head. I barely made it in before she was bomping against me and nuzzling her face into my stomach.

We stayed out for much of the afternoon, tending first to the animals, and then picking through the ever-expanding vegetable garden for supper. He'd bought some fried chicken to go with it, and we sat on the back porch to eat while the sun set on a fiery horizon.

"What did you bring to read tonight?"

Grandpa asked after we'd settled inside for the evening.

He was in his recliner with his feet propped up and a crossword puzzle book in his lap. We both knew he'd only get about three words in before his eyes drooped shut and he started snoring, something I liked to tease him about.

"It's about kids who live in an old boxcar 'cos they don't have parents," I said from my place curled up on the couch.

"S'that so?"

"Yeah, it's for school. They make us read books over summer, but I like it."

"Good, good," he mumbled, his pencil scratching across the page of his crossword.

It was quiet on my grandpa's farm, especially at night. I was used to hearing cars going by, dogs barking, neighbors outside, and all the sounds of suburbia. Out here was nothing but insect songs, the occasional farm animal call, and the wind. It could be a little unnerving at times if I focused too much on it, but when I was awake in the living room with Grandpa nearby, surrounded by soft lamp light, I found it peaceful.

Grandpa had just dozed off and I'd tucked myself comfortably under a blanket, my book propped up against my bent knees, when the pigs started to scream.

I nearly dropped my book. Grandpa rocked forward in his chair, his eyes snapping open. The pencil he'd been holding slipped from his hand and rolled across the floor. I looked to him, my jaw clenched tight with surprise, uncertainty, and fear.

"It's ok, Hazelnut," he said, pushing himself

quickly to his feet. "Probably a coyote sniffing around and scaring the girls. Nothing to worry about."

But he didn't seem entirely convinced of that himself. In all my visits to Grandpa's, I'd never heard Gretel and Fat Babs make that kind of noise: loud, harsh squeals that cut through the evening air. Nothing about it sounded right or normal.

I followed close at Grandpa's heels wile he hurried out of the room and went to his office. He got his shotgun, ammunition, and a flashlight from his closet.

"A-are you gonna shoot it?" I asked shakily.

"Maybe," he replied, grim. "You stay inside."

The shells loaded with loud clicks into the belly of the gun.

"No!" I cried, desperate not to be left alone while the pigs were shrieking so frantically.

Grandpa looked like he wanted to argue, but the loud bellow from one of the cows cut him off. Like the pigs, she sounded panicked. As soon as one cried out, the other two joined in. He told me to stay put again and headed toward the door in long strides. I'd never seen that stony look on his face before. I hesitated a moment, just long enough for one of the pigs to scream again, before chasing after him.

"Grandpa!" I shouted.

"I told you to stay inside!"

"I'm scared!"

He glanced over his shoulder at me, grit his teeth, and nodded. "Stay close behind me."

We followed the squeals to the pig pen. Grandpa handed the flashlight to me, and I shined it around, looking for the girls. Usually they would have come up to meet us when Grandpa whistled sharply, but there was no familiar tromp of hooves over dirt.

Only screaming.

The flashlight beam finally fell across them in the middle of their pen. Fat Babs had her teeth buried in Gretel's ear, and she was squealing and pulling and trying to buck. Gretel was bowed slightly and tearing chunks of flesh from Babs' neck. Both were already bloodied from multiple bite wounds and gouges, their mouths lined with thick, red foam, their eyes rolling wildly.

Grandpa shouted their names, but neither even looked at us; they just kept attacking each other and making the most awful sounds. He grabbed me by my upper arm and dragged me away, toward the cow and goat enclosure, where more bellows and shrieks and moans tore through the night.

Lady, my grandpa's oldest and favored cow, was on her side by the gate, her legs kicking feebly. Two goats rammed into her body over and over again. Off to our side, another goat released an agonized bleat. I found her quickly with the flashlight.

Sally Mae was pinned beneath the trampling hooves of a second cow who kicked and stomped madly at the smaller animal. I screamed and grabbed at Grandpa.

"She's killing Sally!" I cried.

Before he could do anything, the cow reared back as far as she could and brought her hooves down onto Sally Mae's head with a ringing crunch.

Blood poured from the poor goat's nose and ears. She writhed upon the ground until the cow did it again and a third time, and then Sally Mae laid still.

I turned with an anguished cry and took a few steps away. My ears rang with the sound of the hysterical animals and tears spilled in hot streaks down my face. I lifted the flashlight again, trying to find my way home. I just wanted to get inside. I wanted the noise to stop!

Something moved in the darkness a few feet ahead of me, just beyond the reach of my light. I froze.

"Grandpa!"

I didn't know if he'd seen it too, but he grabbed me around my waist and hoisted me up against his side. He started to sprint as fast as he could back toward the house. We passed the pig pen again, where I caught sight of Gretel standing over Fat Babs, rooting through her spilled innards.

The back door was in sight. We just had to cross through the vegetable garden and we'd be behind the safety of locked doors.

My grip on the flashlight slipped slightly as I was jostled about. It angled downwards, illuminating the ground in front of us. I screamed again.

Arms. Human arms, at least a dozen of them, were reaching up from between plants on either side of the path leading to the door. They waved jerkily, their fingers clenching and then unclenching as if grasping at something.

When the light fell on them, they all turned and stretched toward us.

"No." Grandpa breathed the single word in

disbelief.

He stumbled backward and we both fell hard to the ground. I yelped and the flashlight bounced from my hand to land beside me, pointing toward Grandpa. He'd gone so white, so haggard, and his eyes were locked on those reaching arms.

Gradually, through the haze of terror and confusion, I realized that there was a figure standing behind my grandfather. It looked like a man, but taller than any I had ever seen, and so muscular and broad. It took a step toward Grandpa, who was still unaware, and moved more into the light. The head sitting atop its neck wasn't human, but that of a great brown bear with one eye scarred shut.

I knew I should have been afraid. I should have warned grandpa, should have responded in some way, but when I looked into the face of that creature, all I felt was an odd sense of complete peace.

You do not need to be afraid. I felt more than heard something in my head. A voice, a thought, I wasn't sure. It was like nothing I'd ever known. *You are an innocent.*

I wanted to tell it that Grandpa was an innocent, too, but I was unable to speak.

It reached out its large hands and plucked Grandpa off the ground as if he weighed nothing. He let out a strangled yell as he was tossed into the vegetable garden into those waiting arms. I just sat there and watched with that same feeling of peace as the filthy hands closed around Grandpa's body. They began to pull and pull and pull, until the soil swallowed him up along with his screams.

The creature stood and watched until Grandpa and the arms vanished. Then as suddenly as it appeared, it turned and walked back into the darkness.

The moment it was gone, so too was the calm that had blanketed my body and mind.

The 911 operator could barely understand me when I finally got my legs to work and made it to the house phone. I was sobbing and hysterical, and mostly all I could say was, "Grandpa's in the ground!"

Cops and firefighters and paramedics filled the front yard. They thought my grandfather might have had a heart attack or a stroke, and I was too young to know how to explain it properly. It took some time to make them understand that I meant what I said: Grandpa was in the ground.

They dug up the freshly tilled earth of the garden where I'd last seen grandfather. They had to go down almost six feet before they found his body. It was covered in deep fingernail scratches, his limbs nearly torn off at the sockets, buried amongst six others in a mass grave.

I knew the way to Grandpa's by heart.

An hour up the highway, another on small country roads; and then you start seeing signs for the Native American reservation off to the right. A reservation that nine women had gone missing from in ten years.

A reservation that had been ignored when it sought help from the local police department after the first two women vanished while hitchhiking down those small country roads.

A reservation that had been ignored by the

media when its council asked for coverage detailing the disappearances.

Then it's just past the same three billboards, one for a missing person; a Native American woman named Dana Young. She was 21 when she left home to catch a ride into the city after her mom couldn't give her a lift. Her family and friends searched for years, without any real help from surrounding authorities. Every year, they paid to keep that billboard up in the hopes someone would see it and recognize Dana.

They didn't know that she was just twenty minutes up the road.

They didn't know she was lying beneath a vegetable garden that had expanded six times over.

They didn't know the friendly old man, whose house they had stopped at with fliers, who had smiled in sympathy while promising to call if he saw or heard anything, was the same one who had taken her.

Two of the women were never found, but jewelry belonging to them — a wedding ring and a necklace — were discovered in my grandfather's safe. They were the first two to go missing.

The ninth and final woman, who had disappeared only three days prior to my visit and who received nothing more than a small blurb in the local paper, was found. She was clinging to life in a cellar dug beneath the old barn behind the cornfield Grandpa never let anyone near. He said it was unsafe, that it was where he stored his old tools and machinery. He said he didn't want someone walking in and hurting themselves.

No one had ever questioned him.

The woman, Pauline Smith, had carved a single word into the wooden beam she'd been shackled to using only her fingernails and blood.

Airsekui

The cops didn't know what it meant, nor did they care much. They were too busy being baffled over Grandpa's death and my version of events that led up to it. That was their biggest concern.

Not why those women had been murdered.

Not why no one had investigated more.

Not why nothing had been done by anyone off the reservation.

All they cared about was the strange way my grandpa and all of his farm animals died.

I had nightmares for years afterward. The screams I'd heard, the waving arms sticking up out of the ground, and of my grandfather, the murderer who had fed me vegetables grown from the bodies of his victims.

I never had nightmares about the bear-headed man, though. I only ever saw him when my dreams grew too dark and I was so afraid that my own heartbeat pounding against my ribs threatened to wake me. He would appear to me then, just on the edge of my vision, and I would hear those same words I'd heard that night. I would feel the same peace.

You do not need to be afraid. You are an innocent.

It took many years before I was able to look back at that night, at those deaths, and start to piece together what I had seen. I had to dig deep, to go through tons of old articles, to re-read all the horrible things about Grandpa that I'd been trying to forget. I found the answer in a single word that a desperate woman had broken her nails off to spell out in wood.

Airsekui

There wasn't much information, but enough.

It was a name that belonged to a being almost lost in the internet age. From what little I could find, there was debate over exactly what had originally been — a god of fire or a god of war — but his later place in his pantheon was clear. He had been a great spirit, one that was called upon in times of peril.

Pauline Smith, knowing that she was part of an often overlooked and ignored group, had kept her faith. Not in the police, or in the authorities who tossed those smiling photos of others like her aside. Not in the media, who gave her a single paragraph at the bottom of a newspaper page. Not in a billboard that hundreds of people drove by every day without ever really seeing.

She had had faith in something greater, and she had cried out.

And Airsekui had listened.

Spider Girl

When my daughter was young, she liked to make up silly rules for our household. On Wednesday evenings, we all wore a sock on our right foot, but nothing on our left; if someone sneezed, the only polite response was "Godzilla nights"; if you dropped something you were carrying, you had to leave it on the floor for at least ten seconds to see if the gnomes who lived under our fridge wanted it. They were silly things that made sense only in Melody's toddler mind.

My husband, Felix, and I thought it was cute and creative, and we played along since there was no harm in it.

We always knew when a new rule was coming because she would take us both by the hand, regardless of what we were doing, and lead us to the couch. She would sit us down and squeeze herself between us.

"What's up, Sprout?" Felix asked one evening after our four year old dragged us to the living room.

"New rule!" she practically shrieked.

We nodded, solemn and expectant.

"No killing spiders," she said.

"But you don't like spiders," I replied, trying to suppress my smile.

"I do!" It was certainly a change of tune from the last time she'd seen one. She'd cried for hours, even after Felix disposed of it.

"Oh yeah? Since when?"

"I like them 'cos they like me." She glanced up at us, daring us to question such sound logic.

"Ok then." Felix nodded. "Spiders are our friends."

"Yeah!"

After we tucked her in, my husband and I shared a quiet laugh.

"They must be covering Charlotte's Web at daycare or something," I said.

"Must be."

As far as the rules went, it really wasn't such a bad one. I didn't enjoy killing things to begin with, even creepy, eight-legged crawlies, and logically I knew they were good for deterring other pests. Still, I made Felix handle the actual removal from the house. Melody was very careful to oversee all spider extractions (from behind the safety of Daddy's legs), and made sure they were always placed gently in the bushes at the front and back doors.

She even started naming them.

"The biggest is Buttercup; she's black and has long legs and big eyes and likes to sit outside my window. Then there's Spaghetti and Blue and Tomorrow..." she explained from her booster seat while I drove her to daycare.

"There's a spider named Tomorrow?"

"Yup. He's little and stays away from Buttercup 'cos she's the queen spider and he's not allowed near her."

"Right, right, of course."

Most little girls played with dolls or begged

for a puppy. Mine named spiders and made up a hierarchy for them. Lucky me.

Sometimes I'd find her outside in the fenced backyard, crouched beside the bushes, talking to Buttercup and her loyal subjects. Melody told the spiders about her day in a long, rambling monologue, and then ask them how their day was and what they'd done. She never tried to touch them, never disturbed the delicate webs that were woven in the depths of the bushes. She just talked to them.

It was such an abrupt change from the wide-eyed terror she used to experience. About a week after she set the new rule, I had to ask her where her newfound love of arachnid kind came from.

"Buttercup," she said.

"Buttercup? The queen spider?"

"Yeah. She's nice. She protects me."

"She...what? Protects you?" I couldn't stop the baffled frown from crossing my face.

"Yup. From the not-nice."

"W-where'd you get that idea, Sprout?"

"She told me. The not-nice watch from outside, but they're scared of Buttercup. She keeps them away."

"The spider talks to you?"

Melody shrugged nonchalantly. "Sometimes. I wanna go play."

"Yeah, sure. Dinner's soon though."

I watched her scamper off down the hall to her room with a chill in my gut. I wasn't worried about Melody thinking she could talk to animals or even that she picked spiders. Kids did weird, goofy stuff like that all the time. What worried me was that she felt like she had something to be afraid of.

"She called them not-nice," I said to Felix after we'd gone to bed that night. "She said they watch her from outside and the spiders keep them away."

"Kid's got one hell of an imagination," Felix replied sleepily.

"Where would she get that kind of idea from, though? Is she scared of something?"

"You're over thinking it, babe. She's four. She just...says stuff."

While Felix drifted off to sleep beside me, I stayed awake. I stared into darkness, wondering how such a young child would even be able to come up with those kinds of ideas.

Melody didn't seem phased, though, nor did she seem afraid. She was the same happy wild child she'd always been, just with more spiders. I kept an extremely close eye on her, actively searching for any signs that someone might be watching her from a distance. I kept all the doors locked even when we were home. Felix thought I was overreacting, but I couldn't shake that initial chill I'd gotten.

I started following Melody into the backyard when she went out to play. I'd sit with an open, but unread, book in my lap, and I'd watch her. When she wasn't talking to the spiders, she'd bring toys over to the row of bushes and busy herself with playing pretend, completely unbothered by the glossy webbing and its inhabitants lurking only feet away.

Sometimes I'd even catch sight of Buttercup out of the corner of my eye. For how large she was, about the size of my fist, she was an expert at staying hidden.

"Mommy," Melody said one afternoon while we were sitting in the yard, "Buttercup says you don't have to be afraid."

I jumped slightly and looked at my daughter, who was kneeling next to the bushes as usual. Beside her, almost invisible in the shadows, I thought I saw the outline of a very large spider.

"She says that the not-nice won't hurt me while she's here."

Melody was back to her games before I had a chance to respond. I swallowed the tight ball of anxious fear in my throat. I tried to tell myself that it was just make believe, just my daughter and her crazy imagination. That didn't stop all the little hairs on my arm from standing on end.

It also didn't stop me from staring at those bushes and feeling countless little eyes staring back.

Felix tried to be understanding when I broached the subject with him again, but I knew he was still convinced it was just a little kid's nonsense.

"You weren't there. You didn't hear her," I said, struggling to control my frustration.

"I know, I know," Felix sighed. "Can I be honest, babe?"

I stiffened, but nodded.

"I think you're stressed out. Between working and being an awesome mom, you're fried. I think you and I should take a day, just us two, and go out."

"But Melody —"

"We'll call my parents; they'll be thrilled to

watch her."

"I don't know…"

"C'mon, Keira, we haven't had real us time in ages! It'll help you relax, Melody will get to spend time with Nono and Pop Pop; we all win."

He playfully poked and prodded, hugged and cajoled until I relented. I still had my doubts, but I also thought that Felix could be on to something. Maybe I'd been letting my anxiety get the best of me. We made plans for an afternoon river boat ride, followed up with a nice lunch and a visit to the beach. All nice, stress-free things to help take my mind off the fact that my daughter was conveying creepy messages from a spider.

We made arrangements with Felix's parents for the following Saturday, and I spent the rest of the week convincing myself I had nothing to worry about.

"Is it ok if we order pizza for lunch?" Felix's dad asked when they arrived to babysit.

"Don't be ridiculous, Dillon. I brought stuff to make sandwiches!" Felix's mom replied. "Honestly, a pizza."

Pop Pop winked at Melody, who giggled, and shrugged. "I tried."

"Thanks for watching her," I said, giving them both a hug and kiss. I almost mentioned not letting her go outside by herself, and keeping the doors locked and watching for suspicious behavior, but the pleading look from Felix stopped me. He just wanted one nice afternoon; I had to try and give him that.

And I tried, I really did. We sat, hand in hand, on the slow moving river boat, admiring the view.

We talked and laughed over a delicious lunch, but Melody was always in the back of my mind. I could just hear her little voice talking about Buttercup and the not-nice.

Felix sensed my continued unease.

"My parents are with her. She's fine," he said as we paid the restaurant bill.

"I know, you're probably right."

"But you want to skip going to the beach and head right home anyway."

I thought about denying it, but then sagged in my chair. "Yeah," I admitted at last.

"At least we got lunch."

"I'm sorry, babe."

"Not your fault. I know you can't turn off Mommy Brain."

I smiled guilty at him and he rolled his eyes. He leaned over to give me a kiss.

"If only I hadn't encouraged our kid to be so weird," he said.

I actually did feel a bit better during the drive home. Knowing Felix didn't hold my concern for Melody, as silly as he might think it was, lifted a large weight I hadn't even realized I'd been carrying. We talked about how to start distancing Melody from the spiders to make things a little more normal for us all the way home. When we pulled into the driveway, we shared another smile, another kiss, and then climbed out of the car.

We could hear Melody screaming long before we got into the house.

We burst through the door, asking over each other what had happened. Melody was sitting in the middle of the floor, her face red and wet with tears, screaming. Her grandparents were trying futilely to comfort her.

"There was a spider near her outside," Pop Pop said helplessly. "A big one. I thought it might bite her so I—"

"Oh no," I groaned, "you didn't."

While I tried to soothe Melody, Felix explained that the spider Pop Pop had stomped on had been Melody's kind-of pet that she had been very fond of. Pop Pop and Nono were very apologetic, but Melody was inconsolable. She cried for hours, even after they'd left and Felix had sprayed Buttercup's remains away with the hose. She only fell asleep when she was too exhausted to continue.

Melody refused to go outside for a good week after that. She would argue and sob if we tried to make her, yelling that the not-nice would get her because Buttercup was gone. I didn't know what to do. She was so upset, and nothing we said made a difference, even when we tried to tell her that it was all in her imagination. We were all at our wit's end.

Until Felix came home with a paper bag. He put it down in front of Melody and told her that Buttercup II was inside. Our daughter eyed him furiously, but reached in. She came out with a large, stuffed spider with a friendly smile and googly eyes.

"She's going to protect you," Felix said with a great deal of seriousness. "Just like Buttercup did."

Melody seemed uncertain, but after a bit more convincing from Felix, she was hugging the stuffed animal. She told it that she was so glad to have her Buttercup back.

"Think you wanna go outside and show her to the other spiders?"

"No," Melody said. "They all left 'cos Pop Pop squished the queen."

"Oh," Felix said. "Well, what if you bring it out and show them their new queen? Maybe they'll come back."

"They will?" The prospect sparked a joyful light I hadn't seen in Melody's eyes since Buttercup's untimely end.

"Sure!"

With Buttercup II tucked under her arm, Melody darted outside, calling for Spaghetti and Blue and Tomorrow.

I sank into Felix's arms and hugged him tight. "Thank you."

"Sometimes all it takes is a little Daddy Brain to solve a problem." He grinned.

We laughed and he went to get changed out of his work clothes while I went to start dinner.

I chopped up two potatoes before the silence hit me. No jabbering monologue. No giggles, none of the usual noises I usually heard when Melody was playing in the backyard. I wiped my hands on the front of my shirt and went to the window, expecting to see her crouched in front of the bushes.

She wasn't there.

My heart skipped a beat. I went to the door, calling for her. "Melody? Melody!"

There was no reply.

I ran out into the yard, still shouting her name. I dug through the web infested bushes and tore into her little playhouse; they were empty. My voice was becoming strangled as I rounded the side of the house where the fence gate was.

It was still closed and locked from the inside, same as always. Melody wasn't there, but lying at the foot of the gate, her long legs all askew and her googly eyes fixed on me, was Buttercup II.

"Melody!" I screamed again, but I already knew in my Mommy Heart and Mommy Brain that I wouldn't get an answer.

I knew that, without the real Buttercup, something not-nice had happened to my daughter.

Dad's Souvenirs

Dad was a pilot, and it was exactly as cool as it sounds.

He traveled across the globe, bouncing from faraway place to faraway place, seeing just about everything the world had to offer. By the time he was 30, he'd been to dozens of countries across six of the seven continents. It was actually thanks to his career that he and Mom had me and my sister, Josephine. While doing regular flights between the US and various airports in Asia, he became aware of international adoptions and broached the topic with Mom. Mom, who couldn't have children naturally, jumped at the chance.

It didn't bother either of them that Mom would be doing a lot of the proverbial heavy lifting at home while Dad worked. We could go anywhere from three days to two weeks without seeing him, and then he'd come home for a few days before having to fly off again. Mom was left to raise two small kids practically single handedly. He was gone so often when I was young that, for a time, I thought he existed only as a voice in the phone.

Despite his physical absence, Dad always did his best to make sure we knew we were loved.

He called every night, regardless of where he was in the world or what timezone he was in. He would read to us and ask what we've been up to. On those occasions when we were missing him particularly badly, he'd have us snuggle with Mom on the couch with the phone held between us. He retold us the stories of our adoptions: how excited he and Mom had been both times, how he'd begged to fly the next plane out to Beijing where I was born, and then to Mumbai three years later for Josephine to pick us up personally. He talked about how he took one look at our faces and known immediately that we were his little girls.

"And it doesn't matter how far away I go or how long I stay there; I'll always be your daddy."

When that didn't cheer us up properly, there were always the presents to look forward to.

Whenever Dad returned home, my sister and I would tear into his suitcase until we found the three packages tucked away at the bottom: one for mom, always wrapped in deep purple paper, one for me in yellow, and one for Jo in bubblegum pink. While Mom usually got jewelry or clothing of some sort, a handmade piece from the exotic locations, Jo and I usually got toys or picture books. There was always a postcard featuring an iconic landmark to remind us where everything came from.

Because of it, our spare bedroom became a museum of sorts. Mom hung the framed postcards with little date placards and stored the things she thought were too nice or delicate to wear. We weren't allowed in that room unsupervised, she was worried we'd make a mess of it, and the door was kept shut and locked to keep two inquisitive kids from getting into trouble. At first it was a novelty and we wanted in simply because it was forbidden, but as we got older, the spare room with its locked door held less and less mystique. When we got older we no longer cared at all, and the only reason it remained closed was simply out of habit.

Eventually, Dad's seniority with his airline made it so he had more control over his schedule. The international flights became fewer and fewer in favor of domestic ones which allowed him to be home more often. Jo was fifteen by then, and I was eighteen. We were used to his constant coming and going, and we no longer needed nightly phone calls or consolation gifts. That didn't stop him, however.

"You're always going to be my little girl and I'm always going to be your dad, kiddo," he said. Jo rolled her eyes as he handed off his latest package, still wrapped in bubblegum pink paper despite her newfound love for all things black.

I accepted mine with a grin. Jo was going through a phase where everything Mom and Dad did was lame, but I certainly didn't mind still getting the odd trinket, even if most of them ended up unused in some box in my closet. I pulled away the yellow wrapping and tugged open the box to find a ring with a thin gold band entwined around a pair of pearls.

"It's so pretty!" I said, hugging Dad, who looked fairly pleased with himself.

Jo glanced disinterestedly at it, then opened her own gift. For the first time in a long while, her eyes lit up at what she found inside. She quickly tried to play it off.

"What is it?" I asked, curious to know what had caused that rare almost-smile.

She shrugged with practiced dismissiveness

and tipped the box so I could see. Resting upon a bed of tissue paper was a nondescript brass key, old-fashioned and worn. A crimson ribbon was woven through the top of it, turning it into a choker. Apparently Dad had paid attention to Jo's changing tastes, which included a fondness for repurposed keys.

"You like it?" he asked with the same note of eagerness all parents use when trying to deduce the enigma that is their teenager's happiness.

"Yeah, it's fine," Jo replied, pulling the necklace from its box. She held it out to Dad and let him tie it around her neck.

"I found them both in this neat antique shop in New England," he said. "It was run by this strange little old lady; you'd like her, Jo. She said the ring came from some Spanish galleon which sank off the coast down in Florida, but I dunno. It doesn't look that old to me."

"It's a neat story at least," I said.

"Well, the key is even cooler. The lady gave me a warning; she said it can open any door, but beware! It'll show you what's really inside, and know that while you go in, what's inside can come out!"

"What's that supposed to mean?" Jo ran a finger down the length of the key.

"No idea, but she seemed to think it was very important that I know it. Probably just a silly selling tactic to add some mystery and jack up the price."

"You fell for it," Jo pointed out.

"Yeah, well, what can I say? I'm a sucker."

The good cheer brought on by pretty little

presents didn't last long.

Jo had recently become friendly with a group of girls that Mom quickly labeled as "bad influences". They were the same ones who inspired her dark wardrobe and fondness for loud, screeching music. Jo had started sneaking out, and talking back, and her grades had taken a rapid nosedive. It was hard to keep them up when she was cutting more classes than she was attending. Our parents tried talking to her, then yelling at her, eventually even punishing her.

She responded in typical, rebellious teen fashion. She said she hated them before storming off to her room.

It went on like that for weeks. A lot of shouting and slamming doors. Mom cried quietly when she thought we couldn't hear, and tensions on both sides were high. I did my best to stay out of it, determined to get through the final six months before I left for college without getting tangled up in Jo's nonsense. As the trust between my parents and Jo continued to decline, I found myself put in charge every time Mom and Dad left us alone.

"If you can't control her, what makes you think I can?" I complained one night. I'd just found out they were attending a dinner party with some of Dad's pilot pals.

"You don't need to control her. Just make sure she doesn't have anyone over or burn the place down," Dad said.

My efforts to get out of babysitting proved futile. They scurried out the door, blowing kisses back at me as they made their escape into the evening.

After checking to make sure Jo was in her room, I retreated to my own. I had a book report to focus on and I wasn't going to let my little sister's bad behavior affect my schoolwork. I pulled on my headphones, turned on my music, and began the hunt for academic sources to bolster my argument.

I'd only gotten a page into my report when the screams cut through the house: loud enough for me to hear over Ed Sheeran's crooning.

My first thought was that she'd hurt herself somehow and was now bleeding out on the floor. I tore across my room and slid into the hall, calling her name.

There was a whimper, then an unfamiliar woman's voice speaking rapidly in a language I didn't understand. The desperate pleading behind her words, however, was universal.

It was coming from just around the corner, from the spare room that had been locked and unused for so long.

I found Jo standing in its now partially open doorway. Her face was pale and eyes were wide, and beside her was a boy I didn't recognize, looking equally scared. The key from her choker was still in the door's handle, its crimson ribbon dangling limply from its end.

"What the hell, Jo?" I demanded, confused and shaken. I'd worry about who the guy was and what he was doing in our house later; I was more concerned with the screams.

From inside the room, the sound of a woman sobbing and pleading in that foreign language continued. Every hair on my arms stood on end.

"I-I don't know." Jo gaped dumbly. "It was just supposed to be a joke. Dad said the key opened any door and we were just messing with it! Kim, someone's in there!"

I grabbed her arm and pulled her away. The boy stumbled after her. With the two of them behind me, I inched toward the door, my hand outstretched to push it open wider. As my fingertips brushed against its surface, my dad's voice, lower and more menacing than I'd ever heard, sounded from within.

"Shut her up, damn it!" he snapped from the darkness. I immediately froze.

Jo's hand grabbed the back of my shirt. I glanced at her and saw the same frightened bewilderment stamped on her face that I knew was on mine.

There was the sharp ring of a slap. The woman quieted into heart wrenching, subdued sniffles before Dad spoke again. "I can get her out on Thursday's flight, but it's going to cost extra."

"My client is impatient for new girls, he'll pay," another voice, I didn't know, replied. He had a slight accent, maybe Chinese.

"Then I'll make sure she has a seat. You've got an escort for her?" Dad asked.

"Of course," the mystery man said. "The same arrangement as always."

"Not quite." Dad sounded doubtful. "The baby, what'll happen to her?"

"Orphanage, roadside, who cares? I only came for the mother."

There was a brief silence broken only by the woman's continued, plaintiff mumbles. Then Dad's voice: "Contact your guy in Beijing. Have him do up some adoption papers when he makes a passport for the girl. Find somewhere safe for the baby for the next two months until I can come back for her. Your client is paying for all that, too."

"That's not part of the deal!" the other man protested.

"Get me the papers and keep the kid safe, or your client doesn't have a new girl. Not Thursday or any other damn day."

There was mumbled, begrudging agreement. The room went quiet.

"Kim?" Jo was trembling against my back.

"I'm...gonna go," said the boy, who I'd forgotten was even there. He thundered down the hall toward the steps.

Jo didn't even call after him.

I crept forward, my sister still clinging to my shirt, and whispered, "Dad?"

When I got no response, I nudged the door open with my foot. Light from the hallway flooded the room. Aside from all the souvenirs Dad brought home, it was completely empty.

Jo and I exchanged a look, both lost, both terrified. Then we were running as fast as we could back to my room.

We shut and locked the door and tried to call our parents on my cell phone—first Mom, then Dad—but neither answered. We must have dialed them each a dozen times, but each time it went to voicemail.

"I just wanted to show Ethan the room." Jo was curled up at the foot of my bed with her knees pulled to her chest, rambling tearfully. "I wanted to—wanted to show him the stuff Dad brought back. I didn't even think the key would work. I only used it because of the story Dad told us when he gave it to me. I thought it would be funny! What was that, Kim?"

But I didn't have an answer for her. I couldn't even be angry with her for sneaking a boy into the house. I was too rattled.

Neither of us left my room until hours later, when Mom finally pulled into the garage a little after one AM.

Dad wasn't with her.

It was hard to piece together what had happened at first. Mom was so upset that she kept alternating between fury and near-hysterical crying. She paced from room to room restlessly. We trailed after her, too afraid to ask for details but desperate to know more. She finally sat at the kitchen table with a bottle of wine and one of the large glasses which she filled to the brim. She drank greedily before bursting into tears again. I understood her reaction well enough later, even if it only made me more upset in the moment.

There really was no easy way to tell her children that their father had just spent the evening boasting about his long standing involvement with a ring of human traffickers.

What had started as a pleasant supper among friends took a sudden, dark turn. Dad had paused mid-dessert to look across the table at the Filipino wife of one of the other pilots. "I know a guy who would pay good money to have a woman like you," he said.

When she asked what he meant, Dad grinned.

"Guy up north. He likes his ladies young and yellow, so do his buddies. I bet I'd get a couple grand for flying you to him."

Everyone was appalled, but assumed it was a tasteless joke brought on by too much drink. Mom tried to apologize for him, but Dad waved her off and insisted he meant what he said. He asked if his friend was interested in "trading in" his wife for a tidy little sum. He just had to say the word, and Dad could make it happen. A fight had followed, and someone called the cops.

When they showed up, Dad repeated his offer to them as if he expected they'd agree it sounded like a good deal. He seemed honestly surprised when they put him in handcuffs and told him that they needed to ask him some questions at the station.

While Mom spoke, my eyes met Jo's across the kitchen table. I knew she was feeling the same sick churning in her gut that I was. Neither of us said anything then, but we were both beginning to realize what we'd heard upstairs, even if we didn't understand how it had happened.

Jo had used her key to open a door to a room that contained all of Dad's souvenirs from his overseas trips. The room where he'd kept momentos of all the countries he'd visited. The room that had been created as a shrine to all those far off places from which he'd helped rip young women away from their lives and transport them to the highest bidder.

Jo had used her key to open the door, and we'd learned what was really inside that room.

Dad's trial was a swift one; he confessed

everything readily enough. He even seemed proud of it. He'd helped deliver hundreds of women into slavery and abuse over two decades by arranging for them and their escorts to be on commercial flights he was piloting. He smiled about it on the stand.

The thing he was most pleased about, aside from all the extra money he'd made, was the two little girls he had "saved": one from a small village in northern China, and the other from the slums of Mumbai, India.

"We didn't usually take mothers. Our clients didn't want used women, but there were two in particular over the years that the broker couldn't pass up. Beautiful, still young, but they had babies. They were just going to leave the kids behind, come what may, but I took one look at their faces and I knew immediately that they were meant to be my little girls. The same guy who forged the passports and travel documents for the women made me adoption papers for the girls, and I brought them home a couple months later."

He stared at us the whole time he spoke, misty eyed and beaming. I fought back a surge of bile, and Jo buried her face in her hands beside me. Mom swayed in her seat, the color gone from her face. I thought she might faint.

"I love you, Kimberly, Josephine," Dad said. He gave us a little wave. "You'll always be my little girls."

It was the last time we went to court.

It was the last time we saw the man we had called our father.

Jo and I took the choker with its key to the

beach, and she hurled it as hard and as far as she could into the ocean. We stood there and stared over the water long after it sank beneath the waves, gripping each other's hands.

"The lady who sold it to him, she told him that we could get into any door with that key. Whatever was in the room could come out too, remember?" Jo asked softly.

"Yeah," I replied.

"What do you think that meant?"

I shrugged but didn't answer.

I didn't want Jo dwelling on it anymore. I didn't want to dwell on it anymore.

I didn't want to dwell on the fact that so many items he'd brought back for us had been bought with blood money made from innocent, ruined lives.

That we had been bought with blood money.

I didn't want to think about the fact that, if we hadn't accidentally let out the person he truly was, he might still be doing it.

It was hard enough accepting that the man who raised us had been a monster. It was even harder trying to figure out how we'd unleashed the part of himself that he'd hidden so well for so long, or how all it took was one little key that could open any door.

The Lesson of the Tiger

Dad got me started young. It was just Saturday nights at first when he'd wait for Mom to be caught up in her shows, but over time, it became more frequent. Eventually he was at my bedroom door at least two or three nights a week. I'd hear his footsteps coming down the hall, and I would stop whatever I was doing and wait for him to appear. When he did, he always asked the same question with that same smile.

"Hey, Sunny," he'd say, "want to play some Dungeons and Dragons?"

When your dad is a huge nerd and your mom is only slightly less so, it's no surprise when you become one too. By the time I was eight, I had successfully trekked across whole worlds, beaten back hulking monsters of the abyss, and saved countless kingdoms from sure destruction. I was Sunny the Slayer, Ranger Princess of the North Wood!

While we often played properly, with dice and character sheets and manuals spread around the table, sometimes we just roleplayed. I liked playing pretend and Dad enjoyed world-building, so he'd come up with something for my character to do and off I'd go, unconcerned with stats or rolls. It was all about the storytelling.

It was during one such session that Sunny the Slayer ended up in a cave in the middle of the jungle. I'd been traveling to a new town to answer a call for adventurer and had to stop for the night. My only options were sleeping out in the open or in the cave. I opted for the cave.

"You enter and realize you're not alone. A tiger is standing in the back of the cave. It watches you; what do you do?" Dad asked from over his dungeon master's guide.

"I'm a ranger, so I'm going to tame it and make it my companion!" I said quickly. It was the same thing I did with every animal I came across.

"How?"

"I'm gonna charm him!"

"It doesn't work, and he's still staring. What do you do?"

"Um, if my charm animal didn't work, I think it's time to leave Mr. Tiger alone."

"He runs around you and blocks your path."

"I...crawl under it!"

"It lies down before you can get under it. It's still watching you. What do you do?"

"Why's it being such a pain?" I whined, frustrated at this persistent make-believe tiger.

"What do you do?" Dad asked patiently.

"I'm gonna..." I paused and considered kicking it right in its dumb face. As a ranger and animal lover, that just wouldn't have been right. Maybe it was just a lonely tiger and wanted me to stay and be its friend. "I'm gonna pet it."

"It purrs and you have a pet." Dad waited for me to quiet my cheering before continuing. "And now you have learned the lesson of the tiger."

"Huh?" I said. I'd been too busy trying to come up with a suitable name for my new pet to have realized this was one of Dad's Learning Moments.

"Even though you are presented with a scary situation, if you remain calm and friendly, sometimes you are rewarded."

I found out later that my dad had played through the same scenario with his older brother when they were kids. Dad had chosen to attack the tiger and promptly been eaten, ending their campaign.

When he'd asked his brother what else he could have done, Uncle Kev had said, "You could have asked him nicely to move. Sometimes that's all it takes."

As I got older, we played D&D less and less, until it was only a fond childhood memory. The lesson of the tiger remained an inside joke between me and my parents. Whenever I was nervous about something or feeling unsure, they'd remind me to think of the tiger and tackle whatever I was facing with positivity and an open mind.

When it came time for me to move away to college, a forty-five minute drive up the highway, my parents presented me with a stuffed tiger to keep in my dorm.

"Don't forget about us little people while you're off being a big university student," Dad said as he handed it to me.

"I'll try not to," I replied with a smile.

Mom just managed to say she loved me before the tears started. I reminded her I'd be driving home the following week so she could do my laundry and cook my meals. She laughed, wiped her eyes, and pulled me into a hug.

"I've already changed the locks," she whispered, snorting with a giggling sob.

A few more tears, a few more laughs, and then they were walking down the hall to the elevator. It was just me and my tiger in the dorm room.

The semester started smoothly. Classes were easy, covering a lot of the same material I'd learned in Highschool. I made new friends fairly fast, and I learned the ins and outs of freshman college life. I was really enjoying myself, right up until I met Dylan.

He was in my Composition I class, a pre-req for most majors that retaught us the basics of writing. While I found the work to be simple, he struggled a bit, and our teacher asked me to work with him to help him improve an essay we'd done. I was happy to do so—I was an education major after all—and he seemed to appreciate my help.

That appreciation quickly crossed a line into inappropriate.

While Dylan was an alright looking guy, one that I might have even found cute, he lacked a lot of social graces. During our tutoring sessions, he'd sit way too close until his leg was pressed against mine. When we were talking, he'd loom over me, taking one step forward for every one I took back. If I said something he disagreed with, he'd just get louder and louder until I was drowned out and gave up. When that happened, he'd grin and tell me he knew I'd see his side of things eventually.

I could have forgiven all that. Sometimes social cues are lost on people, and I tried to stay understanding even as I told him he was standing too close for the hundredth time. It was just another tiger lesson: stay calm, stay friendly, and he'll learn. That's what I kept telling myself anyway.

What I couldn't forgive was when he started to follow me.

It was subtle in the beginning, just running into him at the dining hall or outside of class. That could have just been coincidence. He'd act surprised every time, but the more it happened, the more transparent it became. His thin smile could barely mask the smug, arrogant pleasure in his eyes at having "bumped into me". I started finding new routes to class, but it never took him long to figure them out and we'd go through the same ridiculous song and dance until I could get away.

I tried to let Dylan down gently. When that didn't work, I tried to let him down politely, but bluntly. He'd huff and stomp off while muttering about what a bitch I was, but then he'd be right back to it, showing up wherever I was the very next day.

I still thought he was mostly harmless. It wasn't like he'd ever gotten violent—just a little overly attached to his tutor. I didn't want to be one of Those Girls who made a big deal out of nothing and get someone with perfectly innocent intentions in trouble. It was nothing I couldn't handle on my own.

Friday nights were often quiet in my dorm. A lot of people went out to clubs and parties, and I'd often be right there with them. One day after class I was feeling a little under the weather and just wanted to get my homework out of the way and then get some sleep. The moment I was back in my room, I logged into my computer and made a Facebook post declaring my hermit status to let my friends know I wouldn't be going out with them.

I was down to my last bit of homework, a few tricky algebra problems that were only making my headache worse, when someone knocked on my door. I stayed quiet, figuring it was the RA or someone who wanted to borrow something. I tried to focus, but they knocked again. Again I ignored it. Then I heard the door knob turning.

I often left my door unlocked when I was in my room and awake, feeling secure enough in a building full of fellow students. No one had ever just let themselves in before. I spun in my chair to see Dylan slipping in, his back to me.

"What the hell do you think you're doing?" I demanded.

I started to stand as he turned around. The switchblade he pulled from his pocket and flicked open made me stop.

"Dylan?"

He reached behind him. The door lock slid into place.

"Hey, Sunny," he said casually, as if he weren't breaking into my room.

We stared at one another for a tense moment, then he moved to my bed and took a seat. He kept the knife in plain view the whole time.

"You know, I've just gotta ask," he said. "I've been nothing but nice to you, and you *still* treat me like shit; why is that? I'm not good enough for you or something?"

He was staring at me with such intensity that I shrank back into my seat. I could scream, I thought, but who would hear? More importantly, who would come? Not that they could get to me before he killed me. The thought almost closed my throat. My next breath was a desperate, shuddering gasp of air. Howling panic threatened to fill my head and overrun any logic.

He was still looking at me, his eyes narrowed, actually expecting an answer.

He's still staring. What do you do? My dad's voice from over a decade ago floated up from the back of my mind. It was the only calm in the storm that was my mind. I latched on to it, forcing myself to focus on the question.

He's still staring. What do you do?

My eyes flicked toward the stuffed tiger that was sitting on my pillow. Looking back to Dylan, I certainly saw the beast within the man.

Remain calm and friendly, I thought with a slow inhale.

"Good enough?" My voice cracked despite myself. "What do you mean?"

"You're not an idiot. Neither am I, Sunny, so cut the crap. You act like you don't even notice all the attention I've given you, but I know you do."

"Well, yeah," I conceded, trying to think quickly, "but I thought we were friends."

"Guys don't want to be friends with girls like you," he scoffed, as if it was the most obvious thing.

"I-I guess I thought that you were just a nice guy to everyone."

That set him off. He started ranting about how girls always tell him the same thing, that he's just so nice, but they aren't interested. He spoke in a low, spiteful tone, snarling and cursing about how "us bitches" use nice guys while we wait for some roided out asshole to mistreat us. He thought I was different, that I would actually give him a chance, but then I started acting like all the rest.

Every insult was punctuated by Dylan driving his blade into my mattress.

I stayed as still and small as possible, my hands balled into white knuckled fists my lap. My nails bit into my palms so harshly that I was sure I was drawing blood. I had to stay composed. I had to stay calm.

"I'm sorry," I said meekly. "I didn't know you felt that strongly about me. I've never dated a guy before and it made me nervous—"

"Never dated a guy?" he interrupted. "You a lesbian?"

"N-no. It's just my parents were strict, and I wasn't allowed," I said. I was sure they wouldn't mind me telling a little white lie about them at a time like this.

"Oh," he said, and he seemed to calm a bit while he mulled it over. He continued to fidget with the switchblade even as he thought. His eyes never left me.

He's still staring. What do you do?

"Have you? Dated, I mean," I asked suddenly. The only thing I *could* do was keep him talking. Make him think I was interested. If nothing else, it would buy me some time.

He let out a short bark of a laugh and was off on another tangent very similar to his previous one, all about how unlucky in love he'd been because girls only cared about money and popularity.

Whenever he paused, I'd find something else to ask about or make a comment agreeing with him. I had to be careful. At one point he thought I was a little too eager and became angry again.

"Don't patronize me!" he growled. He was on his feet, looming over me with the knife clenched in his hand, its tip pointed at me.

I calmed him by claiming this was just such a new perspective for me. In my sheltered upbringing, I'd never heard anything like it before. I knew he liked feeling superior and smarter than me, and I willingly fed into it so he'd sit down again. He cooled enough to perch on the edge of my bed once more. I immediately asked another question to get him going again, trying my best to make my terror look like interest.

Eventually, he started to ask me questions, too. Not from any desire to learn about me, but so he could tell me what was wrong with my family and how I'd been raised. How women like me, the prissy prudes, were just as bad as the sluts.

He was in the middle of one of his rants when my phone's text notification went off on the desk behind me. I tore my eyes away from Dylan long enough to look at the screen.

"It's my dad!" I said.

"Leave it."

"If I don't answer, he'll call the RA to check on me," the words tumbled out in a jumble. "He sends a text every night at 9:30."

Somehow my bluff worked. Dylan told me to sit next to him on the bed while I unlocked my phone.

Hey kid I'll be up your way tomorrow morning.

Lets get breakfast

A lump, hard and jagged, lodged itself in my throat. Sorry, Dad, I wanted to type, but I might not make it that long.

Instead, I wrote, *Have a lesson plan to work on for intro to edu. It's a real tiger. Holed up in my dorm til its over :(*

After Dylan approved, I hit send.

It was a long shot. Just a vague reference that I wasn't even sure he'd catch, but it was the only thing I could think of. I held my breath, waiting for a response.

All I got back was a cartoony tiger emote followed by, *Maybe next week.*

I wanted to cry. It wasn't enough. With whatever composure I had left, I put the phone on my desk and painted a shaky smile on my face.

"Want to watch a movie?" I asked.

Despite all of his ranting and raving about how horrible women are, Dylan was all too eager to cuddle up against me on the bed to stream a film on my laptop. His hands were rough and wandering. I sat stiffly beside him, too afraid to push him away. The knife was resting on his knee, a sharp reminder of what might happen if I try.

At some point he knocked my tiger from its spot on the pillow to the floor.

The movie was barely half over before Dylan started to get more aggressive. He was tugging at the hem of my shirt, sliding his hand too far up my thigh, trying to land kisses whenever I turned enough for him to get even the corner of my mouth. I could tell my attempts to pull away under the guise of shy embarrassment were starting to wear thin. He was getting frustrated, and his temper starting to boil over again.

I'd played out the lesson of the tiger as far as it could take me. Calm and friendly weren't going to save me. I was running out of time.

We both jumped when someone knocked on the door.

"Sunny? You in?" It was AJ, my floor's RA.

Panic and hope surged like twin bolts of electricity through me. I almost shouted for him to come help me, but Dylan grabbed me by the back of the neck and put the blade of his knife to his lips, motioning for me to keep quiet.

"I'm sorry to bother you so late, Sunny, but, uh, there have been some noise complaints. I need you to sign this form to signify I warned you," AJ said through the door.

A tear slid down my cheek.

"I know you're in. I can hear your TV."

After another moment with no answer, AJ said, "I really don't want to have to let myself in."

Dylan's fingers tightened on my neck. He got off the bed, hauling me up alongside him.

"Just sign the thing and shut the door," he hissed into my ear. "I'll kill you if you try anything."

The tip of the knife jabbed against my side. I nodded once.

Dylan stood just behind the door, one hand resting on it in case he had to slam it quickly. The hand kept the knife pointed at me. I took a deep breath, unlocked the door, and tugged it open just enough to peek out.

"Sor —"

I only just started to apologize when the door was shoved violently inwards. I stumbled back and fell against the end of my bed. Dylan, still tucked against the wall behind the door, took the full force of the metal door to his face. There was a sharp cracking sound and he yelped, grabbing at his face with his free hand while trying to close off the room again.

As soon as Dylan made that sound, giving away the fact that he was there, the door swung in again. Faster and harder than it had before, shouldered open by my red faced, furious father.

"He's got a knife!" I shrieked, the only words I could get out before I started to hyperventilate.

Dylan was laid flat against the wall three more times before he dropped his knife. Then a fourth for good measure. Over my dad's shoulder, AJ looked like he was going to be sick while he tried to get campus security on the phone.

Dylan wasn't able to be arrested that night, though. He had to be rushed to the hospital first to find out the extent of damage Dad had done to his body.

After spending what felt like an eternity answering questions and filling out forms for the university and police, I was allowed to leave campus with my dad. I didn't even pack, just got in the passenger seat of his car and we took off.

The ride was quiet for a long time, until Dad asked, "You ok?"

"Yeah," I said. A numbness had settled in my chest. I was sure I'd have a rush of emotions once the shock wore off, but in that moment, I welcomed it.

After another stretch of silence, I turned to him. "You got my text?"

"I got your text," he said grimly. I was never so glad that he'd been able to read between the lines. I should have known he would.

"Why didn't you knock yourself?"

"Figured if you were in trouble, I needed a plausible cover to get the door open. Your RA is a little shit, by the way. He tried to tell me it was unethical. I told him what I was going to do to his face was unethical."

"What if I'd been fine?"

"Then I'd have looked like a real asshole."

"Thanks, Dad."

He just looked at me and smiled.

I learned that night that there are two parts to the tiger's lesson. Sometimes, most times, you are the player and being nice and calm is the better way to go. It will certainly earn you more friends in the long run.

Sometimes, though, you just have to smash a psychopath in the face with a door half a dozen times.

Sometimes, you have to be the tiger.

Daddy's Little Princess

I had been wholly unprepared to be a single father. Carla had been the super-parent, ensuring all of our little Fiona's needs were met, that she was happy and healthy. I felt like a bumbling oaf beside her natural effortlessness, and it made me love her all the more.

When she passed away after a short, aggressive battle with cancer, I was lost. It was easy to pretend at first, when I was surrounded by the support of friends and family, but they slowly trickled back out and returned to their own lives. Then it was just me and my baby girl.

She was a strong, willful child, and I saw her mother every time I looked at her. She had the same smile, the same deep blue eyes and strawberry blonde curls. I loved her and I pitied her, left alone with an ill equipped father and no mother to make up for him.

I was reminded of all my short comings every time she cried, and nothing I did seemed to comfort her. Some nights I'd just sit outside her bedroom door, tears streaming down my cheeks, begging Carla to come back and tell me what to do. I knew that, without her mom, there would always be a void in my child's life. Not knowing how to fill it terrified me.

So I did what I did best and returned to work at my law firm. I couldn't give Fiona her mommy, but I could make sure she had everything else she could ever want. The next few years were spent growing: absorbing smaller offices, taking on new partners and clients, until we were one of the largest firms in the city. All the while I made sure Fiona knew it was all for her.

Anything she wanted, she got. Horseback riding, ballet, tennis, clothes, toys, nothing was off limits. All she had to do was ask, and it was her's. Every day when I came home, I'd be greeted by her tearing down the stairs to throw herself in my arms.

"I missed you, Daddy!"

And I knew it was all worth it.

"Telephone call on line one for you, Mr. Harper." My assistant, Helen, knocked gently on my office door.

"Who is it?" I shoved aside the file I'd been reviewing, a frustrating divorce settlement, and reached for the phone.

"It's Angela."

I dismissed her with a quick nod and picked up. "This is Bill."

"Hi, Mr. Harper, it's, um, Angela." Fiona's tutor always sounded nervous when she spoke to me, and now was no exception.

"Everything ok?"

"Yeah, kind of, it's just...well, I think Fiona fired me? Can she do that?"

I sighed, rubbing the fingertips of my free hand in small circles against my temple. "Is she there? Put her on."

"Daddy!" Fiona said indignantly as soon as the phone was handed off. "I hate Angela! She's mean and stupid and doesn't know what she's doing!"

"What happened, baby girl?"

"I hate her!"

"She's a good tutor, sweetie." And very expensive. "Mrs. Montgomery wouldn't have recommended anyone who was stupid or mean."

"Well she did, and I want her to go away! I don't wanna work with her anymore. I won't!"

She started to cry bitterly. My heart sank. I couldn't stand to hear her so distressed.

"Ok, ok. If you really don't like her that much, we'll find you someone else."

I hung up and dragged a hand down my face, wondering just where I was going to find another tutor. Fiona had never really fit in at school; she'd been mercilessly bullied by the other children and made into an outcast. The teachers were no help. They tried to blame Fiona, saying she was the one causing problems. They even dared to suggest she might benefit from counseling.

"Of course she's acting out!" I had snapped when the principal called me in to discuss the matter. "She's being tormented, and no one will help her!"

She'd looked at me with a condescending frown, like she and her staff knew my daughter better than I did. I could see why Fiona was having such trouble.

The day she came home, crying and screaming that she was never going back, I knew something had to be done. The next week I withdrew her in favor of homeschooling. I hired a private tutor, cost be damned, and turned one of our spare bedrooms into her very own classroom.

Fiona was ecstatic! I hadn't seen her so excited about her education in a long time. The tutor, touted as the best one in the region, lasted a month. The next one managed to hang on just a bit longer, and the one after that only made it through two weeks.

Fiona was a sensitive child with special needs, and the tutors were having trouble meeting them. They didn't know how to speak to her. They were too critical, and didn't bother trying to learn the best method to teach her so that she would respond. I could understand her frustration and had similar experiences during my childhood.

She was asleep by the time I got home that night. I peeked into her room, lit softly by her favorite Minnie Mouse night light, and leaned against her doorframe. I was going to find someone special for my little girl. Someone who would understand her and meet her needs. I would find someone to make her happy. I blew a kiss across the room and let the door drift slowly shut as I turned for my own bed.

Josephine Green was the fifth tutor that I'd interviewed in a week. She provided an impressive resume for someone still in her thirties, and her recommendations were nothing short of glowing. I was still skeptical. People with more experience under their belts had failed Fiona, so how could Josephine expect to do any better?

"Why are you interested in tutoring my daughter, Ms. Green?" I asked plainly when she sat across from me in my home office.

"I've heard that she is an...intense child," Ms.

Green replied carefully. "I have a background in teaching students who require more time and attention than others. I prefer it, actually; I find that kind of one-on-one work to be the most rewarding."

"You've heard, hmm?" I knew that word of a difficult client traveled fast in any profession, but it still irritated me to have it confirmed that my Fiona was the subject of gossip. "I take it you're aware that we've had a bit of a revolving door in terms of tutors?"

"Yes. I'm friendly with many of her former teachers. We work in a small community."

I eyed her for a long, quiet minute. She met my gaze evenly, unflustered and composed. I found myself smiling slightly. Her honesty was refreshing.

"And you came anyway?"

"Like I said, I prefer working with children like Fiona. I enjoy the challenge."

We parted with a handshake and, although I met with a few others after her, I knew I'd already found Fiona's next teacher.

Their relationship had a tumultuous start. Fiona, so used to being abandoned, was resistant to Josephine. She hid behind me on her first day until I coaxed her to her desk. She refused to answer questions, pouted at any attempt to make conversation, and stared resolutely at her lap while Josephine wrote on the dry erase board.

The second day was no better. Fiona threw a fit, scattering her unfinished work across the floor and throwing things around the room. The third day she just flopped herself over the beanbag chair in the reading corner and cried until her face was purple.

But Josephine stayed.

She allowed Fiona to express herself without interruption, waiting until the tears and the yelling had been exhausted to ask if Fiona was ready to begin the lesson. The more it became clear that Josephine wasn't going anywhere, the less combative Fiona became. My daughter started sitting at her desk and engaging with Josephine. She still struggled to complete assignments, but her schoolwork started to improve.

I saw such kindness in Josephine, such gentleness, warmth, and understanding. And for the first time since the death of my wife, I found myself drawn to another woman. I found excuses to stop in when I knew Josephine would be at my home, and to call her after she'd gone for the day. What started as monthly progress meetings became weekly, then almost daily. Our conversations started to shift away from Fiona, and we learned about each other's likes and dislikes, about our passions and lives.

The first time I invited Josephine to stay for dinner, Fiona was ecstatic. She grabbed Josephine's hand and tugged her from the school room to the dining room, chattering happily about what we were going to have. We glanced at each other shyly from across the table like school children while Fiona obliviously rambled, both aware that this meal marked a change in our relationship.

When I finally gained the courage to ask Josephine out on a proper date, all of my Highschool awkwardness came rushing back. I, a man who could deliver impeccable monologues in court, found myself stumbling over words. Luckily, she found it endearing, and she accepted.

It was a whirlwind romance, one we kept separate from Fiona; I didn't want it to affect her relationship with Josephine. Even when Fiona wasn't physically with us, her presence was always felt. She was constantly at the forefront of my mind, although there was a sense of guilt and betrayal lurking beneath my happiness. Josephine couldn't quite leave Fiona behind either, but for different reasons.

She broached the topic of my daughter slowly, treading lightly to test her boundaries. She'd off handedly mention that Fiona had been overly demanding during lessons, or that it seemed she was trying to avoid her work. I'd brush it off, laughing that kids will be kids. Josephine didn't see the humor. It was the only issue between us, and one that I viewed as inconsequential. I knew she'd see that Fiona was just a little needier than most, and we'd be able to move on.

As the months wore on and we became more comfortable with one another, Fiona started to take notice. She demanded to know why Ms. Green was over so often, why I was going out more, and where I was going, and no amount of excuses appeased her. As I had feared, she started to withdraw from Josephine, becoming sullen and refusing to do her work.

Fiona became clingy, wanting extra snuggles during movie nights. She'd ask for just one more story before bedtime, trailing after me around the house. She'd latch on and cry whenever I said I was leaving and she couldn't come. Watching her suffer so was heart wrenching.

"Daddy?" she whispered as I was tucking her in one night.

"Yes?"

"Are things changing?"

"What do you mean?" I frowned down at her.

"A-am I still your little princess?" Her lip quivered dangerously, and I immediately knelt and gave her chin a gentle tweak.

"Of course you are. You always will be."

She threw her arms around my neck and squeezed with delight. "I love you, Daddy."

"I love you too, Princess."

Despite my assurance, things between Fiona and Josephine continued to deteriorate. They came to me separately with complaints about the other. Fiona claimed Josephine was mean, Josephine said Fiona was hostile. Fiona said Josephine was being hard on her, Josephine said Fiona was being petulant. I felt myself being torn between the two people I cared for most, and it ate away at me. I tried to defuse the situation, tried to make them see the other's side, but I could feel things starting to boil over.

It finally came to a head while Josephine and I were in the kitchen making supper together. The silence between us was thick and tense. She was having to work to keep her mouth pursed into a thin white line.

"What?" I finally asked, setting my knife aside. "Just say whatever you have to say."

"What's the point? You don't listen anyway," she snapped back without looking up from the salad she was making.

"Don't be like that..."

"Be like what? Frustrated? Upset? I have tried and tried to tell you how I'm feeling, but you either aren't hearing me or you don't care!"

"Of course I do!"

She slammed the cucumber she'd been chopping and turned to me, her face pinched and angry. "No, you really don't, Bill! You haven't done a damn thing about Fiona! She walks all over you and treats everyone else like garbage!"

"Hey no—"

"No!" she cut me off, her voice rising. "She's spoiled rotten. She has no sense of the real world. She's manipulative and controlling, and she needs to grow up! How do you ever expect her to get anywhere in life when you've allowed her to live like this? How is she ever going to cope in college?"

"We have a while before we have to worry about that," I said defensively, my own temper starting to flare.

"You have two years! She's sixteen, for God's sake! I've dealt with some pretty damaged kids before, Bill, but Fiona takes the damn cake."

We glared at each other, eyes narrowed, hands balled into fists. I wanted to refute her, to scream in her face and tell her she was wrong, but I found I had no voice. I knew I babied Fiona, but she needed it! She was such a sensitive girl, and her mom's death had hit her so hard... How do you tell a five year old that Mommy's gone forever? I had to make sure she'd always known she was loved. I had to fill the void left by my wife. How could I make Josephine see that?

"I did what I needed to! I know she can be difficult..."

"Difficult? She's *broken*! She needs a shrink, not a tutor!"

"Ms. Green?"

The sound of Fiona's voice, so small and shy, from behind Josephine made us both jump.

"Fiona," Josephine turned to face her, "I'm sorry, sweetie, I didn't hear you come i—"

Her words ended abruptly, swallowed by a sharp gasp. She stiffened and became very still. Fiona giggled.

"Jo?" I asked, confused.

She made a wet gurgling sound and slowly, her hands went up to her throat.

"Josephine?" I took a step forward and rested a hand on her shoulder.

She fell forward, out of my grasp. She landed with a heavy thud, face down on my kitchen floor. The straight edged tip of a pair of scissors burst through the back of her neck.

Slowly, I tore my eyes from the fast growing pool of blood spurting from Josephine's neck and looked up. My daughter was standing in front of me, grinning behind a red stained hand.

"Wh-what have you done?" I croaked, "Why?!"

"She was mean," Fiona said, her grin fading. "She was saying bad things about me. She wanted you to hate me! She wanted you all to herself, but you're my daddy!"

She stepped over Josephine's body and wrapped her arms around my neck, her cheek pressed against my chest. When my arms remained limply at my sides, she started to sob.

"You don't hate me, do you?" She hiccupped, "Daddy?"

"N-no," I said in a daze, patting her mechanically on the back, "I could never hate you."

"Am I still your little princess?"

"Of course..."

Her tears stopped, and she sighed contentedly. I stared down at Josephine over the top of her head, horrified. What was I going to do? What could I do? The only thing I'd ever done, I realized, my gut twisting; I had to protect my little girl. I had to get rid of the body, all the evidence. The thought made me sick, and my vision swam behind tears. It wasn't Fiona's fault. I made her like this. I did this. Now I had to fix it.

"Daddy?" she murmured into my shirt.

"Yes?"

"I love you."

"I love you too, baby girl."

Crinklebottom

Crinklebottom had been passed down in my family for the past couple of generations. It's a nighttime companion to help ward off bad dreams and those pesky monsters who live under the bed. In his first incarnation, he was a stuffed brown bear with button eyes that my great grandmother sewed for my grandfather when he was a boy. When my mother was old enough to be afraid of the dark, Grandpa gave her a sock monkey with a bright red fez to sleep with. When it was my turn to inherit my own Crinklebottom, Mom tucked me in with a small blue bunny.

It didn't matter what form Crinklebottom took, his story was always the same: he'd been sent by The Sandman, King of Sleep, to watch over us. Although he might look small, he was a fierce warrior, loyal and courageous and always ready to protect his friend. Having a Crinklebottom helped all the kids on my mom's side of the family sleep soundly throughout their younger years, and it became a cherished memory as we got older. It would be no different for my own five year old daughter.

The first morning Alexia even hinted at being afraid of the dark after a particularly bad dream, I dropped her off at school and immediately set off to the toy store. I was excited to share a piece of family history with her, something maybe she would in turn share with her own children in some far distant future. I spent a long hour going up and down the aisles of stuffed animals. I wasn't going to settle on just any old critter; it had to speak to me.

I passed by the Disney and Pixar section, finding nothing amongst the rows of brightly colored bears. I couldn't find any blue bunnies that looked close enough to mine for me to be satisfied. Eventually, Alexia's love for the bovine kind (she'd been obsessed since she saw some commercial pushing cheese with a talking cow) drew me to a bean filled cow with soft black and white fur. I picked it up, studied its dark, twinkling eyes, and knew I'd found the newest member of Clan Crinklebottom.

Maybe it was a bit silly. My wife certainly thought so, but I pulled out all the stops when it came to getting Cow Crinklebottom ready for Alexia. A colorful gift bag, a couple flowers, even a card from The Sandman himself to explain her new friend. I laid it all out on her bed, garnished with a few chocolate coins wrapped in gold foil, and stood back, pleased with my work.

"Couldn't you have just given it to her like a normal parent?" Marta asked from the doorway.

I scoffed at my wife. "This is not just any toy! This is—"

"Crunklebutt, yeah, you've told me," she teased.

"Crinklebottom," I said, folding my arms over my chest and sticking my tongue out at her, "and Alexia will love it."

"Oh, I'm sure," Marta agreed with a smile,

"but I doubt she'll love getting it as much as you're going to love giving it."

"I'm not giving her anything! It's from The Sandman."

When Alexia climbed into the car that afternoon, I had to really bite my tongue to keep from saying anything. I hadn't realized I'd be quite so excited to pass down the family tradition. Before I spoiled the surprise, I asked her how school was. Off she went, recounting every minute of her day with as much detail as she could muster. It was much easier to keep quiet while she went on and on, barely pausing for breath. All I had to do was make the occasional "Ooh" or "Ahh".

"...And then Maddie told Miss. Spring that Danny put the booger in her hair, but he didn't!" Alexia threw her hands up as if this was the most scandalous thing to ever come out of kindergarten.

"Ooh?"

"Yeah! And Miss. Spring believed her, but then I said she was a big, fat liar, and then Maddie started to cry, but I didn't care because she was being a big, fat liar and Danny didn't do that!"

"Well, it's good to be honest, but next time, why don't we avoid name calling, ok? Looks like we're home, kiddo. Why don't you go change and then we'll take a look at your homework folder."

She ran inside, shouting a hello to her mom as she passed, and disappeared into her room. I had to quickly hide the grin that spread across my face when she squealed loudly and came racing back, the gift bag crushed to her chest.

"Daddy, Mommy, look!"

She clambered onto the couch and bounced

eagerly in her seat while she waited for us to join her. When she was sure she had our full attention, she opened the bag and pulled Crinklebottom from it with a dramatic flourish.

"Oh, wow! Where did that come from?" Marta said. She winked at me over Alexia's head.

"I dunno! It was on my bed!"

"Was there anything else in there?"

Alexia dug around in the bag and came up with the card. She tried to offer it to me or her mom to read, but we told her to try it herself. She gripped the card tightly in both fists, her little face wrinkled with deep concentration.

"Alexia," she read slowly, "this is C-C-Cri..." She frowned and looked up at us.

"Crinklebottom," I offered over her shoulder. It wasn't fair to try and make the kid read a made up word.

She giggled at the name. "Crinklebottom. He is your new friend," she went on with the slow, monotone precision of someone still learning to read. She discovered Crinklebottom's purpose and, much to her delight, that she didn't need to be afraid of the dark anymore. She was absolutely thrilled with the little cow and his story. She spent the rest of the evening parading him around, introducing him to all of her other stuffed animals.

Although we didn't usually allow her to bring toys to the dinner table, we made a one-time exception for our guest of honor to celebrate his first night on the job. When it came time to go to bed, she apologized to Lord Watermelon the lion, her oldest and best loved toy to date, and moved him aside to make room for Crinklebottom.

"So, you think you need a nightlight tonight, kiddo?" I asked.

She chewed her lip uncertainly, but finally nodded. "It's Crinklebottom's first night here. He's a little nervous."

"Of course; he still has to learn his way around."

The nightlight only lasted a couple more nights. Soon Crinklebottom took Lord Watermelon's place of honor atop Alexia's pillow during the day, and at her side when she was sleeping. The poor old lion was sent to The Bin with all the other has-been stuffies, and he wasn't seen again. Marta was a bit upset about that— Watermelon had been a gift from her late mother— but she understood that a five year old's attention could only be held for so long.

Crinklebottom became more than Alexia's nighttime protector; he became her best friend. She held entire one sided conversations with him, took him everywhere she could, and spent hours playing with only him. Marta and I didn't think much of it. Little kids had imaginary friends all the time, and our girl's just happened to have a cow body. Then her teacher called.

Miss. Spring and the school counselor, Mr. Bellstein, sat across from us with a grave air. They had a small pile of papers stacked face down in front of them. When they asked if Alexia had been behaving oddly at home, I was put on edge. I could feel Marta stiffen beside me.

"No... why?"

Mr. Bellstein picked up the papers and fanned them out across the desk, five in total. He sat back, watching us closely for our reaction. Marta and I exchanged an uncomfortable, uncertain glance, and leaned forward to see what had caused such a display.

"Alexia has been drawing some rather...unsettling things," Miss. Spring said, adjusting her pink framed glasses.

Each paper had a large, black creature taking up most of the page. In the childish scribbles, I could make out what looked to be a pair of curved horns, two overly large yellow orbs for eyes, and a giant mouth lined with jaggedly drawn teeth. In one, the creature was holding the hand of a little stick figure girl with a purple triangle dress and blonde hair, like Alexia's. In another, it was sitting on the end of the blonde girl's bed, its yellow eyes staring flatly out at me. In the third, the beast was clutching a smaller monster, all black except for lines of red spurting from what I assumed was its neck.

"Have you asked Alexia about these?" Marta's voice was shaky.

"Yes," Miss. Spring said, "she said that it's her friend. She called it Crinklebottom?"

I sputtered, trying to mask my laughter behind a cough. Marta didn't look nearly as amused.

"It's just a character from a story that Adam's family tells. Crinklebottom protects kids while they sleep."

"Is there age inappropriate imagery included in this story?" Mr. Bellstein asked.

"No," I said, swallowing my smile, "she's just got a very active imagination. She walked in on me watching 300 last weekend; I'm sure that didn't help."

They advised us to keep an eye on her, and to monitor her for any unusual behavior, signs of withdrawal, or avoidance. We agreed, apologized for her pictures (which I thought were pretty good for someone so young), and signed the papers saying we'd been made aware of the situation. On the ride home, Marta looked back at Alexia who was humming quietly and staring out the window.

"We saw some of your art today," Marta said.

Alexia perked up. "Did you like it?"

"It was great, kiddo!" Marta frowned at me, so I added, "but why did you make Crinklebottom so big and scary?"

"'Cos he is big and scary!"

"I thought he was a cute little cow."

"Nope." Alexia looked out her window again. "He's big and scary, and he eats the bad monsters. He likes the crunchy ones the best."

Marta sighed and shook her head. "No more scary movies with Daddy," she muttered under her breath.

We tried to ask Alexia to avoid drawing Crinklebottom in the future, at least at school, but she was a stubborn child and she wanted to draw her friend. Crinklebottom started making appearances on the back of worksheets, and in all of her arts and crafts projects. She even drew what she claimed was his handprint, three long clawed fingers on a fat palm, on her desk. We got another call over that one. No matter how much we tried to dissuade her, she kept drawing. Sometimes it seemed innocent enough, just a girl and her monster hanging out, but those were becoming fewer and far between.

The more we told her no, the more prominent Crinklebottom became. And the more violent. She said he liked to eat. Many of her pictures depicted him mid-meal, usually dining on a smaller creature with plenty of red crayon slashed across the page. Sometimes he'd be picking up cars and throwing them into fiery buildings. Other times he'd be hiding under another child's bed while they cried big, blue tears.

When I saw that one, I pointed to Crinklebottom. "What's he doing under there? He only protects kids!"

Alexia shook her head adamantly while coloring in one of his eyes. "Nope, only me."

I sat across from her and laid my hand over her's so she stopped drawing. "Crinklebottom is a good guy, kiddo."

"Yeah, good to me. He doesn't like the other kids. They're mean."

"Mean?" This was news to me.

She told me that the other children started noticing her art. They were telling Miss. Spring and their parents that she was scary. They didn't want to sit next to her because they were afraid of her pictures and Crinklebottom. It was the first time I'd seen my baby girl cry over something other people had said, and it broke my heart. I took her into my lap and stroked her hair while she hiccupped and sniffled, wondering aloud why people didn't like her or her friend.

"You know what? I know how we can make this better," I said, falsely bright. "Why don't you bring Crinklebottom to school and show them he's just a sweet little cow? Then they won't be afraid of him. Maybe then you can start drawing him as he really looks, huh?"

"But, Daddy," her lower lip wobbled with the threat of more tears, "I do draw him like he really looks!"

"But he's a cow, honey."

"Nu uh, he's like in my pictures! When I asked him how come, he said it's so the other monsters are scared of him."

That was pretty well thought out for a five year old. I swallowed hard and kissed the top of her head, concern crowding like storm clouds in my mind.

It took some convincing, but Alexia finally relented and brought Crinklebottom to school with her for Show and Tell. I thought that having her explain that he was actually a cow would help her shake the Crinklebottom she'd created in her mind. I learned later, however, while sitting in the same office with Marta, Miss. Spring, and Mr. Bellstein, that she had barely managed to say his name before Miss. Spring asked her to sit back down. Alexia had refused and argued that she wanted to share her friend. Miss. Spring took the cow and sent Alexia to time out.

"It's disruptive," Miss. Spring told us. "The more she brings it up, the more upset the other students become. I can't allow it."

"She was just trying to show her stuffed animal," Marta said quietly.

"This Crinklebottom nonsense has to stop," Miss. Spring said sharply. Even Mr. Bellstein seemed surprised by the severity of the usually soft spoken woman. She was glaring at us, wordlessly blaming us. "Alexia's behavior is affecting my entire class."

"We'll talk to her," I said coldly. To see the teacher that Alexia had been so fond of speaking with such disdain raked against every protective parental chord I had. Marta placed a hand on my arm and gave it a squeeze.

"We're sorry she's been disruptive," she said, "but if a few pictures from an otherwise well behaved student is enough to have this effect on you, maybe you should reconsider your career choice."

We left, slamming the door in their gaping, stammering faces. At home, Alexia went straight to her room where we could hear her muttering to herself, or maybe to Crinklebottom. I'd never heard her sound so angry.

"Do we give her space?" I asked Marta helplessly. "Do we go in? This is new territory, Captain."

She shrugged, equally at a loss. We sat in the living room, listening to our daughter's tantrum. When her grumbles and stomping faded into silence, we crept to her room and peeked in. She was lying on her stomach on her bed, entirely engrossed with her drawing pad and box of crayons. I knocked softly.

"How you doing, kiddo?"

"Ok," she said without looking up.

"What're you drawing?" Marta asked.

"Crinklebottom and Miss. Spring."

"Oh? Can we see?"

She nodded and sat up, holding out the pad to

us. There was Crinklebottom, same as always, but this time he was holding just the triangle outline of a stick figure dress. Around him, the stick figure's limbs were scattered across the ground in deep red circles. Featured prominently up front, directly at Crinklebottom's feet, was the stick figure's decapitated head. It was wearing a pair of pink framed glasses.

"Alexia, what is this?" Marta sat beside her, and I could see the fear and worry flashing in her eyes.

"Crinklebottom," Alexia said.

"But it looks like he's done a very bad thing. Why would you draw this?"

"Because it's what he did. He told me so."

"What?" I crouched in front of Alexia, her words echoing in my ears.

"After we left. He was mad at her; he said she was a very naughty monster and he had to protect me." She said it so dismissively that I knew she didn't truly grasp the meaning of her words. "He waited until she was alone in the classroom and he punished her for being so mean to me."

"You shouldn't say things like that, Alexia!" Marta was trying very hard to sound in control and undisturbed.

"But it's true! He even brought me a present!"

"Alexia..." I didn't know what to say. We had leapt from new territory to being entirely out of our element, and it was happening way too fast for me to find any kind of footing.

"I'll show you!" she slid off the bed beside me and reached underneath it. She felt around a bit and, for a brief moment, I was sure she wouldn't find anything. How could she? It was impossible.

She held up a pair of broken, bloodied pink eyeglass frames.

From The Basement

When Aunt Norma asked me to house sit, I was hesitant. She lived in a large, old Victorian set out in the woods, the kind of place that gave me the chills just driving by. The thought of being alone inside it, surrounded by her antiques and hunting trophies, had beads of nervous sweat breaking out across my forehead. When I told Dad that I was thinking of saying no, he scoffed at me.

"Don't be ridiculous. Your aunt is relying on you; she hasn't had a vacation in years! You're going."

He was a big proponent of the picking-yourself-up-by-your-bootstraps theory, believing that if you just sucked it up and forged ahead, you'd get through anything. It didn't matter that I'd been diagnosed with an anxiety disorder and almost had a panic attack on the way to the house. In his Professional Dad opinion, I was just being a big baby and it was time grow up.

"I really don't want to do this," I said pleadingly. "What about Marco or Anna?"

"What about them? You should be flattered that Norma asked you. It's a big house, lots of expensive things in it, and she trusts you to look after it while she's away, not Marco or Anna."

"Mom, please!" I tried to appeal to her protective maternal instinct, but she frowned.

"I'm sorry, Cassie, but I think your dad's right.

You need to get out of your comfort zone a little. This will be good for you."

I could feel the tears of frustration starting to well despite my best effort to keep them in check. Dad sighed, disappointed. "You're too old for this behavior, Cassandra. Your aunt's only going to be gone for a few days. Go pack, we're leaving in an hour."

The drive over was quiet and tense. I knew Dad was annoyed and that just made me feel worse, more broken. I wished so badly that I could be the child he wanted me to be, that I could be normal have him be proud of me. Instead, I sat in the backseat, hugging my overnight bag and trying desperately to ignore the churning in my gut. Dad kept his eyes fixed stonily on the road ahead.

Aunt Norma's driveway was a long and winding slope up a small hill. We rounded the curve to the house and I shrank in my seat at the sight of its uneven roofline rising in the distance. It was a three story monster of deep green, scalloped shingles, rusty red trim, and large windows, dark against the overcast day.

I'd hated the place ever since I was a kid and my brother, Marco, had locked me in the tower room at the top of the house. The memories of how helpless and trapped I'd felt still clung to me, making the crowded rooms seem cramped and filled with shadows that the too-dim lighting never touched. I'd never been alone in it before, and the thought of having to be now sent tiny needles of fear prickling up my arms.

"Come on, Cassie," Mom said with her best smile, the kind she reserved for times when she needed to convince the kids everything was okay. "Norma left yesterday, so you'll have the whole place to yourself."

"Can you stay with me?" I asked her. Even with my anxiety washing over me in waves, I was ashamed. The look Dad gave made me want to shrivel up and disappear beneath the car seat.

"It'll be fine, sweetheart. You're gonna have a great time! You know Norma keeps the best food stocked, and she has that huge TV with all the channels!"

"She's 18, not 8, Donna," Dad grumbled, pulling my bag from my arms. "You've been here a thousand times, now knock it off and get out of the car."

Hurt and embarrassed, I hung my head and shuffled after them. Mom hugged me to her side sympathetically, but I knew that her patience was also thinning. Part of her believed Dad was right. I wanted to apologize and tell them I'd get better, that I could just get over it, but I couldn't force any words past the lump in my throat.

Their goodbye was brief and barely saw me over the threshold. I stood in the doorway and watched their car disappear back down the drive. I stayed there for a long while after they'd gone, my breath shaky, feeling small and alone in the mouth of a cavernous beast. I could only bring myself to enter fully and shut the door behind me after the rain started to fall.

Aunt Norma was something of an eccentric woman, and it was reflected in her home. Instead of family portraits, she had taxidermied creatures displayed prominently along her walls. Some she'd killed herself during hunting trips, others she'd just seen and liked enough to purchase. Her favorite, a snowy owl fixed in permanent flight over the door to her living room, stared balefully down at me.

I tried to distract myself by setting up camp in front of her large television, which stood in stark contrast to the rest of the room. The sleek black flatscreen and its DVD filled entertainment center dwarfed the stiff, overstuffed furniture that looked like they could have been house originals from the early 20th century: an odd combination that spoke of Norma's love for antiques, but also for modern comforts.

It worked, for a while. I was able to relax just slightly with the noise of a movie filling up the quiet. I still checked constantly over my shoulder, feeling the occasional rush of butterflies if I thought I heard anything unusual. I employed the breathing techniques my therapist had taught me, and I stayed rooted on the couch. I liked to think Dad might even have been proud of me, had he seen how hard I was trying.

The day was waning though, and whatever weak light that had been coming through the clouds outside was swallowed by darkness. Aside from the living room, the house had turned pitch black.

My stomach rumbled. I wanted to ignore my hunger, and I might have been able to if I'd eaten anything else that day. Nerves had kept my appetite firmly suppressed, but the moment they relented even a little, it groaned and gurgled back into life until all I could think about was food. Food, and the fact that the kitchen was down a long, narrow hallway now shrouded in shadow. I hovered in the living room's entryway, my fingers scratching nervously along my forearm, an anxious habit I hadn't broken yet.

"Maybe two dozen steps," I said aloud, trying to reassure myself that the journey to the kitchen wasn't a journey at all. It was just a short walk.

With my phone gripped tightly in my hands, it's screen pointed outwards to illuminate the hall, I managed to take a single step forward. The floorboard beneath me squeaked in protest. I had to fight back the urge to go running back to the couch.

"I can do this. I can do this."

I shut my eyes, pictured the hallway as brightly lit, and charged. I slid into the kitchen and caught myself on the doorframe, laughing, proud. I'd done it! With the light switched on in the kitchen, I allowed myself to feel a sense of triumph. I realized it was silly, but I didn't care. Dr. Jones always said to celebrate the victories, no matter how small. I shimmied my way to the fridge for some dinner.

"Cassiiiieee."

I froze. It was like ice down my spine. I argued with myself, one half of my brain trying to convince the other that it was all in my head, that I hadn't just heard my name.

"Cassiiiiiiieeeeee."

But there it was again. I was certain that time. Slowly, I turned my head toward the basement door. I'd been so busy dancing around that I hadn't noticed it was slightly ajar. From somewhere down below, in the thick blanket of shadows, a thin, reedy voice, was whispering my name.

"Cassandra!"

I screamed and threw myself at the door, slamming it shut with my whole body and turning the deadbolt into place. No sooner had I managed to get it closed than something thudded against the other side. I screamed again and tore out of the kitchen, back to the living room, where I immediately called my mom.

"Deep breaths," my mom said soothingly. I'd never been so happy to hear her.

"Somethings in the house with me, Mom! Please, come get me!"

I heard my dad in the background, "Is that Cassie? Oh no. Give me that." There was a shuffling sound, then Dad's voice, "What's going on?"

"Something's here! Please let me come home!"

"You need to get a hold of yourself. These outbursts, you're too old for them! It's time to realize it's your over active imagination. You're fine." He didn't sound angry, just tired. I couldn't hold back the sob that bubbled in my chest. "Cassie, I love you, but this is good for you. You'll see."

Then he hung up.

I curled on the floor beside the couch, my knees hugged to my chest, and I cried. Any sense of accomplishment had vanished, replaced wholly by an aching, hollow aloneness. Except I wasn't alone. I looked back down the hall toward the kitchen and shuddered.

I didn't want to leave the living room with all of its light and noise from the TV, but my bladder betrayed me. I waited until I couldn't stand it anymore, then a bit longer still. When the threat of relieving myself with or without my consent became all too real, I was forced from my nest onto the floor. I didn't have time to hesitate despite the knots in my stomach pulling tighter and tighter. The bathroom was down the hall, halfway between the kitchen and living room. I waddled as fast as I could, all my senses on high alert.

I didn't hear the crying until after I finished and was in the hall again. It was soft and plaintive, and coming from the basement. I held my breath, terrified and shivering in the dark hall, torn between bolting and being stuck in place. Every so often, between the distant sobs muffled by the locked door, I'd hear my name.

"Cassiiiiieeee."

It sounded so pained and needy, which only made it more terrifying. When I was finally able to rip myself away, I was only too happy to drown it out by turning the TV up.

Sleep didn't come that night. Every sound, every shadow out of the corner of my eye, was the thing in the basement coming for me. I was cocooned in blankets on the sofa, my phone clutched in one hand and the fire poker from the hearth beside me. I was shaking and crying quietly, praying for daylight.

The knocking started just after midnight. A series of dull, irregular thuds from the basement.

Thud.

Thud.

Thud.

It echoed throughout the house. Each one sent

a new jolt of terrified electricity shooting through me. I buried my head in the blankets and fought not to call my parents. Dad would just get angry anyway.

Enduring this was torturous. Exhausted and too frightened to think coherently, I ran from the living room and up the steps to the closest guest room to lock myself in.

I sat in the giant bed, rigid and tense, ears strained like a rodent being stalked. I couldn't hear anything from downstairs, but that didn't mean I could relax. The night dragged endlessly on, and it was only once the gray pre-light of dawn started to push back the darkness that I got any sleep.

Ravenous hunger woke me only hours later, and I had to make the trip to the kitchen. I kept the fire poker with me and did a thorough visual sweep as I entered. My heart beat hard and fast against my ribs, and I was ready to turn tail and flee at a moment's notice. The basement door was still shut, still locked, and everything was just as I had left it.

I was only there long enough to make a couple quick, sloppy PB&Js and wolf them down with a glass of milk before I went outside. It was a brilliant, sunny morning, and I needed to get out of the house. If it felt cramped before, it was claustrophobic now. I breathed deeply, repeating to myself that all was well and I was ok. I walked along the cobblestone path leading around the side of the house.

Norma let her large yard run wild, saying she loved the freedom it represented. The grass grew tall, weeds were as plentiful as flowers, and the

trees stretched wide and open in every direction. I
would have missed the basement window, set low
to the ground and half concealed behind an
overgrown bush, except for the sun glinting off it. I
paused and scratched my arm, struggling
internally.

I wanted to look. I didn't want to look. I did. I
didn't. I needed to know. I was scared. But the
window allowed me to peek in without actually
going into the basement, and I eventually crouched
beside it. The glass was dirty on both sides and I
had to wipe away a layer of grime before I could
even begin to see inside.

It was dark. All I could make out was a mass
of shapes: all of Norma's things that didn't fit in the
attic. I didn't see anything moving. Didn't hear
anything. After a moment, I stood up again.

"Maybe Dad was right," I said doubtfully.

I turned away with a shake of my head.
Something behind me rattled the window's glass
from the inside.

It took some convincing and some crying and
some screaming, but my parents showed up a half
hour later. Dad marched past me, straight into the
house. I followed on his heels.

"Please, Dad, don't go down there!" I begged.

"No! It's nothing. You've let your damn
imagination get the best of you, and I'm going to
show you!"

I grabbed at his wrist, but he shook me off
roughly. Mom took my hand and tugged me gently
back to her, but I was hyperventilating. The room
was spinning, and I pulled away to stagger into the
kitchen.

"Dad!" I had to hold the fridge handle to stay on my feet. "Please!"

But he opened the door and he went down, never once looking back.

"Jesus Christ!"

Mom flew past me at the sound of Dad shouting. "Tony?!" she called down to him.

"Jesus Christ, oh God!" he was still shouting.

There was loud scraping. It sounded like banging metal, and my dad yelling for us. I managed to get across the kitchen and, with small, trembling steps, I followed Mom into the basement.

Dad was hunched over with his back to us, mumbling rapidly. Even Mom paused on the final stair, her posture tense.

"Tony?"

He turned to us, his face a white mask of horror. I'd never seen my father so shaken. It was almost enough to send me reeling backwards.

"Donna, help me!"

"What is it? What's wrong?"

He moved aside. Mom and I gasped.

Aunt Norma was facedown on the basement floor, pinned beneath a heavy set of steel shelves and everything that had been on them. Old books, sporting equipment, and various odds and ends had spilled around her. Beneath the dark hair that had fallen across her face, her skin was shockingly white. I could have sworn I saw flecks of red around her mouth.

Was she breathing? I couldn't tell. I felt sick, awash with dizziness. I looked away, unable to stomach the sight. With my eyes turned to the floor, I became aware of about a dozen balls, golf and tennis, scattered around the bottom of the stairwell.

With a slow, sinking, I pushed myself up and walked mechanically to the basement window. Another few balls were lying beneath it.

"Oh...oh no..." I breathed, realization setting in like a sharp blade.

Norma had never made it to her vacation. She must have come down to the basement to get something. She'd tried to pull it down, but the whole shelf came with it. That was why the door had been open. The voice, thin and pained, had been her's, calling to me. It was her that I'd heard crying in the night. She must have been throwing the balls that fell around her at the stairs, then at the window, trying to get my attention. And I'd ignored it. I'd been so scared, so wrapped up in my own head, that I'd not even checked.

Mom and Dad scrambled to get Norma, who had yet to move or speak, out from under the shelf. I sank to the floor, my hands covering my face, and let the guilt dissolve me into tears.

Little Old Lady Magic

Mom changed after Dad died.

The heart attack was sudden while washing his car. He was only 64. I found him when I got home from school, but it was too late. The doctor said he went quickly, like it would be some kind of consolation to a sixteen year old. I just wanted my dad back, not his empty attempts at comfort. My mother was far more open to the gesture and had a good, long cry on his shoulder beside her late (by an hour) husband. At least the doctor had enough sense to look embarrassed by the display.

It was the first time I really noticed just how selfish she could be.

Dad had been a good barrier; he'd shielded me from the type of woman Mom really was. I imagine part of it was her own doing. Dad had kept her happily wrapped up in expensive clothes and a three story McMansion with his investment banker salary, and she had no reason to rock the boat. Thinking back to all the times he'd been the only one to attend my horseback riding competitions and dance solos, making excuses about Mommy not feeling well, it became clear that he'd been sparing my feelings.

She just didn't want to go, and he did his best to make sure I didn't know it.

I asked myself a lot how I never noticed before. I'd always known she was a little vain, a little self-absorbed, but that came part and parcel with a lot of my friend's moms and hadn't seemed out of place. I guess it boiled down to the willful ignorance of childhood: I simply hadn't wanted to.

The last clump of dirt had barely been tossed on his grave before Mom was on the phone with his life insurance provider, sobbing about how she hated to think of money at a time like this, but she did have a daughter to think of, you know. I sat across from her at the dining room table, at once disgusted and, admittedly, a little impressed. If she hadn't made it as a bored trophy wife, she certainly could have tried her hand at acting.

I tried to give her the benefit of the doubt at first; everyone grieves different, and maybe focusing on finances and the like was her way. That lasted for all of two days before she started going through Dad's things.

The clothes in their giant walk-in closet went first.

"They're perfectly good suits, Calla." Mom grabbed an armful from the rack and dropped it into a nearby box. "Your father would be happy to see them go to someone less fortunate."

It might have seemed like a generous gesture, had she not almost immediately filled the space with a brand new wardrobe for herself.

His photos were the next to start disappearing.

"I just can't bear to look at him, Calla," she said while plucking frames off the mantle. "It's too painful right now."

Another seemingly understandable move for a grieving widow to make. Or it would have been, if she didn't replaced them all with pictures of herself and her gaggle of equally botoxed and bottle-blonde girlfriends.

His collection of antique hunting rifles, his golf clubs, the sportscar he'd spent the last two years restoring himself, all disappeared in a month.

The only signs that my dad had ever lived in the house at all were in my room, tucked away in the back of my closet under my bed. I'd saved his wedding ring, something I was sure would be pawned off if Mom could find it. I'd managed to get my hands on some of his vinyl records too. None of his favorite ones, though; for some reason, those seemed to be the first to go.

The home I once loved, where I had felt loved, quickly became the world's largest shrine to my mother.

Even that might not have been so bad if she hadn't brought her brother to live with us.

Unlike my mom, I never cared for Uncle Blake. There was just something about him, a constant ooze of used-car-salesman, that got under my skin and put me off from the get go. Dad tolerated him well enough—he was his brother-in-law, after all. After one too many requests for a loan on this or a "sure thing that just needs a couple thousand dollars for deposit" that, Dad put his foot down and Blake stopped coming around so frequently. It was the only time I ever saw my dad really stand up to Mom.

Fat lot of good it was doing me now.

I started looking for any and every excuse to get out of the house. I spent more time with my friends, and at the dance studio, and the gym than ever before. When I wasn't doing any of those things, I was out jogging.

Our neighborhood was a semi-rural one: a gated community of equestrians who owned acres of land for their horses. It was peaceful to run along the side of the road, past well-manicured pastures and stylishly rustic barns. A lot of my neighbors had lived there a long time, same as my family, and I was friendly with most of them.

Mrs. Grady had been an exception, but that changed when I started jogging.

She was an older woman who lived at the end of the cul-de-sac in what was probably the largest house on the largest piece of property. Unlike a lot of others in the neighborhood, she always looked a little frumpy with fly away gray curls and baggy, comfortable clothing. She had what Mom liked to call a resting bitch face.

Whenever we saw her, Mom made a point not to wave or even look in her direction, muttering about "such a woman" taking up the most expensive lot.

It didn't help that she had two dogs who barked and clawed at the tall wooden fence whenever anyone went by. I never saw them, I don't think anyone did, but it was generally agreed that they must have been huge and mean from their sound. There was always the slightest hint of a strange smell hanging over her backyard, almost like rotten eggs. Just the kind of pets someone like Mrs. Grady would be expected to own.

After hearing nothing but negativity spewed toward the older woman, I'd unconsciously internalized a disdain for her. I took a page out of mom's book and pointedly stared straight ahead whenever I went by her house when she was outside, which was most evenings, as she did all her own yard work. Another oddity that set her apart from the majority.

It was during one such evening run that I finally had my first real encounter with Mrs. Grady.

I'd gotten into an argument with Uncle Blake over something small and stupid, and I'd headed out to put some much needed space between us. I was fuming, stomping my feet with every step, distracted by all the nasty names I was coming up with for my uncle in my head. I didn't notice the pothole in my path until I rolled my ankle in it.

I went down with a surprised, pained yelp. Behind me, Mrs. Grady's eight foot fence began to quiver as her dogs pawed at it, barking wildly. They had the deep, bone vibrating barks of very large canines. Of all the lawns to have fallen into, that one probably would have been my last choice.

"Snicker, Doodle, hush!" a voice snapped from the depths of the rose bushes outside Mrs. Grady's front door.

The dogs immediately quieted save for a few whines and the sound of snuffling along the ground.

The elderly woman disentangled herself from the plants, wiping her gardening gloves on her already dirt stained capris. She saw me sitting in the swale at the edge of her yard and came bustling over with a frown. At first I thought she was going to yell at me for daring to trespass, and I braced myself with a snappy retort if my own.

Instead, she removed her glove and offered a

hand to help me up.

"Oh, dear, took a bit of a spill did you?" she asked.

"Uh, yeah, sorry." I didn't know why I was apologizing. It just came out.

She laughed, accentuating the deep lines of her face, and I was surprised by how warm and grandmotherly she looked. "Here, let's get you up. Are you hurt?"

"I don't think so," I said.

I let her help me to my feet and put some tentative weight on my twisted ankle. It was a little sore, but nothing that wouldn't wear off in a day or two. Mrs. Grady watched with an astute purse of her lips. After she was satisfied that I could support myself, smiled.

"Seems you're ok," she said. I nodded. "You've been running a lot lately; I see you almost every night now."

"Yeah, training for the track team at school," I replied. It was an idea I'd been toying with, so it wasn't a total fib.

"That's real good, to keep busy after such a loss."

I hadn't expected her to mention my dad's death at all, much less so bluntly. I just shrugged and looked down at my feet, trying to subtly swallow the lump that sprang into my throat at the thought of him.

"He was always so nice," she continued, "and so proud of you."

"Y-you knew my dad?"

"Of course!" Mrs. Grady said. "We lived near each other for almost fifteen years: hard not to trade the odd hello. He'd stop by every now and again on his way home from work and check up on me. He was always talking about his little Calla."

Tears filled my eyes, and I wiped them across the back of my hand. Dad never mentioned speaking to Mrs. Grady, but I guess it made sense. Mom wouldn't have liked it much.

"If you need anything, to talk or just get away for a while, you can always come by, alright?" Mrs. Grady gave my arm a quick squeeze.

"I don't think your dogs would like that much," I said, trying to keep my voice light. It cracked anyway, both from the raw pain of my dad's death and the unexpected kindness from this woman who was practically a stranger.

"Snicker and Doodle? Oh, ha! They're just a couple of old hellhounds. They won't give you any trouble, don't you worry."

Hellhounds. The term of endearment seemed suitable for the noisy, territorial pair. I thanked her and turned to start jogging home. She stayed where she was, watching me with that same grandmotherly smile.

While I appreciated her offer, I hadn't really thought I'd take her up on it. I figured I'd stop on my way past sometimes if she was outside, just to check up on her like Dad had, but that was all I was expecting. And that's all that it started as, the occasional pause in my run to trade a few minutes of small talk. Those few minutes started to stretch though, and our curbside chat moved further and further up the driveway until we were sitting in her garage on a couple of folding chairs, sipping iced tea.

Mrs. Grady became like the grandma I'd never had, right down to the sage advice and sugar cookies that she liked sending me home with.

I still never saw Snicker and Doodle. They remained locked in the backyard behind their tall fence, but instead of barking when I came up the drive, they'd whine happily and Mrs. Grady would give me chunks of rare beef to toss over for them.

"They're good boys," she'd say with such affection, "but it's best they stay back there. Never know what kind of trouble a couple hellhounds might get into if let loose!"

My visits to her house were my happiest times in the months following Dad's death. They offered me an escape from the outside world, from my house and mom and uncle. I could forget my role as the perfect, straight A, involved-in-every-activity-possible, rich girl that everyone expected me to be.

Mrs. Grady was understanding, patient, and quirky. She really didn't fit into the mold of our little neighborhood, and that was exactly what I needed. Our little visits didn't go entirely unnoticed, however. Mom had started to pay attention to where I was disappearing off to and, to my surprise, she wasn't entirely displeased when she confronted me.

"This is great," she said, cornering me as I came inside after a visit to Mrs. Grady. "How close have you gotten to her? Have you gone inside?"

"What? Why?" I tried to push past her, but she stayed in my way.

"What's the condition of the house like? Still good? I'd hate to have to put a lot work into it because that old bat hasn't been keeping it up."

"What are you even talking about?" I demanded.

"Your uncle and I have been talking, and we think a bigger house would do a world of good for all of us. You know there isn't a bigger one than her's in this community. Your father's life insurance payout would more than cover whatever she could ask for."

I stared at her incredulously. "She's not selling."

"There's more than one way to get a person out of a house, Calla," Mom said.

The look on her face, some dark mix of greed and determination, made my skin crawl. I finally got around her and hurried up the steps to hide out in my room. I didn't know what my mother and her skeevy brother were planning, but I was sure nothing good would come from it.

They didn't make me wait long to find out.

Their first attempt came in the form of animal control. I saw the big white van with the city's logo at the end of our street when I got home from school. I was quick to change into my running clothes so I could head down. The animal control officer was just walking out of Mrs. Grady's house, cookie in hand, when I arrived. She smiled when she saw me and invited me to join her in our usual spot for some iced tea.

"What was he here about?" I blurted out gracelessly.

"He couldn't remember," Mrs. Grady said pleasantly.

"Seriously," I said. "Are the dogs ok?"

"My old hellhounds? Of course, why wouldn't they be?"

"Because...animal control?"

She clicked her tongue and handed me a glass. "I told you, he couldn't remember why he'd come by. Nice man, bit of a sweet-tooth."

No matter what I asked, her story didn't change. It didn't really make sense either; how could an animal control officer forget why he'd come around? Mrs. Grady just chuckled.

"Must be my little old lady magic, huh? Makes it so nobody wants to pick on us."

That night, Mom all but confirmed that the officer's presence hadn't been a mistake.

"I know neighbors have been complaining about those mutts for ages," she sniffed dismissively. "It was about time someone did something."

Uncle Blake huffed in agreement. "They shouldn't be allowed here. It's too nice of a neighborhood for big, mean dogs."

It didn't take them long to realize, however, that their first attempts at making Mrs. Grady pull up stakes hadn't been successful. I found them muttering about it over glasses of Dad's whiskey, but they fell silent when I came into the room. Whatever their next step, they were being careful not to let me in on it.

Shamefully, I didn't tell Mrs. Grady what they were trying to do. I was too afraid it would damage my relationship with her and I'd lose my sanctuary in her garage. It was selfish and self-serving, and I prayed her little old lady magic would hold up enough to ride it out. In the meantime, I did my best to make it up to her in other ways by helping around the yard and bringing her trash barrels in and out.

Every week for the next few weeks it seemed my mom and uncle had some new and devious trick to pull. Cops were called with noise complaints, the HOA was called for any minor infraction they could think of, the city received complaints about the supposed state of her house. Inconvenience after inconvenience, all done to make Mrs. Grady feel unwelcome, threatened, and intimidated.

All done in the hopes that it would become too much for her and she would move away.

The final straw was the social service worker who showed up with complaints that the elderly Mrs. Grady couldn't take care of herself anymore.

I was helping Mrs. Grady trim back the roses when the worker pulled up. Mrs. Grady didn't look the least bit shaken or surprised when the woman introduced herself and explained why she was there.

"Can we go inside?" the worker asked.

"Sure," Mrs. Grady stood and motioned for her to follow.

I sat back on my heels, the clippers clutched in both hands, and watched them disappear behind the front door.

They emerged again barely a half hour later, laughing and chatting like old friends, and I was able to relax. Mrs. Grady waved the worker off and waited for her car to turn back down the lane before turning to me. Her smile had faded into the shadow of an expression and, while she still spoke as sweetly as ever to me, there was a hard edge to her words.

"Do you know why she was here, Calla?"

Slowly, I shook my head.

"Apparently there's been some concern about my ability to live on my own."

"That's ridiculous!" I said.

"Isn't it?" she tugged her gardening gloves back on and knelt beside me again to continue pruning. "Will you do me a favor, dear?"

"Y-yeah," I agreed, suddenly nervous.

"Tell your mother and that brother of hers that I'd like a word. They can come over anytime."

"My mother?"

"Yes," she met my gaze. I averted my eyes to the ground. "I know what they're doing."

I looked up again sharply, then sat in stunned silence. I wanted to protest, but I knew in my gut that it would be useless. She knew, there was no doubting it; I could see the cold certainty in her face. Finally, I just quietly asked, "How did you know?"

"My little old lady magic," she answered cryptically.

My lower lip trembled and I bit down on it. "I'm so sorry!"

"Oh, dear, shh, shh," she pat my knee. "It's not your fault, you didn't do anything. We both know what kind of people they are. They're cruel and selfish and think only of themselves; they don't care who they hurt. I prefer to deal with their kind in person."

Considering my mom and Mrs. Grady had never spoken, I wondered just how she knew. I didn't ask though, I had a feeling I already knew the answer.

Little old lady magic.

Mom and Uncle Blake made every excuse under the sun not to meet face to face with Mrs. Grady, until I finally called them out on their cowardice.

"We're not avoiding her, Calla," Mom scoffed. "We just have no reason to speak with her."

"Because you know she's going to call you out on your bullshit," I said.

Mom gaped at me, rolled her eyes in disbelief, and gaped again, until Uncle Blake stepped in.

"Fine, we'll go," he snapped. "We have nothing to be ashamed of."

We piled into Mom's Mercedes and drove slowly down to Mrs. Grady's house to where she was watering her garden. She watched us pull up from beneath the brim of her straw hat and, once we were parked, set her hose aside. Snicker and Doodle were oddly silent as we stepped out.

"My niece said you have a problem with us," Blake said with his usual tact.

Mrs. Grady removed her hat with all the grace of a practiced hostess and inclined her head politely. "I believe it might be the other way around."

"What are you implying?" Mom asked sharply.

"I'm not implying anything, dear. I'm saying that you have an issue with me."

"Why would we give two shits about you?" Blake demanded.

"Are you really going to make me say it out

loud?" Mrs. Grady sighed. "Fine. You want my house."

Blake tried to loudly deny it while Mom whirled on me, hand already raised. She brought it down with a resounding slap against my cheek, then another.

"What have you been telling her?" she hissed.

Before I could react, Mrs. Grady physically stepped between myself and Mom and took hold of Mom's wrist.

"Calla didn't tell me anything," she said. "She didn't have to. Now, before you make any more of a fool out of yourself, why don't we go inside and discuss things further."

I could see the naked, hungry greed in Mom's eyes spark almost instantly. She'd been waiting for ages to get a glimpse inside Mrs. Grady's home, and now was her chance. She wrenched her arm from the older woman's grasp and straightened her blouse with a single nod. Blake followed suit. Mrs. Grady motioned for them to head for the door, but when I moved to follow, she gently stopped me.

"I'm going to take care of this. You have nothing to worry about anymore."

I tried to argue, but she gave me a firm shake of her head and told me to go home.

"But, my mom—"

"It's fine, Calla. I'm going to take care of things."

I stood on the walkway, staring after her and feeling a bit lost. Mom and Blake were whispering back and forth while Mrs. Grady pushed open the front door, completely unaware of and unconcerned with leaving me behind. An odor drifted out from inside the house, like sulfur and old fire and rotten eggs. Mom put a hand over her nose, but still stepped past Mrs. Grady when she invited them in.

"Smells like shit," Blake said as he crossed the threshold.

From deeper in the house, out of sight from the door, I heard a pair of long, rumbling growls that vibrated down to my bones even from that distance.

Snicker and Doodle, Mrs. Grady's dogs, the ones she always called her hellhounds, were inside.

Mrs. Grady started to close the door.

"What the fuck is tha—" Blake tried to say. It turned into a scream that rooted me in place, making it impossible to move or cry out.

Mom soon joined.

In the sliver of doorway that had yet to close, I saw Mrs. Grady turn her head toward them. As she did, her mouth started to open, and open, and open...

Like a snake about to consume its prey.

The front door clicked all the way shut, and the sounds of screaming, snarling, snapping teeth and tearing flesh were swallowed up. I was left alone to stand in the silence that followed and the fading afternoon light.

My Brother's Voice

I should have known better than to pull off on an unlit, backwoods road. It was my first instinct when I noticed my car pulling to one side with the telltale limp of a flat tire. I groaned, hitting the heel of my hand against the steering wheel. I could change a flat without a problem, but after so many hours of nonstop waitressing, I was exhausted and did not want to be fiddling around in the dark.

I wanted to drive the rest of the way home, still another half hour, on an increasingly flat tire even less. With my phone's flashlight leading the way, I reluctantly got out to inspect the damage. Mercy, my poor old girl who ran half on gas, half on divine power's good grace, was lilting obviously to one side in the back.

"How did I not notice that when I got in at the restaurant?" I kicked the tire grumpily and trudged to my trunk for the jack and spare.

I was bent over the spare, struggling to get it out, when headlights from behind illuminated my car. I half turned, one hand lifted to shield my eyes, and tensed as someone pulled over behind me and stopped.

"Kerri?"

The driver's familiar voice put me immediately at ease. I waved, enthusiastic and hopeful that maybe I wouldn't have to do the work alone. Greg, the restaurant's bartender and everyone's favorite drinking buddy, came over with a concerned frown. "Everything ok?"

"Got a flat, probably from the construction over on Hamilton."

"Need any help?"

"Sure! Could you get the spare out? It'll be good enough to get me home and over to the shop tomorrow."

I turned to move the jack out of the way when the first blow came down, hard and fast, on the back of my head. I didn't even really register it before the second came and everything went black. I faded in and out for a while after that; there were slashes of red light, the sound of wheels on gravel, the smell of stale cigarettes and booze. I was in a small, dark place. My head was pounding. I felt around clumsily, not yet realizing what was going on. Everything was painfully loud. Was that wind rushing by? Was I moving? My thoughts were hazy, still half scrambled, and in a dreamlike fog I started to piece together what had just happened.

"Greg?" I croaked, my throat dry with fear.

I was getting more coherent by the second and the panic was setting in. I tried to stretch out, to sit up, to move, but I couldn't. I was completely enclosed. The trunk, I thought numbly. I'm in the trunk. His trunk. I lay very still, my breath coming in quick, shuddering gasps, and tried to think. The pain, the noise, the fear—all shadowed my thoughts, consuming rationality and reason. The only clear thought was of my brother Leo. A conversation I'd had with him once, a long time ago while at our parents' house.

I didn't even remember how it started. Just

that we'd been watching TV, maybe a true crime show. Maybe that's how it came up. I'd laughed, I remembered that, and said, "If something ever happened to me, you wouldn't be able to do anything about it."

He looked at me then, and there was no trace of humor in his usually bright face. Somehow, in the span of a single sentence, the warmth and softness that I had always known in him had hardened into iron wrought by a decade behind the badge. "I'd take the case. I'd find you."

I paused, still half joking. "You couldn't. Conflict of interest and all that."

"I'd take the case."

There was such a finality in his tone, an unshakeable certainty that dared someone, anyone, to challenge him, that I could only nod. It was the only time I'd ever seen him as Detective Cooney and not my older goofball of a brother.

Tears burned in my eyes at the thought of him. Large, loud, impossible to ignore, a good cop and a better man. I wished with everything in me that he could be there with me, to protect me as he always had. He couldn't, not this time.

This time, the only thing he'd be able to do is take the case. But I knew that, even if he was allowed, it probably wouldn't matter. How many stories had I heard over the years about girls who go missing and never turn up? Or if they do, it's only their body. I didn't want him to spend forever looking, and I didn't want him to bring me home to our parents in a bag.

In the back of my mind, it struck me as absurdly funny that I was being taken to who-knows-where in the trunk of a car in the middle of the night by a coworker I thought I knew, and one of my biggest concerns was how it was going to affect my family.

I started to shriek with laughter and tears and terror. I beat my hands and feet against the roof of the trunk, throwing myself wildly around. I vaguely remembered something about punching out tail lights and sticking your hand through the hole, so I tried to figure out how to do just that. Then we stopped.

I could hear crickets in the stillness that followed. Then squeak of his car door, and the crunch of leaves under his feet as he came around the back to the trunk. I always hoped that, if anything like this were to ever happen to me, I'd be brave; I'd fight like a cornered animal with teeth and nails and the fury of someone hell bent on survival. When he opened that trunk, I huddled as far back as I could and wet myself. He grabbed me and yanked me out like I weighed nothing, was nothing, and threw me to the ground. My eyes darted around: a shack, woods, a long dirt driveway, and nothing else. The trunk had felt less claustrophobic.

His fingers closed on the back of my neck and he hauled me toward the door. If I went inside, I was never coming out. My screaming barely seemed to bother him. He even looked amused. The door was pushed open and I was dragged, kicking and clawing uselessly, over the threshold.

There was a cot with a filthy mattress in one corner. I was forced onto it and tied to its metal frame by heavy ropes which bit roughly into my wrists. The smell, oh god, the smell. Old piss, sweat, horror. It told a tale of other women before me; I couldn't begin to guess how many. Greg leered down at me, his bearded face at once familiar and a stranger's. I stared at him through unblinking, wide eyes. He crouched beside me, and his breath was hot against my cheek. "I got tomorrow off so we could have some fun."

He slapped me hard when I started to scream again. "Knock that shit off."

From his pocket, his cell phone started to ring. Given the odd hour, he seemed surprised.

"Oh, it's the boss man," he said lightly. "I better take this."

He shoved an old rag from under the mattress in my mouth and I gagged on the acrid taste. He chuckled at me, patted the cheek now swelling from his slap, and took the phone outside. My parents must have called our boss when I didn't come home, I thought, my eyes squeezing shut. Mom could never sleep until she knew I was back. I could hear Greg adopt a sleepy sounding tone, saying oh no, he hadn't seen me on his way home. Why? Oh dear, no, he'd gone the opposite way to go camping for the night. Big fishing plans tomorrow. On and on, all lies.

My thoughts went again to Leo. How would he find me? What would he have to learn about my last night alive? What would he have to tell my parents? Greg Halloway's awful smirk trailed behind each question. Somewhere, a tiny voice, almost indiscernible from the rest of the mess, filled my head with my brother's voice.

I'm coming. Hold on.

I cried at the cruelty of my own mind and its wishful thinking. I cried for my brother and my parents. I cried for myself and for the life I'd never get to lead.

People do unspeakable things in the dark when they think they're alone. Greg kept doing unspeakable things long after day had overtaken night. I stared at the tarpapered ceiling and wished myself away. The pain grew into a fire, burning over every inch of my violated body, and then to icy numbness before erupting once more with the latest flick of his knife or the shifting of his weight.

Every time I cried out, in the back of my mind, my brother's voice.

I'm coming. Hold on.

I screamed at the voice, demanding it shut up, telling it to stop taunting me. No one was coming, but it kept repeating itself. And it was getting louder.

I'm coming. Hold on.

Greg was taking his time, but the cuts were starting to get deeper, less careful, and I knew he was almost done with me. How many hours had it been? Enough for the sun to look like it was starting to set through the shack's single window. I found myself drawn to that window and the rays of golden light that streamed through it. Even as Greg started to get up, his already bloodied knife held tight in his fist, I remained focused on those last few strands of sun still reaching toward me.

I'M COMING. HOLD ON.

The window exploded inward. Greg leapt up, stunned, staring at the black hood of the Ford Explorer where the wall had once been. Standing beside it, a man, tall, bald, wrought from iron.

"What...?" Greg asked dumbly, unbelieving.

Leo's pistol was already up, but he was looking past Greg, to me.

"I almost didn't believe it. I thought it was a nightmare and then Mom called..." He said, his voice choked. For a moment there was fear, and relief, and so much love written on his face as our eyes met. "I don't know how, but I heard you."

I sagged against my restraints, sobbing pitifully, wanting to run to my brother, wanting him to take me home. Greg moved, little more than a flinch, and Leo's eyes were back on him. All else was lost behind a mask of black, terrible fury. "I heard everything."

I hadn't noticed the radio in Leo's other hand. He raised it to his lips. "Dispatch, this is Detective Cooney, badge number 7362, Walsh County Police Department. I located missing person Kerri Elizabeth Cooney. She was still with her assailant. A struggle ensued, he attacked me with a knife. We need an ambulance six miles down Old King Road as soon as possible: one female in need of immediate medical attention, one male, deceased."

Greg's mouth fell open. He dropped his knife. "I'm unarmed!" he said desperately.

"I'm not," said Leo.

He cocked back the gun's hammer and took steady aim.

The Little People

Grandma Eileen came into some money in 1962 after the death of Grandpa Joe. She used it to move herself and my father far away from the only life they'd ever known, from a small village in Ireland to a bustling U.S. city. She made a name for herself there as a seamstress, selling her craft to "the high society folk". Dad got himself a couple of business degrees and started helping out on the operation side of things, and it was through his work that he met Mom.

By the time my brother, Allen, and then myself, were born, Grandma's solo operation had grown into a family run corporation. She oversaw a handful of dry cleaning and fitting shops with enough employees to run each.

We were a tight-knit family and, since Grandma would have been on her own otherwise, all lived together in a large, two story house. My parents remodeled the second floor into an apartment so Grandma would have her own space away from the rambunctious activities of two young boys. When my parents went out, Allen and I tromped up the stairs so she could watch us. This inevitably lead to arguments over incredibly important matters like who got to sit in the big red recliner, what to watch, and who got to snuggle Priss, Grandma's sweet Maine Coon.

It seemed to me that Grandma always sided

with Allen, which he lorded over me with a smug smile while I was left sulking and petulant. When I tried to tell my parents about the obvious favoritism, they just said that Grandma loved us both equally.

In addition to her obvious bias, Grandma had also always been a little eccentric. Dad said it was left over superstitions from the Old Country, omens of bad luck and the like. When she sat us down one night while we were visiting the apartment, I wasn't concerned.

"Never speak to the Little People," she said gravely. "If they ever make themselves known to you, don't acknowledge them. Don't even look at them. Do you understand?"

"Why?" I asked at the same time as Allen. "Who are the Little People?"

She regarded us with an almost panicked expression. "No questions. Just listen and do as I say, okay?"

I squirmed nervously under her intense scrutiny and managed a stiff nod. Allen furrowed his brow uncertainly, but finally did the same. Grandma remained thin lipped and serious throughout our visit, her eyes darting to and from the front windows at the smallest of sounds. I was relieved when my parents came home and we were free to go back downstairs. Our subdued behavior for the rest of the night didn't go unnoticed and, when Dad was tucking me into bed, he asked what was wrong.

"What's a Little People, Dad? Grandma was talking about them." I paused, hesitant to make myself seem like a baby. "She made them sound scary."

He chuckled and I immediately relaxed. How bad could it be if Dad was so dismissive?

"They're just a fairy tale, kiddo. Let me guess, Grandma was saying to ignore them or something, right?" When I nodded, he said, "She used to say the same to me when I was your age. It's just one her stories that she brought over from Ireland, don't worry about it. You get some sleep now. Love you."

Reassured, I was able to fall asleep quickly and peacefully. Grandma's warning about the Little People didn't trouble me again and, soon enough, I had forgotten all about it.

"I want to pet Priss now!" I whined at Allen, who had been hogging both the recliner and the cat all afternoon. He stuck his tongue out at me and hugged Priss closer to keep me from trying to take her. I balled my hands into fists and breathed heavily through my nostrils, as if my frustration would do anything but make my brother keep Priss from me even longer.

"Grandma!" I finally shrieked, "Allen won't let me play with Priss!"

I heard her clucking her tongue from the kitchen. She poked her head in, but her ire seemed more aimed at me than Allen. "What have I told you about yelling in this house, young man?"

With no help coming from her, I grumbled something about going to play outside. I stomped my way down stairs and out to the backyard. I plopped myself down with a huff and began plucking blades of grass and tearing them to shreds. I'm not gonna cry. I'm not gonna cry!

"You ok there, child?" someone asked.

I jerked around to find the speaker. Half hidden in Grandma's rose bushes was the tiniest person I'd ever seen. I thought I'd been mistaken at first, that it was a trick of light and shadow, but no, there was certainly a man there. Standing at no more than two feet, he was dressed in delightfully bright colors from head to toe, all of which seemed just a hair too big for him. His hat, a floppy thing with a tinkling bell on the end, kept sliding down over one eye.

He grinned at me and offered a flourishing bow which sent his hat to the ground and revealed a shiny bald head. I giggled despite my nervousness, watching him scramble to pick it up and set it back in place.

"You seemed sad just the now." There was a sweet lilt to his voice, the kind Grandma had. "Are you alright?"

I bit my lip and started to get up. It wasn't his smallness that unsettled me—a child's mind is very accepting—it was the fact that he was a stranger. My parents' lessons about Stranger Danger were not unheeded.

"Wait!" He held out a hand. In his palm was a perfectly smooth, round rock that changed colors as he moved it about in the sunlight. "Take this, it will help you feel better."

I was fascinated by the stone and took a step forward, but stopped myself before I reached him. "I'm not supposed to take things from strangers." I felt a touch of pride at having remembered that.

"Right you are, lad, right you are! So let me introduce myself so that we can be friends, aye?

My name is Coilin. I don't usually come out when you folk are around, but you seemed so sad that I wanted to do something for you. You'll let Mr. Coilin give you this nice present, won't you?"

It was just a stone, a very pretty one, what harm could come from that? And he was so very small. I checked to make sure we weren't being watched and hurried over to take the gift. He dropped it into my open hand and cheerfully encouraged me to give it a good look over. Feeling more at ease, I sat in front of the bush and thanked him for the rock.

"Why don't you tell me what was troubling you before, child."

I frowned sharply, my mood darkened by the reminder of Allen and how horrible he was being. I closed my fist around the stone. "My dumb brother always gets to do whatever he wants and Grandma just lets him," I complained, and was gratified when Coilin tilted his head sympathetically. "He's mean to me, but he gets away with everything!"

"Oh aye, I understand. I have brothers too, you know, and sometimes I feel the same way."

It felt good to finally be able to talk to someone who understood. "It's not fair!"

"Not at all!" Coilin agreed. "Do you know something...I think I can help you!"

"You can?"

He nodded so eagerly that the bell on his hat jingled. "It sounds like your brother could use a little taste of his own medicine, hmm?"

That sounded exactly like what he needed. I leaned forward, excited to hear Coilin's idea.

"Take that stone I gave you and put it in his

shoe!"

I couldn't hide my disappointment; that didn't sound like it would be a very effective way to exact my revenge.

Coilin tapped his index finger to the side of his nose. "Don't worry, lad, trust Mr. Coilin."

That night, I did as the little man in the bush told me. With some measure of regret because I hated giving it up, I put the rock in my brother's shoe. I didn't know what to expect, and spent a sleepless night waiting and wondering. It felt like I had just managed to fall asleep when Allen started to scream.

I rushed from my bed and came sliding into the hall at the same time as my parents, who looked only half awake but wholly troubled. I followed them to Allen's room where he was standing on his bed, pressed against the wall.

"What's the matter?" Dad demanded.

"My shoe! It's in my shoe!"

He was deathly pale and trembling, his eyes wide like saucers. While my parents tried to coax him down from the bed, I leapt at his shoe and picked it up, eager to see what had caused such a fright. When I tipped it, only the stone I'd put inside tumbled out. Although confused, I was quick to pocket it in my pajama bottoms and hold the shoe up innocently.

"You want your shoe, Allen?"

"There's a spider in there! I saw it crawl in! It's huge! Kill it, Dad!"

I left while our parents scoured the room for signs of the giant, shoe dwelling spider and hurried back to my own room. I sat on my bed and plucked the stone out to sit in the middle of my palm. I gazed at it wonderingly, gleefully, and knew that the man in the bush was responsible for what my brother had seen. It made me feel like I'd made a powerful friend.

I went back to the bush that afternoon and crouched in the same spot I'd been in the day before.

"Mr. Coilin?" I whispered. "Mr. Coilin?"

There was a rustle and the tinkling of a bell, and then the small, grinning man was standing before me again.

"Hello again, child!" he said cheerfully. "Did you do as I told you?"

I nodded, unable to hide my pleased smile.

"Wonderful! Do you feel a wee bit better now?"

"Yes!"

"But surely one little prank isn't enough, is it? Not after all he's done to you."

This time I was slower to agree.

"This afternoon, when you're eating your meal, put the stone under his chair."

"But what if someone sees it?" I asked.

"No one will, I promise."

Again, I trusted in the little man and his advice. I tossed the stone into place before taking my own seat and waited with baited breath for Allen to join me. Mom made us grilled cheese for lunch, usually my favorite, but today I merely held the food in my hands and watched. My brother sauntered in and took his place across from me.

"What?" he asked, frowning when he saw me staring.

"Nothing," I said, quickly taking a big bite of my sandwich.

He rolled his eyes at me and picked up his grilled cheese. He managed three bites before he threw it, gagging, back on to his plate.

"Mom!" he cried.

"Yes, honey?" She was washing up in the kitchen.

"There's bugs in my food!"

"What?"

She was beside Allen almost immediately, inspecting his sandwich with great concern.

"I don't see anything, honey."

"There were worms, Mom! And ants!"

"Are you playing a joke on me, Allen Maxwell?"

"N-no," he sputtered, deflating completely when she put the plate back down. He saw for himself the only thing on it was a partially eaten grilled cheese.

Mom excused me once I was done, but she kept Allen at the table to talk about what he thought he'd seen. I pretended to have dropped something by his chair on my way out as an excuse to get my stone back, but neither took much notice of me. I could tell they were both a bit worried, but I didn't let that bother me. I was finally getting back at Allen, and that was all that mattered! I slipped quietly back outside and reported the second success to Coilin.

He clapped with delight at my news, which made me puff up with pleasure.

"Now tell me, my boy, does that make you feel like you're even?"

"No," I said, almost crossly. "Tonight we're going to Grandma's. She's always liked Allen more. I want to...to make her eat bugs or something too!"

"Of course." Coilin nodded gravely. "I believe I could be of some help there, lad, more than just worms betwixt some bread. Bring your granny and your brother out to this very spot tonight and we will give her exactly what she deserves."

We shared a conspirators' smile and agreed that I would return that evening after supper.

It was easier than I thought to get them outside. Allen was feeling fidgety and nervous, and that was making Grandma anxious. After a tense dinner, during which Allen kept looking through his food for insects, I asked if they wanted to go outside and walk around the yard with me. Allen seemed hesitant, but Grandma hurriedly agreed on both of their behalf.

After making sure Priss was lounging safely inside, the three of us tromped out to the garden. We made the rounds to each of Grandma's flower beds, Allen and I listening politely while she explained what plants were what. All the while, I had my sights set on the rose bush.

I heard the tiniest of bell tinkles from somewhere in the tangled depths, and I knew Coilin was there. As agreed, I nonchalantly dropped the stone by the bush and called my brother over to look at something. I didn't know exactly what Coilin was going to do, but if it were anything like his previous two pranks, it was going to be great.

"I don't see anything," Allen said irritably,

peering into the bush.

"Look closer!"

Grandma noticed our unusual interest in her roses and had started to come over. When she was just beyond arm's reach, the stone at my feet flashed bright gold before its surface faded into a murky black.

I fell back in surprise. Allen tried to as well, but something had him around the wrist. A vine from the rose bush, thorny and cruel, was biting into his flesh. He cried out and clawed at the vine, but another shot out and took him by his other wrist.

"Grandma!" We both screamed. She tried to tear at the plant in vain, bloodying her palms and fingers on the thorns.

I hugged Allen around the waist, trying to drag him back, begging Coilin to help. The vines continued to twist and turn up Allen's arms until they were lost from sight. Grandma beat against the bush, wailing like a banshee from one of her stories. Allen looked to her, his eyes glassy and his pale lips flecked with blood, and then he was gone, yanked impossibly into the bush. Grandma collapsed to her knees in front of it, reaching for the spot where Allen had been.

"Coilin!" I shouted. "Help! Help Allen!"

At the sound of his name, Grandma turned to me, and I saw such fear, such anger, in her expression. I thought she was going to strike me, and maybe she was, but the sound of a tinkling bell froze her solid.

"Consider your debt repaid, Eileen O'Hara," Coilin's voice sounded from somewhere far away, much too far to be in the bush. Then there was silence.

Grandma Eileen came into some money in 1962 after the death of Grandpa Joe. A death she had arranged with the help of the Little People. All they had asked for in return was to give up the love of her first born son. She agreed and celebrated the end of her abusive, alcoholic husband before taking her money and fleeing to America. She thought she managed to escape, but the Little People are patient, and they do not forget.

She knew they had found her again; she heard their whispers outside her window. She didn't know how, not after so much time, and she tried to warn us, but we didn't listen. It wouldn't have mattered anyway; the Little People came to collect, and collect they did.

Dad's relationship with Grandma was never the same after Allen disappeared. He said he didn't blame her, that he knew she would have died before she let anything happen to my brother. There was no warmth in his eyes anymore though, no affection.

We sold the house barely a year later. Grandma wasn't invited to join us in our new home. They told her the new house was too small, but the truth was, it was just too hard for my parents to see her. With nowhere else to go, she ended up in a retirement community where she remained, alone, until she passed away in her sleep some time later.

Mom convinced Dad to collect her things and provide a proper burial as a way to say our final goodbye. That's when we found how little

Grandma had kept: only a few photographs, some clothes, and a murky black stone that had reminded her of home.

Moomaw's Curses

When you're a scrawny, awkward kid from a poor family, you're going to be teased. A lot. It's just one of those inescapable universal truths that nobody questions. You may expect it to remain almost exclusively a peer-thing: something that your classmates do when there aren't any adults looking. Even if the teachers happen to agree with what the others are saying about you, they're not supposed to join in or encourage it.

Not everyone gets that memo, though.

Ninth grade was a particularly rough year for me. At fourteen, I was still one of the shortest guys in my class. I wore thick glasses that gave me an owlish appearance, and the only clothes I owned were hand-me-downs from my much larger brother that made me look even smaller than I actually was. Saying I made an easy target was like saying Michael Jordan was kind of ok at basketball.

I wanted to complain to my grandmother, Moomaw, about how embarrassed I was just to be me. I knew she was doing the best she could with what little she had though. After my parents divorced and both skipped town, she'd been saddled with two teenage boys that required her to go back to work as a cleaning lady after five years in retirement. She never griped about it, so what right did I have?

I like to think that I held up pretty well in the

beginning. I didn't want to bother Moomaw with my problems, and I knew my brother Devon wouldn't care one way or another. I kept them bottled up instead.

When Kelsey spent a few days convincing me she liked me, then laughed in front of all her friends when I finally asked her out, I stayed quiet.

When Glenn shoved me in his gym locker with his unwashed PE outfit and held it shut until I started to gag, I stayed quiet.

When my lunch was stolen, when I was forced to give over my homework to be copied, when my art project was torn up, I stayed quiet. I thought if I didn't react and just kept my head down, they'd get bored and move on.

And then Mr. Farkle started.

He was a young teacher, fresh out of college and all too eager to be liked by the popular kids. When he noticed that I was a favored target for teasing, he joined right in. It started out subtly enough with him asking me to go to the board and solve a problem he'd written high up where I couldn't reach. Once could have been a fluke, but after the third time I had to struggle in front of the class's barely concealed laughter, I knew it was intentional.

He ignored me when I had my hand raised to answer a question, but call on me when he knew I didn't know what he was asking. He kicked my bag whenever he walked by, no matter how far I tried to tuck it under my desk, and tell me off for being careless with my things. He was open and generous with his praise, but only had disparaging remarks for me.

I still stayed quiet. I just tried to do better and show him that I was just as good as any other student. No matter how hard I worked, though, nothing changed.

My grades, which had always been exceptional, started to drop. Food lost its appeal, as did simply getting out of bed. My stomach ached constantly, my head throbbed, and I was always on the brink of breaking down into tears.

It didn't take long for Moomaw to notice.

"What's wrong, Brad?" She had come to wake me for school, but when I just rolled over, she sat next to me and rubbed my back.

Her voice and touch were so gentle and warm, something I'd been lacking from anyone else for so long that I couldn't stop the tears from falling. Through messy sobs, I told her about Mr. Farkle and what he'd been doing. Storm clouds gathered in Moomaw's eyes. She mimicked spitting at my floor when I was done.

It was what she always did before she recited one of her curses.

"That man," she said, "may he find a fly in every one of his meals!"

Moomaw didn't believe in wishing ill on others. When she was upset, she'd think up something benign, but annoying, instead. Usually they made me laugh, but that morning, I wanted far worse to happen to Mr. Farkle.

"Don't you worry, Brad, I'm going to take care of this for you."

Before I could beg her not to get involved, she'd stomped out of the room.

Mr. Farkle's behavior did change a bit after

that. He now ignored me completely except to grade my work with almost painful pettiness, taking any excuse to mark me off. He must have told some of the other kids that I'd gotten him in trouble, because suddenly I was being pelted with spitballs and crumpled paper throughout class.

I just bit my lip, clenched my fists, and tried to endure it as best I could. I even managed a small almost-smile when I saw him waving irritably at a fly buzzing around his open soda bottle a few days after Moomaw's "curse". Any enjoyment I got out if it was quickly squashed, though, when a wet, sticky wad of paper hit me in the back of my head.

There was a brief respite from the abuse when Mr. Farkle was out sick for almost a week and we had a no-nonsense substitute. Being able to complete my math work in peace was almost magical.

It didn't last. When Mr. Farkle returned, he was in a worse mood than I'd ever seen him. He'd lost a lot of weight while he'd been out, and his skin was pale and drawn. Dark circles rimmed his eyes. Severe food poisoning, we learned.

"Bugs all over everything in this damn school," I overheard him telling his little groupies. "It's no wonder I got sick with how often I've been having to brush them off anything I eat."

I thought of Moomaw's curse again, quietly delighted in the coincidence.

He must have sensed that I wasn't exactly upset he'd been out, because it wasn't long before I was on his radar again. The brunt of his foul temper was unleashed in a rant over how I needed to pay attention in class after I couldn't figure out a problem quickly enough. He screamed until my face was burning with shame and tears had built up in my eyes. I tried to discreetly wipe them away, but he saw and sighed with disgust.

"Go to the girl's room if you're going to cry, Pierro," he said.

The class giggled and whispered behind me as I hurried out.

Moomaw was livid when she found out.

"That man," she was shaking with anger, "may his shoes fit poorly and pinch his toes! You sit tight — I'm going to call the school."

She bustled into the kitchen, and I heard her speaking in a sharp whisper to whoever was unfortunate enough to answer. If I had thought of it at the time, I might have told Moomaw about the amusing timing of her fly curse and his food poisoning. My mind was too filled with self-pity and sadness to focus on anything else though.

"We have a meeting with Mr. Farkle and the principal tomorrow," Moomaw said once she'd hung up.

But the meeting didn't occur as scheduled. Mr. Farkle had been walking down the stairs to reach the principal's office when he tripped on his untied shoelace and stumbled down the last few steps, twisting his ankle and hurting his foot.

The next time I saw him, he was on crutches and his foot was in a black medical boot. He propped it up on a stool to teach, and the ends of his bruised toes, too swollen to fit comfortably into a shoe, were just visible.

I reminded myself to mention it to Moomaw that afternoon when she came down to school for the meeting. I figured she'd get a kick out of the timing of the accident, but the seriousness she carried herself with when she arrived told me it would be better to just stay quiet.

Our conference with the principal did not exactly go well. Moomaw and Mr. Farkle were almost shouting over each other about what was going on in his classroom.

"He's a lazy trouble maker!" Mr. Farkle said.

"You're a horrible teacher!" Moomaw replied.

They went back and forth until Ms. Haggarty, the principal, had to step in. The conversation didn't become any more productive than that and, when it ended, exactly nothing had been accomplished. Ms. Haggarty did agree to check what other math classes might be open to me, but she couldn't make any promises. In the meantime, Mr. Farkle and I would have to try and maintain a "professional relationship".

"That man," Moomaw mimed spitting before slamming her car door, "may his car stall at an inconvenient time!"

"It's ok, Moomaw," I said quietly.

"No, it's not," she said. "Don't worry, we'll figure something out."

The drive home was quiet. Moomaw fumed the whole way, and I just did what I did best: I stayed quiet and kept my head down.

I didn't sleep at all that night. I was too afraid of what the following day would bring. No doubt Mr. Farkle would take out his anger on me and try even harder to ensure I was miserable. I appreciated Moomaw sticking up for me, but the cost was going to be way too high.

I was already up and dressed when Moomaw knocked on my door at 5:30 the next morning.

"I'm up," I said, trying not to sound too upset about it.

"Can I come in?" Moomaw asked through the door.

"Yeah."

Her expression was grim as she let herself in to sit beside me on the edge of my bed.

"I have some unfortunate news, Brad," she said. I nodded for her to continue. "I just saw on the news that your teacher, Mr. Farkle, was involved in an accident."

"Ok?" I said slowly.

"He was driving home last night and got a flat tire. It was dark, and he was standing next to his car when a truck came down the road. It didn't see him in time and, well...Mr. Farkle didn't make it."

I gazed at Moomaw, my mouth hanging open and my eyes wide. I struggled to find the words for all the thoughts racing in my head.

They kept circling back to one thing, though. The last thing Moomaw said about my teacher the night before.

"Your curse," I stammered, "you wanted his car to stall and his shoe not to fit and the flies!"

"What?" she looked baffled, so I reminded her of her curses and told her everything that had happened to Mr. Farkle after each one.

"Y-you wanted this to happen, didn't you?"

Moomaw tutted her tongue and smoothed my hair away from my face. "Of course not, Brad! You know I don't wish ill on anyone!"

"But—"

"You know me better than that, young man. Now finish getting dressed and come downstairs for breakfast."

"Everything you said happened, Moomaw," I said earnestly as she got up. "How?"

"You think an old woman's silly words could kill a man?"

"I dunno," I said doubtfully, knowing how dumb it sounded. "Maybe?"

She paused in the doorway and half turned to me. "No, dear, that's ridiculous. It wasn't what I said that hurt Mr. Farkle; it was what was listening that did."

"What?"

She just smiled and walked out.

"Moomaw?" I called after her, but she did respond.

She just left me sitting in my room. I stared at where she'd been long after she'd gone, very confused, and more than a little afraid.

The Past Repeats

Sage had always been a very normal kid, except for the stories. It wasn't that they were disturbing or horrific: they were just unusual. Sometimes they seemed exactly like the kind of thing you'd expect from a little girl, but other times, I'd have to look at her and wonder how she came up with such things.

It started when she was four, shortly after her deadbeat dad split, leaving the two of us on our own.

I'd just finished reading her a bedtime story and was tucking her in with a goodnight kiss when she yawned, smiled sleepily. "You'll always be my mommy, right?"

"Of course," I said.

"Good. I'd miss you if you weren't. You've been my mommy for a long time."

"Yup, your whole life," I replied, smoothing her hair back.

"All my lifes," she murmured into her pillow.

Her eyes fluttered shut, her breathing deepened, and she fell asleep while I sat next to her. Kids really do say the darndest things.

I didn't dwell on it; it was just an off-the-cuff remark by a child with a very active imagination. The same child who, a few weeks before, had told me that rainbows are unicorn slides and clouds are their trampolines. Sage didn't even seem to remember saying it the next morning. She didn't mention it anyway, which was pretty much the same thing as she had a tendency to say whatever popped into her head.

I thought it was a one off thing until we were watching a show with princesses in poofy dresses.

"We used to dress like that," Sage said casually.

"Oh yeah?" I asked with that indulgent parent tone used when a kid is about to tell a tall tale.

"Yup, yours was blue and mine was red, and we wore them a lot."

"We must have looked very pretty!"

"Yup, but I didn't like mine 'cos it was hot and you didn't let me play in it," she said. "You used to-used to be a lot meaner."

"I was?" I played along and raised my brows in surprise.

"You didn't let me do a lot of stuff."

"But I'm better now?"

"Yeah," she giggled, "you're nicer now!"

"Well that's a relief!"

It was certainly an odd conversation, but one I attributed to the TV show that was on. It had a "mean" mom with lots of rules, a daughter who was getting into trouble for bending them, and a lot of the stuff she was claiming we had done. It was kind of cute, really.

Until it started to become a more frequent occurrence.

She'd see sor hear something and it would "remind" her of something we'd done together in a previous life. Foods she'd never tried, places she'd never even heard of, pictures of clothing and items she had no way of knowing about; she claimed to have memories of them all. I made up excuses for it, convincing myself she must have heard about it on TV or at daycare. It was the only thing that made sense.

"Honey," I said with a laugh after she asked if I remembered teaching her to use chopsticks back when we had black hair and lived in the mountains, "where do you come up with this stuff?"

She shrugged. "I just remember."

"You've got some imagination."

"Imagination is for not real stuff, though," Sage said with a frown, "right?"

"Yeah."

After a moment of thought, she shook her head. "It's not imagination. I remember."

She seemed a bit upset that I was doubting her, but I was starting to become unsure about encouraging her stories. I worried she might lose sight of the line between fact and fiction and start confusing herself. I also wondered if it was all some kind of coping mechanism to deal with her dad's departure. While she seemed fine when we first talked about it, maybe her stories were somehow a cry for attention or her attempt to make sense of things.

A few nights later as we cuddled on the couch, I gently broached the subject and asked if she missed Daddy.

"No," she said, "he never stays."

"What?" I sat up a bit to glance at the impassive expression on her face.

"Daddy always goes away, every time, and

then it's just me and you. I like it when it's just me and you."

"Every time?"

"In all the lifes, Mommy," she said with an exasperated huff.

"Oh."

I veered the topic away from all our previous "lifes", and we settled back down. Sage was soon absorbed in the movie we'd been watching again, but I was distracted and concerned. She seemed so convinced that these previous lives, which always mirrored our current one, had actually happened. It didn't seem healthy.

After I put her to bed, I turned to the internet for answers. It was hard to know where to start.

my kid thinks she remembers past lives
young daughter has false memories
is something wrong with my child?

I tried them all, eventually finding other situations like mine. Sage was far from the only kid to claim to have these kinds of memories and, in most cases, it seemed completely harmless.

They'll grow out of it, sites assured me. *Children are just little sponges who soak up everything and process it in creative ways that adults don't.*

That made me feel better. It also supported my theory that Sage was just constantly taking in information, things I obviously missed, and incorporating it into her "memories". I breathed a sigh of relief and slept a bit easier that night.

Still, I didn't want to feed into such behaviors. It was my job to teach her what was real and what wasn't, and I felt like I let her down. Her fifth birthday was coming up, so I decided we should focus on that instead of her stories. Every time she tried to bring one up, I'd redirect her back to the present and planning her party.

It was frustrating for both of us; she felt shut down, I felt like I was crushing her creative spirit, and for the first time, Sage wasn't her normal, cheerful self.

The night before her birthday party, I was seated on the edge of her bed, trying to read her a story. She was fussy and uninterested.

"What's wrong, Sage?" I asked at last.

She just rolled over, her covers pulled up all the way to her chin.

"What is it, baby girl?"

"I don't want a party," she grumbled.

"Why not? I thought you were excited."

"No."

"Why not?" I asked again.

"You never believe me," she whispered. It was like an icy knife to my heart.

I rubbed her back in small circles and told her to try me.

She peeked over her shoulder, her little face creased with uncertainty. When I smiled encouragingly, she turned a bit more toward me.

"I don't wanna party 'cos it's always my last."

"Your last party?"

"My last birthday."

Chills trickled down the back of my neck. I assured her that wouldn't be the case and that she would have lots more birthdays. She didn't seem convinced.

Her party the next day went off without a hitch. She and her little friends ran around, laughing and squealing, and I was glad to see her relaxing enough to enjoy herself.

Admittedly, I was able to enjoy myself too. One of the kids had been brought by their single, handsome uncle, Taylor, who stuck around to chat. He was funny and charming, and he helped me keep the children wrangled. By the time the cake was rolled out and the presents opened, we'd exchanged numbers.

It was the first time I'd even looked at a guy since Sage's dad left.

After all the guests had gone and I'd cleaned up a bit, I found Sage sitting under the kitchen table, despondently dragging a comb through her new doll's hair.

"What're you doing under there, birthday girl?" I crouched beside the table and grinned.

I was surprised to see tears in Sage's eyes when she looked up at me.

"Nothing."

"Hey, come here, what's the matter?" I gathered her up in my lap and snuggled her close. "Did something happen at the party?"

"You met him," she said. There was a note of resignation in her voice that seemed far too old for her.

"Met who? Mimi's uncle?" I immediately thought I knew what was wrong; she had seen me talking to Taylor, was missing her dad, and was now worried Taylor might replace him. Wasn't that every kid's nightmare?

Sage just pulled away from me and stood up. "You never believe me," she said sadly.

"You haven't even told me what's wrong."

"I did. Lots of times, but you never listen."

I watched her trudge off to her bedroom, more concerned than ever.

Sage remained distant and solemn for weeks. I tried talking to her and taking her out to do fun things. I tried meeting with her daycare providers, and I was even careful to avoid talking about or to Taylor when she was around, but nothing seemed to lift her spirits.

"She just doesn't want Mommy moving on," Taylor said dismissively. "Kids are selfish like that. She'll be fine."

I wanted to believe him and tried to act like everything was normal with Sage, hoping she would perk up. Every time my phone went off though, Sage glanced at it with this resigned, knowing expression that unsettled me.

It was getting to the point where I thought I might have to consult a child psychiatrist. I couldn't really afford it, but I would have to manage if that's what my baby needed.

Before we went that route, though, I decided to try and get her to open up one more time.

I called Sage out of her room after dinner one evening and had her sit beside me on the couch. She stared down at her lap, vacant and uninterested.

"You have to talk to me, honey," the plea came out more desperately than I had intended, but I couldn't stop it. "I can't make things better if you don't tell me what's wrong."

"You never believe me," she whispered.

"Stop it, Sage! Stop saying that! I'm here, I'm listening! Help me understand!"

Her lower lip quivered, but she looked at me from beneath her lashes.

"He's going to hurt us, Mommy. He always does."

"Who?" I knelt on the floor in front of her and grabbed her hands between mine.

"Taylor," she said.

"Baby, I barely know him! Right now, he's just a...a sort of friend. Why would he hurt us?"

"Because he always does."

According to Sage, we'd been mother and daughter for a long time. We'd lived lot of lives, in a lot of places, as a lot of different people, but it always ended the same. Mommy met a man and he was bad and he hurt us.

"Once he put a knife in me, here," she pointed at her heart, "and then he did it to you, too, but more times."

She told me how he held her under water in a wash tub until her chest burned and everything went dark. How he'd thrown her off a mountainside, and how she'd screamed and screamed until she hit the ground. Her throat was slit, she'd been shot, been hung. She had hurt, she had cried, and she had died.

And, every time, I died, too.

"I tried to tell you," she said, her voice wavering, "but you never listened."

"You've got to know that those aren't real memories, Sage," I said gently.

She just stared at me. There was such fear in her eyes, such sadness, that my breath caught in my throat.

"He's gonna hurt us, Mommy," she said.

There was no conviction in her voice, just defeat.

"I won't let him."

"That's what you always say."

I don't know if it was the weary, hollow expression, or the weighted slump of her tiny shoulders, but as she slid off the couch to go back to her room, I found myself believing her. It was ridiculous and irrational and maybe even a little crazy, but I knew that, even if it made no sense, my daughter was telling me the truth.

When that stoney certainty in my gut didn't fade after an hour of sitting and thinking, I texted Taylor and told him I couldn't see him anymore.

I didn't expect the barrage of calls and texts that I received in return. At first, he was curious and pleading, but it quickly turned to anger, then fury. He started calling me terrible names, saying that women like me were the problem and he knew I'd regret being such a tease. I didn't understand why he was lashing out so horribly; we hadn't even gone out on a proper date!

I told him he had issues and blocked his number.

It could have been coincidence, his sudden and violent turn in personality. Even if it was, Sage had still recognized a darkness in him that I hadn't, and warned me against him. I was just grateful I'd listened.

I set my phone aside and curled up on the couch with a glass of wine. It had been a rough night to say the least, and I needed some quiet time to process my thoughts and the strange, frightening things that Sage told me about our past lives.

I let the sun fade completely, throwing the

house into darkness, and didn't bother turning on any lights. I found it peaceful to sit there alone, no noise, no interruptions, just me, my drink, and my thoughts. I leaned back, letting my eyes drift closed.

From the foyer, I heard the soft rattle of my door knob.

My eyes popped open and I slowly turned toward the noise. It rattled again, the cautious sound of someone checking the lock. I set my wine glass aside and crept across the living room to peek around the corner to the door.

The knob rattled again, followed by faint clicking noises. Someone was trying to pick the lock, I realized. My heart leapt. Goosepimples rose across every inch of my skin, and I pressed myself against the wall, biting fiercely down on my lip to keep from crying out.

I didn't know how long the lock would hold. It was just an old junky thing my ex kept meaning to replace, and I doubted any of the doors in my house would do much to keep out a determined prowler.

For a split second, I thought about trying to make it back to my phone and calling the cops. I'd even half turned toward it, but then I thought of Sage. My little girl, scared, feeling alone, isolated, and convinced her fifth birthday was going to be her last.

Something awoke in my belly, a hot, furious, terrible creature that was far less afraid than it was angry. This person was trying to get into *my* house, threatening *my* baby?

Sage told me that, in all my incarnations, I

never once listened to her. Well I was listening now, and if a bad man, Taylor or otherwise, wanted to get to my child, they were going to have to get through me first. And I wasn't going to make it easy.

My ex hadn't been good for a lot of things. In fact, I think he only ever did two things right by me: Sage, and the aluminum baseball bat he'd left in the front closet.

I don't know what Taylor was expecting when he finally managed to unlock the front door: maybe that we'd already gone to bed, maybe that he'd find two sleeping, defenseless targets for the knife he'd brought with him.

What I do know is that he wasn't expecting me to be waiting for him just on the other side, bat raised above my head, and a complete willingness to use it.

Cops arrived to find him sprawled in a pool of his own blood in my foyer. He was still breathing, but barely, and he had to rushed to a nearby hospital. I let the officers take me outside for questioning while one of the policewomen sat with Sage, who had mercifully stayed in her room. I handed over the bat, gave my statement, and proceeded to vomit all over their shoes.

They were disgusted, but understanding.

I was advised to get a hotel for the rest of the night as the entryway to my house was now a crime scene. I didn't argue; now that the Mama Bear within had gone back into hibernation, all the blood on my floor was almost enough to have me throwing up again.

I took Sage out the back and we found a cheap

motel a few minutes away.

"You ok, baby?" I asked her as I tucked her in beside me in the bed.

"Yeah," she said, laying her head on my shoulder.

I inhaled deeply, still shaken, and held her tight.

"Mommy?" she asked quietly.

"Yeah, baby?"

"What happens now? I never got to this part before."

I swallowed a tired sob that was half residual fear and half relief. "I don't know, but it's gonna be ok. We're gonna be ok."

She nodded, but still seemed unsure. "You'll still always be my mommy, right?"

"Of course," I said, kissing the top of her head and giving her a squeeze. "For all of your lifes."

ABOUT THE AUTHOR

S.H. Cooper is an author of things both horror and wholesome. After getting her start as part of Reddit's NoSleep community, she has since contributed her stories to horror fiction podcasts, a multi-author anthology, and published two collections of her work. When not writing, she enjoys spending time with her husband and animals in their home state of Florida.

Learn more and check out her other books:

Corpse Garden

Love, Death, and Other Inconveniences

Facebook: www.Facebook.com/Pippinacious

Twitter: Twitter.com/MsPippinacious

Tumblr: Pippinacious.tumblr.com

Please remember to
leave a **review on Amazon**!

It's the best way to support the author and help
new readers discover her work.

HAUNTED HOUSE PUBLISHING

Read More horror at:
TobiasWade.Com

Check out our other horror collections
and read more for free.

Made in the USA
Middletown, DE
02 March 2019